# More praise for
# *Dead South*

"Solid prose, conniving characters, and an under-current of humor will leave readers eagerly awaiting Cecile's next adventure."
—*Library Journal*

"Even more waggish than Cecile's debut (*A Sudden Death at the Norfolk Café*)."
—*Kirkus Reviews*

"The perfect read for a busy weekend."
—*Mystery News*

By Winona Sullivan
*Published by Ivy Books:*

A SUDDEN DEATH AT THE NORFOLK CAFÉ
DEAD SOUTH

# DEAD SOUTH

## Winona Sullivan

IVY BOOKS • NEW YORK

An Ivy Book
Published by Ballantine Books
Copyright © 1996 by Winona Sullivan

http://www.randomhouse.com

Library of Congress Catalog Card Number: 96-94818

ISBN 0-8041-1513-3

This edition published by arrangement with St. Martin's Press.

Manufactured in the United States of America

First Ballantine Books Edition: April 1997

10  9  8  7  6  5  4  3  2

To Edmund and to all our children.

The interested reader will find a glossary at the end of the book identifying foreign terms or unusual words.

# 1

THE Florida hurricane season wouldn't end until November, but so far no great storms had roared across the Caribbean. The calm, hot weather continued well into October. Up north, tourists were making plans to come down for the winter; some already had. One, in fact, had already arrived. A handsome gentleman, a man who had worked hard for some time at his chosen career, was in place at a cheap Miami Beach hotel looking for some well-deserved excitement. His name was Bradley Locke.

On that October night Bradley drove across the causeway to Coral Gables in his rental car, an oversized Lincoln. He parked on the street near the International Bank of Trinidad. He locked the car and emerged into the steamy night street, looking behind and beside him as he had been trained to do fifteen years before. There could be live surveillance. Not that being careful had ever mattered. In all his years with the Agency he had never been accosted. He had never even been tested. He wished, sometimes, that he would be.

That was on his mind as he entered the Hotel Place St. Michel bar, first passing through the lobby, glancing at the dark mahogany hotel desk before he entered the lounge. He picked a seat at the end of the bar near the small bowl of mixed crackers and pistachio nuts.

Three hours later he had downed five Blue Lagoons and had entered into deep conversation with a good-looking Panamanian national seated beside him who had been drinking Cuba Libres. In all his years Bradley had been the complete good agent: discreet, cool, sober. Tonight he made the dangerous discovery that acting out of character was exciting.

"Castro, he's not going to be around forever," the Panamanian was saying in a soft voice. "You see, anyone can go there. Boats go every day, in, out, smuggling in fresh pork, taking out cigars. It happens. Eighty percent of our drugs here come outta Cuba. I know what's gonna happen when he's gone."

Bradley looked smug. "You think?" He raised an eyebrow carefully, a tough trick after a few drinks, but a trick he had mastered. "I know about all that," Bradley said. "I know."

"You don't know nothing," the Panamanian scoffed.

"I know everything," Bradley insisted. What the heck, he thought, this guy doesn't even believe me.

"Like what?" the Panamanian asked.

Bradley shrugged. "Lots. What do you know?"

"I was a *sapo*, you know *sapos*?" the Panamanian asked.

"Noriega's little private cops, right?"

"I was one of them." Olimpo nodded modestly.

"Nasty bunch," Bradley murmured into his glass. He sounded wise, all-knowing.

"Where you from, anyway?" Olimpo asked. A tinge of respect had begun to show in his voice. Bradley's subtle allusions apparently weren't lost on him.

"Washington area. In the Beltway."

"Government man," Olimpo nodded.

"Didn't say that." Bradley picked out the last pistachio and chewed it slowly. His lips were feeling numb. Bradley would have noticed the difference in Olimpo's tone had he not been drinking all night.

"So, what's your name?"

"Bradley. Bradley Locke."

"Olimpo Olarte-Rodríguez. That's me. From Panama."

They sat for a moment in silence as though mulling this new friendship.

2

"How come you know about down here?" Olimpo finally asked. He motioned to the bartender to bring another round of drinks.

Bradley shrugged. He shouldn't be talking to anybody about anything, but he had begun to like Olimpo. All the foreign nationals in Miami hated the Castro regime. They called Castro *"hijo de puta,"* son of a bitch. It was common knowledge. It didn't matter what he said. "I know what's going to happen, that's all."

"No kidding. You got contacts?"

Bradley didn't answer. He'd said enough. Nothing really, just hints. No facts. Drinks arrived.

"How come you know that stuff, like what's going to happen?" There was major respect in Olimpo's tone now.

"No reason." Bradley heard his own words and felt proud. He hadn't said anything, hadn't betrayed his trust. "I know people."

"Like in Washington."

"I live there."

"You government?"

Bradley shook his head. Enough was enough. He reached for the bowl of munchies and picked out three crackers. He entirely missed the speculative look on Olimpo's fine features.

"Very important man," Olimpo said quietly, almost to himself. Then, "You like women?"

"I like women," Bradley agreed. "You?"

"Oh, yeah, women and chocolate. Hash, you know? You like chocolate?"

"No. Don't do drugs." Bradley took a long pull on the drink.

"Then, do I got a woman for you," Olimpo said.

Bradley felt a tingle up and down his spine. It was the one thing his life was missing just now. A woman. "I'm fussy," Bradley said. It came out, "I'm fuzzy."

Olimpo started to smile. "I know a beautiful woman, and you are such a stud, *guapo*, she's clean, beauti-ful, goes to church twice a week, maybe even marry you,

3

eh? You got no family? Wait until you see Marta. My sister-in-law."

"I would like to meet Marta," Bradley said very carefully. "I got to get back north soon."

"You come to my place," Olimpo smiled. "You wanna come now?"

Bradley tried to look doubtful. He tried to feel doubtful. Instead, he looked at Olimpo and saw the very clean-cut features, soft curly hair, and pleasant smile of a man who understood him. And there was the possibility that a good-looking Latino would have a sweet sister-in-law. "Maybe I'll take a little time. Just a few hours, okay?"

"Sure. You come with me. I drive you out, drive you back. No problem."

They paid up and left the bar, then waded out into simmering Florida night air, air thick with the sound of chirping crickets, the odor of rotting mangos and car exhaust. Bradley walked in a dream. This was paradise. People paid a hundred fifty bucks a day for this.

"Where are we going, Olimpo amigo?" Bradley asked.

"Hey, we drive in my car, okay? I have a rental."

"We go in my Mazda," Olimpo explained. "I know the way, the road gets bad out there. My place is out behind the Redlands. It's real private. You're gonna love it. I get you back home with plenty of time."

Bradley should have known better but this had been a long time coming, the escape from reality, the freedom, and the fact that back at the CIA he had been feeling seriously unappreciated. He went over it all in his mind as Olimpo drove south. All the things he'd done for the Company as a CT, a career trainee doing the kind of job that was supposed to be fun, he'd spent filling in papers and developing computer files. All that training had resulted in four years in Bolivia chasing a subversive group that eventually blew itself up, no thanks to him. More of the same had followed. Then his wife had left him. The system wasn't living up to its promise.

Tomorrow he had a late afternoon flight to Wash-

4

ington, D.C. After this vacation, he'd go back fresh. A new start. A new woman in his life. He knew more than any of those bastards on his staff; he was a Latin America expert and knew every move of every politician, doctor, lawyer, and general in the Caribbean as well as points south. He was smart and he could shoot straight and he deserved Marta, whoever she was. Miracles did happen. Bradley chuckled to himself over the way his trip was turning out. Olimpo's sister-in-law just might be real nice. Another prize. Bradley Locke thought about a good woman. It was time.

The streets were clear at night. Olimpo drove fast. Twenty-five minutes later they arrived at a crumbly cement block structure. "Eh, my house. We got a nice place, good drinks, very cool here, *guapo*."

"Where's Marta? She look like you, Olimpo?"

"Yeh, good-looking like me."

Olimpo didn't give Bradley a chance, spilling words out like warm orange blossom honey and fresh coconut patties. "Eh, *guapo*, Marta will be over in a little bit. I make a telephone call," Olimpo said. "You have a drink? Here, I make you my special chocolate rum. You never had it before. Drink it fast, it slides down good."

Bradley sat down at an unpainted, battered wooden table and was given a heavily loaded chocolate rum. In one of his better moments he would have been hesitant to drink anything so sweet and brown. He passed out within minutes.

Olimpo Olarte-Rodríguez dragged the unconscious agent into a back room and tossed him on a bare cot. Olimpo looked down at Bradley, who was snoring slightly, and nodded in satisfaction. He lugged in a jar of water, a bowl, and a bucket. Comfort items. Then the Panamanian left, locking the door carefully behind him.

Two large palmetto bugs watched as Bradley tossed and grunted in his drug-induced sleep. His face was covered with sweat, his shirt soaking. The temperature in the room was eighty-nine degrees, the humidity close to the same. There was no air-conditioning.

The braver of the two bugs moved up close for a look around the man's white sports coat. The large bug crawled into the man's pocket and found a doughnut crumb. Moments later the second bug wandered up to the man's face and stared, bug-like, before hopping off.

Bradley Locke slept on.

# 2

DURING the first week of Bradley Locke's captivity, CIA Headquarters became aware of Bradley's disappearance. Panic came with the realization that the agent had a vast amount of critical information in his head about planned future operations on the big island ninety miles from Florida. Whatever happened out there, Cuba was central for future and current drug traffic, and the power balance in the Caribbean.

It took the Agency another full week to collect a report from their man in Miami, who was able to discover next to nothing about Bradley Locke's disappearance.

Something had to be done, Agency personnel decreed. But it was a domestic issue. This presented a serious problem because technically he was just a missing person. By rights they should call in the FBI. How totally embarrassing.

A meeting was held in a conference room in the Caribbean Operations section.

"Year of work down the drain if we don't find him. Everything compromised," said Dan "Bobo" Quickwater, CIA Operations Director, pacing on the thick rug. This was *his* meeting. Things had to be sorted out. "You all know the deal. We found Locke's rental car, found out he'd been drinking, and came to a dead end right there. *Nada*. The man's gone. We can't even legally investigate this, damn it."

"Bradley Locke? Let him go. He's a cipher," the

man beside Quickwater said, smiling faintly. His name was Zile.

A third man, Damien Drail, shrugged. "Cipher, yes, but what if they get into his brain? One hit with scopalmine and our entire strategy is dead. Plus names. We can't afford any quick solutions, Zile."

A woman, Darcy Crown, nodded in agreement. "Send out a contract agent. Someone not us. Someone good."

"Not us who's good? There's no such person." Quickwater laughed softly. "Anybody have a suggestion? Who's got a salvage man?"

"Pete Ireland?" Darcy suggested. "He did great stuff in Panama."

"He's a serious drunk these days, arrested for DUI last week. I heard from Klondacki about him," Quickwater said. "Wasted man."

"Elena Contreras? She's good," Zile suggested.

"Was good. She's dead," Damien Drail put in. Damien was their current Ops Cuba Officer and was up on who was current in Miami. "We need someone unknown. Raúl Santiago's great but everyone knows him down there. Same with Gabriel Huff. Besides, the underground hates him since he dumped on Mas." Damien paused. "Miami's like third world. We need a Romero that nobody knows." He thought a moment longer, then he grinned, giving his even features a rakish twist. "The nun," he said. "The one my wife, Helene, knew? Didn't you run her for an agent when she was a teenager, Dan? Wasn't she good?"

"Cecile? That one? She joined a convent," Quickwater said. "Not a chance. A nun?"

"Nuns get raped. That's all." Zile shrugged. He looked happy at the thought.

Dan Quickwater didn't like that. He had known the nun before she was a nun. "She might have the right connections. But she's been out of it for years. No experience. Cecile probably wouldn't touch it."

Damien grinned again. "Not so. She became a private

8

investigator. My wife kept in touch off and on, but since Helene died four years ago, I'm not current on this nun. But the nun is probably still a private investigator. She has the right background. She may be good."

"A woman." Darcy Crown nodded. "I like that. Tell us about her."

Quickwater looked back for a moment. He could almost smell Switzerland's crisp air, see the lovely mountains, the valleys. "Cecile Buddenbrooks was great when she was young," he began, then thought some more. Beautiful girl, he'd had a crush on her, but she hadn't known. He'd been so young. Quickwater was older now, with venerable gray hair, long past the crush. Back then, Cecile had infiltrated a spy ring. She'd been a schoolgirl at a fancy boarding school. God knows, that had been crazy. But the kid had been brilliant. "Cecile was always in the right place at the right time. I liked her. We'll check her out. We'll have another staff meeting tomorrow morning on it. There's a rogue agent out there. Or something. We've got to pull him in." He tapped on his chair arm impatiently. This was still crazy, but it could work. "Damien, get in touch with the Boston Office. See what they can get on Cecile." Dan Quickwater felt an old rush, his face wrinkled in a smile. He'd love to see her himself.

Damien saw the look. "I'll get right on it."

Boston was having a cold spell. Unusual for October, the temperature had dropped to below thirty degrees for the past three nights, sending furnaces into spasms. Sister Cecile, of the Order of Our Lady of Good Counsel, had spent the days working in a soup kitchen in Dorchester, a part of Boston that splashed out like the body of a ripe pear, filling the western space along the Southeast Expressway. She had scrubbed floors, mopped tables, and washed the door frames.

At least the work kept her warm. Today she was covering the kitchen walls with pink paint that had been donated by the local True Value Hardware Store. The paint smell mixed with institutional pine scent and onions.

This was all in preparation for a city inspector who was due for an unannounced visit some time soon.

"We've got to pass inspection," she muttered to Sister Germaine, the convent cook who donated her time for two days a week. "These people need a place to eat."

"And good food," Sister Germaine added. She was peeling onions and tears were running down her cheeks. "Eh, look," she whispered. "Behind us is the inspector. *Il est ici!*"

Both nuns felt a brief moment of fear that the soup kitchen would have to close. It wasn't a religious affiliated charity, being run by the Afro-American Society of Abbot Street, but the nuns had become an integral part of its operation. They fed every denomination and color. The nuns liked that. But neither of them liked the looks of the man at the door. Simultaneously they each began to pray, silently, as they turned back to their work.

He stood there by the open kitchen door, watching the nuns. His eyes rested for a second on Cecile's cheek, a very attractive cheek with smooth, classic cheekbones. He didn't see how she tightened her grip on her brush and whispered out of the corner of her mouth to Sister Germaine, "There's green mold in the sink."

With one eye Cecile saw Germaine casually begin scrubbing the sink. With the other she glanced back at the stranger. He was slick, and there was an ominous bulge under his coat. It might be a wad of eviction papers, or perhaps a gun. In this neighborhood, city inspectors came prepared for every contingency. More than one carried a gun.

The stranger looked down at a photograph in his hand. "Sister Cecile Buddenbrooks?"

Sister Cecile had her back to the man at that moment. He sounded bad. Eviction, that was it, and it couldn't

10

come at a worse time with the winter influx of hungry, homeless people that had already begun.

Cecile put down the paintbrush. "I am she." The nun turned slowly.

"Sister, my name is Damien Drail. Could I speak with you privately? Quickwater sent me." He held out a hand, smiled, and walked forward.

"Who?" She ignored his outstretched hand. "Quickwater? Bobo Quickwater?"

"Bobo?" Did he have the right nun?

She forced a casual chuckle. "Daniel, of course. It's been a long time." Sister Cecile's mind was racing from the shock of hearing a name she hadn't heard in years, not, in fact, since she had been a teenager. Bobo? Amazing. She shook Damien Drail's hand, finally. "You're his friend?"

Damien Drail didn't answer the question. "May we speak?"

She nodded. "This way. Please follow me, Mr. Drail. Excuse us, Germaine."

She passed him, glancing down at the photograph he was holding in his left hand. It was her! Her high school graduation picture to be exact. Her past was coming back to haunt her. She would have to compose herself, immediately.

Cecile took in a lungful of the chilly air and folded her hands, nun-like, leading him into an almost round room. The desk was covered with boxes. Cases of canned beans and strawberry preserves were stacked crookedly against thin walls. A chair was piled with cartons of canned asparagus. Cecile sat on the peas.

"The beans are solid," she said. She was polite, aristocratic, and suddenly in command. There was no doubt who she really was, the daughter of a multi-millionaire industrialist from Connecticut, who had forsaken her father's obscene amounts of money to become a nun.

Damien Drail sat on canned beans. "You worked for Daniel Quickwater."

11

"Once," she agreed.

"Once," he almost whispered. "You worked for CIA then. You were a student at that school in Switzerland, and you made friends with an agent from the other side. Four years with us." He smiled grimly. "The youngest contract agent we ever had. You're a legend."

"Oh," Cecile said, suddenly embarrassed. "And Bobo remembers? Daniel, I mean." She smiled weakly. She had called him Bobo then. She'd had a crush on him. "How is he?"

"Fine. He remembers you. Actually, I first heard about you from my wife, Helene Waitt. You know she died of cancer? She was the only one at your school who knew you were with CIA. She spoke of you often."

"Helene? I was so sorry when I heard of her death." Cecile spoke slowly. "We kept in touch for years. I loved her." Her face glowed with remembrance.

"I loved her too," Damien Drail said. He didn't talk for a moment. "Really, it's because of her that I'm here. A job came up and I thought of you."

"It was a long time ago," Cecile said. "You need me now? I've been in the convent for years."

"We need you again as a contract agent. No danger," he added with an upward twist of his lips, "and some money. We would pay the going rate plus expenses."

"After all this time," she mused. It didn't sound right, somehow. "Why me?"

"When the situation came up, I remembered Helene had told me you had become a private investigator. We can't use our own people on domestic issues. Company policy. Daniel Quickwater agreed you'd been good. We checked your license. You have experience. You understand how we work." Damien smiled suddenly. "You still have some friends left in the Agency, after all this time. But I'm curious. Why a PI?"

"I am a nun *and* Private Investigator," she said firmly. "Nuns need to work these days. Living expenses are high. Nuns need to eat. We pray better on beans and

12

chicken than on bread and water, no matter what you may hear." She smiled a dazzling smile, setting Damien Drail back a step. "And we have the retirement problem. Old nuns need care. Care costs money."

"Helene said you were very well off."

"My father didn't want his money following me. He didn't like religion."

"What happened to all the money?"

"Do you really need to know?" She heard herself use CIA buzz-words. It made her shudder. It had been so long ago.

"Just curious."

"I can use the money for non-religious things. For my secular career I have a non-denominational credit card. My earned fees, on the other hand, go to the convent. Tell me about this job."

"First, do you know anyone in Miami?"

"Miami?"

"Maybe another nun?"

Cecile closed her eyes and thought. "Miami. Oh. Yes. Actually, an old friend who started in the Maryknolls. I believe she's down there now, in another order."

"Maryknolls? Perfect." Damien appeared satisfied. He reached into his pocket and pulled out a wad of papers. The bulge wasn't a gun after all. He walked over to her and from the papers he took a wrinkled photograph of Helene, himself, and a child. He handed the picture to her, credentials of some sort. The little girl was about four years old with streaky blond hair. "See? Helene and Leonie, my daughter. She's twelve now."

Cecile stared. "Lovely child. Of course. Helene sent me a birth announcement years ago. Where is the girl now?"

"At school in D.C. Her mother's been dead four years."

Cecile shook her head. Beautiful Helene was gone. She had left a pretty child. "Tell me about the job?"

"Go to Miami and find an agent who's disappeared

13

there. Your having a friend in Miami, particularly a former Maryknoll nun, should open a lot of doors with the underground, but they won't come near us. They would you, because you're a nun. The missing agent's name is Bradley Locke." Damien's expression became impassive. "You must find Bradley Locke."

"I see," Cecile said. It couldn't be so simple. "Tell me again why you can't use your own people. It doesn't quite make sense to me."

"This is a domestic issue. Not our jurisdiction."

"But the FBI is very good at these things. Haven't they been expanding their areas?"

He looked uncomfortable. "Our people and their people don't always work well together. We had a lot of discussion about how to handle the situation. It's unique, possibly embarrassing. CIA doesn't need being embarrassed again at this juncture. The missing man has important information in his head. *Very* important. We *must* get him back. Intact."

"By that you mean alive and brain cells in order." She looked at his serious expression and felt something vibrating inside her. Fear, maybe. "I charge three hundred dollars a day plus expenses."

"Fine. You'll be primarily on your own. I would be running you from Washington."

"When would I start?"

Damien was shuffling papers. "Soon." He frowned, then looked at the nun as if he had just made the worst mistake of his career in co-opting such a woman. He took the plunge. "Now. We want you to start immediately. Today."

Sister Cecile sat still for a moment.

"Tomorrow. I have to set up the convent to run without me. As far as my pay goes, I'll collect my working receipts, you people will reimburse me for all expenses. My daily fee should go directly to the convent."

14

"That's acceptable. I have everything with me. We can do all the paperwork. May I brief you now?"

"Please."

Sister Germaine was working on another heap of onions when Cecile returned from her conversation with Damien Drail. Cecile found her paintbrush and dipped it in the can, carefully wiping the drips off on the edge. "Old friend," she said. "Isn't it amazing how people turn up after years and years?"

It was strictly a rhetorical question, but Sister Germaine noticed that Sister Cecile's first stroke of paint looked very shaky indeed.

Damien was worried. Sister Cecile Buddenbrooks was good-looking, but possibly too much of a nun for the job. She didn't seem very tough. "Damn," Damien muttered as he left the soup kitchen. They needed the nun, particularly with her Maryknoll connection. Maryknoll missionaries had long been on the forefront of South American movements. This Sister Cecile knew the right people. He hoped.

The agent walked away toward downtown Boston, turning his collar up against the chilly wind. He shrugged, relieved to have the job done. Now, if only he could arrange to see that nun again on a personal level, life would be very interesting indeed. The nun was a knockout.

15

# 3

BRADLEY Locke had awakened the first morning of his captivity and puked over the edge of the filthy cot. The palmetto bugs watched from a distance, nodding between themselves. Bradley hadn't seen them yet. He was groggy and sick from the drug Olimpo had slipped him in his chocolate rum. But Bradley knew he had been had. What a fool. And what exactly had he said? He started to shake his head, but it hurt. What on earth had he said to that guy? And where was he?

Bradley rose slowly to check out the space. He discovered that he was in a high-windowed, screened room with a tightly locked door. The walls were green. The windows were narrow. No way out. The room had an impenetrable door with only a small swinging porthole at the bottom, suitable for a small animal. He saw bugs the size of dinosaurs. His floor was a jungle. Bradley stomped wildly and squashed one. The second bug made a dive for a crack in the wall.

"Hey, what the hell goes!" Bradley shouted after he tried the door. "Lemme outta here! I got things to do! I gotta go back." Then Bradley was quiet as he realized the implications of his predicament. He had to be cool and figure out what was going on. He knew too much to mess around. He kicked the dead bug into a corner. If that bastard, Olimpo, ever figured out he'd grabbed a CIA agent, Bradley's life wouldn't be worth a dime.

"Damn," Bradley whispered, then tried again. "Hey, Olimpo, I'll buy you ten women, you let me outta here.

Ten! You hear me?" Sweat began pouring down his face as Bradley rattled the door, smashing his fists on the wood. There was no answer, and nothing gave except a little blood on his knuckles.

When he finally calmed down, Bradley discovered that he had a bucket for a toilet, a bowl, and a jar of water for washing and drinking. He climbed up on the cot and opened the window, a window that was merely a screened slit with feathers stuck in the cracks. It gave him the creeps. Chickens? Everything about this place gave him the creeps. He spit a feather out of his mouth.

Eventually Bradley cleaned up his vomit, using some newspapers from a huge pile in one corner of the room. He stuffed the soiled papers out the cat door, and he began his new life.

The only words Bradley ever heard during the next two weeks were words informing him that he could slip the toilet bucket out for a dump, and the jar out for fresh water. Bradley Locke was thoroughly stuck while Olimpo and his close friend, Bajito Suárez, made serious plans.

Olimpo Olarte-Rodríguez knew that he had a valuable asset locked in his back room, but he had a problem. How to cash in Bradley Locke? The best bet, he decided, was to sell Bradley Locke to Fidel Castro himself. He began to ask around.

None of Olimpo's South Florida network had any advice on how to go about the sale to *El Señor*. And Olimpo had an extensive network. Olimpo Olarte-Rodríguez was the leader of an oddball group of insurgents who dealt drugs, Voodoo, and bicycle parts on the Miami River. Bajito Suárez was his thinking man, the one responsible for Olimpo's great ideas and rhetoric, but Bajito was appalled at this new twist in their life. What to do with a captured *Anglo*?

Bajito wracked his brain. He had an excellent brain, unquestionably. He was a very short Cuban Balsero whose goal in life was to get as rich as all the rest of the North Americans and become the brains behind a new Caribbean Trilateral Commission. Olimpo had similar ideas; it was his methods that were currently in dispute. With Olimpo to front for him, Bajito had seen the future clearly. Until this.

"You never should have," Bajito said. "You should have called me from the bar. Maybe you should have asked our man, Dirty Bobby, for advice. He works right there at the Hotel Place St. Michel, too. See, I hate Castro's guts. So don't we all. We almost kill ourselves getting off that damn paradise island, and now what? Who you gonna send back to make a deal with *El Señor*?"

"I stole him so we could get money," Olimpo said for the fiftieth time. "Castro would give his gold teeth for this man."

They were in the front room of Olimpo's place eating taco burgers. Bradley was safe in the back room, separated from them by a storage room where there was a small bed and several bales of marijuana waiting for a price rise. "Dirty Bobby's no help. He's not subtle, anyway," Olimpo defended himself. "We deal with this ourselves. We gotta send an envoy to Cuba."

"You gotta be crazy. Who's gonna go there? We can't even let him go, we're dead," Bajito squeaked. He had a high voice to go with his small stature, a fact he frequently and loudly blamed on the lack of proper nutrition under Castro's regime. "Just when we were getting some money together. Shit, Olimpo. I done some checking on this Bradley Locke. The guy's on a fucking vacation. So all this talk he's making is just a lot of talk. He's probably some salesman from Toledo, Ohio, taking a trip to the beach. I say we stick him, put him in a canal some place for the alligators."

Olimpo had never heard of Toledo, Ohio. "He knew names, Bajito, he knew stuff. Like he said he knew *stuff*. I said I was a *sapo*, and he *knew*. How many dumb

18

Anglos know about Noriega's *sapos*, greatest force ever? How's the man know that? I tell you, he's gold. I asked him if he's government and he got real quiet, like he's a big government mouth. He got that look. Now we just get to the right people we collect big money."

"I gotta think about this, Olimpo. Maybe we got a long term asset, maybe not. We soften him up a little longer. Don't talk to him for a while. He'll talk when I figure out what we're gonna do."

During the weeks of discussion Bradley Locke waited, safe and solitary except for one Palmetto bug he left alive for company. It crept out from the crack in the wall when it grew dark and shared Bradley's dinner every night: food from Taco Bell. Bradley's only real worry was that his female Manx cat, Bismarck, would grow lonesome ...d bored in the kitty kennel where she had been parked. After a few days of captivity Bradley had begun to identify strongly with Bismarck. His litter box was changed once a day, food was pushed in, he was behind bars. Bismarck, no doubt, would prowl her enclosure by the hour, limited by tiny walls. Bradley did the same.

To keep in shape Bradley did ten push-ups every morning and then read the *Miami Herald*, foraging through a five foot high stack of old issues piled in one corner of the room. CIA had never trained him for this. He took to ripping out The Far Side cartoons, memorizing obsolete sports records, and learning recipes from the food pages. He thought about things in the comics to tell Bismarck. He memorized punch lines, reciting them to the huge yellow and brown bug who frequently lingered next to a crack in the wall. Anything to keep sane, he told himself more than once. Anything.

Meanwhile Bajito learned something more about their captive through the Panamanian ex-*sapo* who was known as Dirty Bobby Ortez, or the Dirt Man. Bajito reported his news to Olimpo.

"Dirty Bobby thinks he's super *sapo*. And Dirty Bobby

tells me there was some kind of cop looking for that Bradley Locke we got, snooping around Hotel Place St. Michel."

"So?"

"Private cop, that's what Dirty Bobby says." Bajito started to move around the shack, his high-heeled cowboy boots tapping on the cement floor in a dance pattern. "Dirty Bobby thinks he's fucking smart because he killed people for lunch in Panama."

"The Dirt Man did that," Olimpo said knowingly. "Very close to Noriega." Olimpo was proud of knowing Noriega himself, but his own association with the *sapos* had been very peripheral. The *sapos* were Noriega's secret police and were responsible for unprecedented acts of terror. Olimpo had merely procured girls for Noriega's orgies.

"The Dirt Man crazy about blood, see," Olimpo said. "So you gotta watch it with him. I don't trust him, but we need him. People know we got Dirty Bobby on our side, they don't screw us."

Bajito shrugged. "I say we feed the *gringo* to alligators some place. He's not safe."

"Now you're talking crazy, Bajito." Olimpo took a long and final drag of hashish before stubbing it out on a plate covered with chocolate cookie crumbs. "You know how much money government's got? We make a deal with Fidel, or maybe even deal with the U.S. Government, I mean, maybe we buy Guyana with the money we get." He paused, trying to think. "What you do is tell the Dirt Man to set up a deal with this private cop he saw. Say he heard of the problem from friends, he maybe arranges a trade for some money. Simple, right? We trade the man for money. Meanwhile, we send a man to Cuba and make a deal there. Two deals going. We can't lose. Get it?"

Bajito got it. "Okay, Olimpo," Bajito said finally. "We tell Dirty Bobby to get some money from this cop in his bar before we give out any information: up front stuff.

20

But what's he gonna tell the cop for information? We don't want to wreck our group, Olimpo. We got power plans, money plans. I don't like this stuff. Who we gonna send to Cuba?"

"Find a Canadian. They go to Cuba. We're talking major money," Olimpo said firmly. "You gotta think big. That's the trouble with you, always thinking small. Why you think I brought this man home with me? We're gonna trade him for lots of money. Why the fuck you think I did this?"

Bajito gnawed on a dirty fingernail. "Yeah, sure, Olimpo. I'll go talk with Dirty Bobby. But he's gonna want to kill him. Wait and see. Might as well kill him now, save some trouble."

"No trouble. You'll see."

# 4

"PAUL, How's your condo in Miami?" Cecile spoke into the convent telephone. She had reached her lawyer, Paul Dorys, whose office was on State Street in downtown Boston.

"Just fine. How's the convent in Dorchester?" Paul's day was made. He loved hearing from Sister Cecile. He had been in love with her for years and still proposed marriage on a regular basis. The sweet sadness of their youth gave him no right to her now, but somehow she was still there and she always would be. Paul was permanently in love.

"Can I use your Miami condo for a while?"

"If I can come too."

"I thought I'd bring Sister Raphael."

"No need to do that."

"I'll stay at a hotel, then."

"Don't be silly. Bring Raphael. Who's watching the convent while you're gone?"

"Sister Germaine."

"Good." Paul propped his feet up on his desk. The sand of his past had just run through his fingers, again. Cecile was such a part of him. But in the current reality, it had been a busy week at his law firm, with no letup in sight. Paul would have left it all and gone to Miami with Cecile. "Why are you going to Miami?"

Sister Cecile began on her story, a story vaguely based on reality. Paul could tell by her tone that something was going on. "Our mother superior in France, Mère Sulpicia,

22

has ordered me down there to get the nuns' retirement home started. We have enough money to break ground somewhere. We just don't have the ground yet. I may be down south for some time."

"I didn't know you were going to be in charge of the retirement home." Paul frowned. It meant Cecile would be out of Boston for too long. "When do you plan to leave?"

"Tomorrow."

"Flights are cheaper with a week's notice."

"It doesn't matter. I'll put it on the credit card."

"You must have a case down there, or are you cheating on Daddy's will?"

There was a long silence. Then, "Daddy never understood."

"You're cheating on the will?"

"No."

Paul thought quickly over Cecile's problem. Her multi-millionaire father had been clear in his will: not one cent of his money could have anything to do with his daughter's religion or her vocation as a nun. Old Jerry Buddenbrooks had been an avowed atheist and had been heartbroken by his daughter's decision to become a Catholic nun. She had rejected everything he believed in. Or didn't, as it were. Paul, as her lawyer, had been able to get around the will by using a credit card system whereby Cecile could charge anything of a non-religious nature, and access the millions of dollars. The expenditures were checked by an impartial bank trustee. Cecile used the card to pursue her profession as a private investigator and stock Boston's nondenominational soup kitchens, kitchens like the one she had worked at that very morning.

"Well? What gives?"

"I'll be using the credit card as stipulated."

"So you *won't* be buying land for the retirement home for the nuns?"

"I plan to."

"You have a case?" He was curious. It wasn't like Cecile to keep secrets from him. And bringing Sister Raphael was suspicious. Raphael was in her seventies, but blessed with a terrific mind. She frequently helped Cecile with her investigative work.

"I can't say. Really, Paul. Trust me."

"And you're actually bringing Raphael?" He tapped on the telephone in mild disbelief.

"This is all very hard to explain."

Paul could hear the strain in her voice. She wouldn't lie. She couldn't. Best not push.

"Paul, could you make two reservations for Miami International Airport, and have a car reserved for me there?"

He sighed and shook his head as if she could see him. "Be glad to."

"And, one more favor."

"Sure."

"Don't order a Porsche for me this time. I get so embarrassed."

Paul laughed. "Anything you say. Have a good trip."

"Thanks, Paul."

"Your humble servant." He didn't like this at all. What wasn't she telling him?

"It will be a lot of running around at first," Cecile murmured, talking more to herself than to Sister Raphael. The two nuns were in flight. The American Airlines 747 was relatively quiet as it headed south from Boston's Logan International Airport. Beside her, Sister Raphael grunted in assent. She was as suspicious of Sister Cecile's motives as Paul had been. Much as she liked the thought of going to Florida during October's chilly days, Raphael knew her younger friend had something besides the retirement home in mind.

"What's going on, Cecile?"

"The retirement home. I told you. There are churches

24

locating in shopping malls these days. Maybe we can buy a shopping mall and turn it into a retirement home."

"No. I mean *really* going on."

Cecile gave up. There was no way she could fool her old friend, and no reason to, either. "All right. We're on a case, Raphael. I'm working for the CIA and your job is to help keep my cover by doing the work on the retirement home." Cecile blasted it out all at once, knowing the old nun could handle it.

"Oh."

Sister Cecile felt infinite relief. "Yes. There's work to be done. I guess you should know everything." Then Cecile explained, her voice muffled by the hum of the engine. She went back as far as she dared, revealing her early work for the CIA, her current job, and her current worries. "Government work is always dangerous because of the money. Governments have so much money it makes people crazy. And misplaced idealism. That's the other problem." She pressed her lips together firmly. She looked quite beautiful in her skepticism of the current world order.

"As long as the job is ethical and the pay is real," Raphael murmured. "Tell me about the missing person."

"Bradley Locke is a long-time agent. He won a week in Miami Beach from a cat food company. The man dotes on cats. He has a Manx cat, and people who have worked with Bradley claim the cat is an obsession with the man. Because of the cat, they assume he didn't disappear voluntarily. That may be a mistaken assumption, of course, but in any case, Bradley boarded the cat three weeks ago, when he went to claim the prize. He was last seen on Thursday, the first week of October. He was to come home the following Sunday. He's been missing over two weeks. He knows too much stuff the Agency doesn't want to be let out. Plans for Cuba. Names of people in place. Critical dates."

"They don't care if he's dead, then. As long as what he knows doesn't get out."

"Damien didn't say that."

"He wouldn't. So he's been missing about two weeks," Raphael reiterated. "And the entire CIA can't find a simple agent in Miami? I'm glad I don't pay taxes anymore if that's how they spend our money."

"You *may* be paying taxes, Raphael. I've signed you on as my assistant, six hundred dollars a week."

"Oh." That took a minute to sink in. "All right. What else should I know?"

"Not much. Bradley spoke a little Spanish, did his job, no children, he divorced some time ago, and he lived alone except for the cat."

"A moderately good man," Raphael nodded. "Fine. I'm on. But, Cecile, we really don't know anything *real* about this man." Her old brain had shifted into gear as questions formed. "Could he have foreign contacts we don't know about?"

"That, I'm going to discover."

The two nuns were silent. Sister Raphael pulled out her rosary beads and began to pray, and shortly after she was sound asleep, lulled by the droning airplane engine. Sister Cecile prayed too, using her fingers to count the Hail Marys. She had just started on the third Glorious Mystery when the plane passed over a small house near the everglades where Bradley Locke was eating his twenty-seventh burrito and sipping his fifteenth warm Mexi-shake.

Not too many minutes later the plane settled down with a bump at Miami International Airport.

# 5

THE jet landed with a thud, then a series of bumps.

"Thick air," Cecile noted as they settled down on the runway.

"Thick food," Raphael murmured, opening her eyes.

They stepped out into Miami International Airport, pushed through crowds, retrieved their luggage, and headed out to the sidewalk in front of the terminal, gasping at the sweet, warm breeze as they passed from air-conditioning to the tropics. There was a hum in the air: bugs, airplanes, the buzz of international danger. Sister Cecile felt it, but she didn't say anything. She worried about Sister Raphael, old and tossed into possible peril, dragged into the city of Miami, a strange, almost third world city where anything could happen. "Paul said someone would be here with a car for us. A nice little rental car. Somebody should be holding a sign. I distinctly said no Porsche, Raphael. He's done that to me before." Cecile dropped her luggage onto the sidewalk. Then she looked behind her, back at the terminal. No danger. They were two nuns in blue skirts and white blouses. Nuns were invisible.

"I think an off-white habit," Raphael managed, wheezing from the torrid air. "Blue absorbs the sun."

"You'll get used to it. The car should be here. Right outside the American Airlines terminal, Paul told me. Someone will have a sign and the car." Cecile looked up and down past the shuttle buses until she spotted a bright

27

red machine with a man before it holding a sign that read, "Sister Cecile."

"I'm afraid I see it, Raphael. I really think it's a Ferrari Testarossa. Do you believe Paul would do this to me? He knows how I feel about conspicuous consumption."

"I always liked Paul," Raphael said and pulled up her luggage. "He may be doing this for a reason. You may *need* a fast car, Cecile."

"The Testarossa is definitely high performance," Cecile grunted as she picked up her bag from where it stuck to some melted gum on the pavement. "The car has major acceleration. You're right, Raphael. Maybe Paul knew what he was doing. Maybe he was just being thoughtful. Although he hasn't a clue we're down here on a case. He thinks it's all for the retirement home."

"Knowing him, he guessed the truth. Besides, he likes cars like this," Sister Raphael said.

"You've driven this kind of car before," the car agent said matter-of-factly after the nuns had introduced themselves. "At least that's what they told me at the agency. The manual is in the glove compartment. There are a lot of new features. The AC is on. I left the engine running, so the car will be cool."

"Just what I wanted to hear," Raphael sighed and began walking around to the passenger side.

The man continued to talk about some of the innovations while Cecile let her eyes roam over the vents and grills. Few changes have been made in the car since production began after the car's debut at the 1984 Paris Salon. It was not a car she had actually driven before, but she knew sports cars. Paul, bless him, had done it again. She would have felt better in a small American utility car, but this is what she had. God willing, she wouldn't need all that speed. On the other hand, she thought, running a hand over the bright red surface, it just might be dangerous. She could be spotted anywhere in this machine.

Clambering in required some agility because the cabin was low, but Raphael made it easily enough. Cecile bumped her head on the roof.

"Here we go," Cecile murmured and settled in, rubbing her brow. She put her hands on the steering wheel where the three alloy spokes were placed so her thumbs cradled the two upper ones while her hands rested on the leather rim. It could have been made for her. Money, she thought, could buy almost anything. Almost. "Even Ferraris can bring you closer to God."

Raphael peered out the tinted window. "Don't drive that fast, please."

"That wasn't what I meant."

The nose dropped so low it was invisible from inside.

"I'm ready," Raphael said. Her head was back, eyes open, hands clutching one another as Sister Cecile accelerated, pushing the old nun back against the seat.

Cecile made surprisingly good time to Paul's condo on the beach, unintentional rubber laid at each stoplight. Paul's place was on the third floor of a high security condo overlooking Miami Beach. The living room was huge and cool and the message box by the telephone was blinking.

"Paul must be making more money than I suspected," Cecile mused, looking around. "He told me he'd have a friend stop by and make the place ready. And there's a computer here, too, Raphael. And a fax machine."

"There are three bedrooms," Raphael's voice came from behind a door. "I'll be unpacking in this one. I'm taking the small room; it's only about the size of the convent chapel."

"Paul likes nice things."

"He does," Raphael agreed, still speaking from the bedroom. "He likes you."

"I keep telling him things aren't important," Cecile said, ignoring Raphael's words. She sat down on a huge couch, poked a button, and listened to the message on the answering machine. It was a greeting from Paul, asking

29

her to call him if there were any problems. There weren't, so she didn't. Although she should, she told herself. She really should call Paul. Later.

The nuns unpacked and finally were able to sit in the living room, drink sparkling water, and look out the glass wall at the ocean skyline. Huge clouds stacked up to enormous heights. Strange horizontal lightning flickered sideways in the distance. This was no Boston sky.

"Can't we just take a vacation?" Raphael asked. "A retreat, maybe?"

"Later," Cecile said. "I have to call the local CIA agent, a Felipe Klondacki, who did the initial report on Bradley Locke. Damien told me about him, and I read Felipe's report at my briefing." Her eyes were half closed as she ran over, in her mind, what she was really doing here. "You have a lot of work ahead of you, Raphael. You're in charge of buying the convent retirement home. While you do that, I will find Bradley Locke. We're being paid."

"I'll keep my eyes open," the old nun said. "Wide."

"Good. Now, that Testarossa. It's so obvious. I'm going to rent a little cheap car."

"Right," Raphael said. She was very serious, but her cheeks were growing pink with excitement.

"I'm really counting on you, Raphael."

"I'll be happy to drive that red car," Raphael said, "if it's too much for you."

"I can handle it," Cecile said firmly. "However, there may be times. I expect if you showed up in that thing to negotiate for convent land, the price of the property would triple."

"A serious consideration," Raphael said.

"And now I'll call Felipe Klondacki."

# 6

FELIPE Klondacki had just completed a deal with some local drug pushers. He had pocketed five hundred dollars cash, not much money considering the size of the deal, but he hadn't given the dealers much in return for the money either. Only a day to get out of town. It was a game he played and he always celebrated his little victories by drinking a Key Lime Hopper on the screened patio of his Kendall town house. The Hopper was his favorite drink.

He had just settled back when his cordless telephone began to ring. He ignored it. The temperature had already dropped from a daytime high of eighty-eight degrees to the mid-seventies. The humidity was seventy-eight percent and it was rather fine weather for an October Friday in Miami. He didn't need any telephone calls. Felipe let it ring and sipped his drink.

Disregarding the occasional small deals, Felipe was a good agent. He was sixty-four years old and looked forward to retiring soon, perhaps here in Miami. His coal black hair had turned gray ten years ago, his children had grown and married, his wife had died in her sleep in June of 1992, and he was generally tired. His official job title was Resident Legal Technician at a federal agency dealing with import and export licenses. That was his cover. In fact, he had a lot to do with observing and recording Cuban exile activity in Miami's inner city. And playing games with the locals. There was always something new.

"Shut up, telephone."

He finally answered the telephone on the tenth ring.

*"Hola,"* he said.

"I'm looking for Felipe Klondacki. This is Sister Cecile."

"Oh, yes, sure, was expecting you. I'm Felipe. How you doing?"

"Good. May we get together tonight? I'm anxious to hear all you have."

Friday night? Not a nice thought, working. The Miami Hurricanes were on the tube and he'd been looking forward to watching the game after his drink. "It's late," he said.

"I know, but things are urgent. I don't mind the hour."

Felipe shrugged. "Okay. Louie's Outdoor Restaurant at eight-thirty. We talk, eat. Know where it is?"

"No."

"Where you coming from?"

A few minutes later Sister Cecile hung up the telephone. "Louie's Outdoor Restaurant at eight-thirty," she said.

"I wonder if they have tacos there," Raphael mused. "I saw a lot of frozen burritos in Paul's freezer. I'll put one in that microwave for myself as long as you'll be eating out. But, Cecile, how does one use a microwave?"

"Sister Germaine wouldn't consider having one of those," Cecile said. "Work of the devil, Germaine says. I've never used one."

"I've always felt they must cause cancer," Raphael agreed, "but all young people seem to live by them. My nephew uses his for everything. I guess the burrito package will tell me what to do."

"I'm sure."

Sister Cecile arrived at Louie's at exactly eight-thirty, pulling up with a lurch because she hadn't quite gotten the feel of the massive twelve-inch molybdenum cast-iron disc braking system mounted within each wheel. The sudden stop threw her back hard.

Every set of eyes at the outdoor cafe turned to the Testarossa. Not that such a car was rare in this part of the world where every third vehicle seemed to be a Rolls or a Mercedes, but fate had opened up a parking space directly in front of the cafe. The car looked good. So did Sister Cecile. She had dressed for the car and wore an ankle length, blue cotton skirt, and a white blouse with the gold cross. She had left off her veil. This way she did not resemble a nun. It was her private detective disguise.

Felipe Klondacki was sitting at a table under a huge purple umbrella. He had told her to look for a man in a white hat; he was looking for a nun. He did not expect to see what he saw as she approached, a lovely woman in a long skirt emerging from an unreal car. Cecile walked confidently up to his table and sat down. "Felipe?"

"Uh, yup."

"I'm Sister Cecile. You are Mr. Klondacki?"

"Yes, Felipe, please." He half rose from his chair, then crashed back down.

She sat. "Felipe, let's order something and talk. I feel there's so much you can tell me. I'm hoping to get this disappearance cleared up."

Felipe was a pragmatic man. How else could he have put his kids through college? He was back in form after a momentary breakdown. "Maybe. I'll tell you all I know, then we take a run over to the Place St. Michel and you can see for yourself. How's that sound?"

"Excellent. Now, what is that you're drinking?"

Cecile ordered a Cuba Grande Platter, containing a selection of everything from black beans to coconut fried plantains, and a strawberry Margarita. Over food and drink Cecile quizzed Felipe. "You went to this bar where Mr. Locke was last seen. And nobody had seen him?"

"Oh, sure, he was seen. Had six Blue Lagoons. I tried one and they're a tough drink."

"So he was potted?"

"You mean, drunk?" Felipe flashed a gold tooth. "Yes. Very limber when he left."

"Right, yes. Who did he leave with?"

"The bartender described a tall Latino. You read the report, didn't you?"

"Yes. Maybe you've thought of more?"

"I questioned all the staff and that's what I came up with. One of the kitchen help might have something. He said he might have remembered the face. Said to come back."

"Did you?"

"That's what we do next. It's your case now."

"Right."

"Want me to drive? I know the way."

"I can handle it. Thanks."

They went in the Testarossa. She drove.

"You filed a very complete report with Damien, or whomever," Cecile said as she shifted into second gear. "Except you didn't mention he was drunk, nor anything about the possibility of this other person."

"I don't put drinking in records. Records last. Don't want to do our subject out of job." He paused significantly. "If we ever find him."

"We'll find him. Have you ever met Bradley Locke?"

"U-uh," Felipe mumbled, distracted. He was running his hand along the English Connolly leather upholstery and moving his feet back and forth on the Italian wool carpet. There was plenty of leg room, even for his length. He could hardly believe it. Even the air inside this car was different.

"Do you know Bradley?" she repeated.

"No, actually, I never met the man," he said. "I just followed leads and got lucky. Bradley Locke's rental car was found near the Hotel Place St. Michel, so I checked possible places in the Gables area. I hit gold at the hotel bar. You read the report; you know Locke never returned

34

to his own hotel. And I don't think he just walked. Not with what he knew."

"He has some critical intelligence."

"So they say. I did my best but I've been here too long. Everyone knows me so I didn't push my search. But someone like you? You can just slide right in and ask. Fresh cover."

"I hope. I hope he's still alive."

"I hope he keeps his damn mouth shut."

Cecile shook her head, wiggling the gearshift. "I couldn't get out of second gear on my way over here. Now, how do you get to this bar? Is it in Coral Gables?"

"Uh, yeah, we want to pop off at Ponce De Leon Boulevard. Take a left here. Maybe we can get you out of second." Felipe stretched back to enjoy the ride.

Not too many gears later, Cecile pulled up outside the Hotel, parking directly in front of the building. Maybe it was the car that caused others to fade out as it approached; Cecile had never had such luck with parking spaces. This time she managed to emerge from the car gracefully, having almost worked out the entry and exit problems.

They walked to the main door on Alcazar. Clearly, Bradley had not been slumming. It looked like a club in Boston or maybe the Pierre in New York: brick, awnings, big tinted windows. Inside Cecile saw ceilings arched with strange angels in shells for lights, and a mahogany bar to the left. Her kind of place she thought, at least the type she had favored before she had taken her vows.

They pushed by the lobby and settled into seats in the bar room. "Mineral water, please," Cecile murmured. Felipe began fumbling for his cigarettes. "But, please feel free, Felipe, maybe they'll have those lime hooker things you had at the other place. I'll pay with my credit card." She looked at Felipe uneasily, wondering how much he had drunk before they had started out. His voice had become slightly louder as they had conversed in the car.

Behind the scenes, the entire staff of the Place St.

35

Michel was chatting about the client with the red Ferrari Testarossa, because the night chief had arrived at the same time the car had pulled up. "Big tipper," someone said, *"Muy rico."* The discussion in the kitchen was in Spanish, but the word for Ferrari was universal. Slick cars were a dime a dozen in the Gables, but this car had a serious mystique and meant there was heavy money somewhere. Maybe a movie star. Maybe Sylvester Stallone's new girlfriend.

One at a time the kitchen and wait staff peered out or ran around to the front of the hotel to catch a glimpse of the car. Dirty Bobby, Olimpo's compatriot, came around from the kitchen and looked at the couple in the bar, the owners of this machine. He recognized Felipe at once as the man who had come looking for Bradley Locke. The man who smelled like cop. The gray hair, the loose jowls, the gold-toothed smile. And a Ferrari. Holy shit, he thought. Money! He rubbed his hands together. Pay dirt. Olimpo had actually made a killing.

Dirty Bobby Ortez licked his lips. He loved killings. It was time to make one of his own.

# 7

JUST to make absolutely sure it really was a Ferrari Testarossa and not a cheap imitation Japanese car, Dirty Bobby went out the back door and around to see for himself. He moved fast, graceful for a heavy man. He wasn't supposed to leave the kitchen, but these people and that car were his. Besides, he had plenty of salads made and they didn't pay him enough. He tried to make up for it by eating everything in sight as he worked, but it was tough to keep eating all the time with the *maricón* he had for a boss. He would have quit this job already except he liked the connections in Coral Gables. A lot of money moved through this bar.

Dirty Bobby walked right out the kitchen door, around the back alley, and out front where he stopped and stared at the car. "Son a bitch," he whispered reverently. "Son a bitch."

After drinking his fill of the car, Dirty Bobby went back to the kitchen and pulled out a pile of lettuce to break up. The couple had to be here investigating Locke's disappearance, and he was their man. Dirty Bobby was about to cash in. He stuffed a tomato into his mouth and chewed. He knew just what to do next, because Olimpo had passed the word. Olimpo gave him a lot of respect because of their history in Panama, but on the flip side, Dirty Bobby would do anything to please Olimpo.

Dirty Bobby ripped lettuce leaves for a minute, deciding

37

just what it was he wanted to say to the rich people, then he waited until there was a lull in the kitchen.

He scooted around and through the door behind the bar and raced up to Cecile and Felipe's table.

He stood there, breathing heavily, as a lettuce leaf dropped down in front of Sister Cecile. "Meet me out back in fifteen minutes. I got some very important information for you," Dirty Bobby said to Felipe, then he backed up, spun around, and vanished.

"There's your man," Felipe chuckled. "Bless my Mama's Mexican luck. The one I was telling you about, Cecile. Your possible link. I have instincts in this business. Good instincts." Felipe glanced down at his watch to check the time. "Name's Bobby Ortez. Joe the bartender, that tall guy, picked up on the description at first, then that fat one, Bobby Ortez, came out. He's got something, somewhere."

"Tell me more about him. Bobby Ortez? Exactly what did he say? Who is he?"

"I asked around. He's known. Got a reputation for being tough, they call him the Dirt Man. He's bad news. He works part-time in the kitchen; he said he was here that night and caught a glimpse of Bradley and the guy he was with. Thought he might have recognized the Latino. But you have to be careful," Felipe advised. "Ortez may be lying though his teeth. Could be just after money and didn't see anything. Don't forget, he's kitchen help. Probably does drugs. I'll make the introductions and pass him over to you. Like I said. They all know me."

"Good job, Felipe. I hope it doesn't bother you, doing all the donkeywork on this case and just handing it to me."

"It's your case," he said. "I'm involved up to the armpits in a lot of other things."

Conversation stalled at that point. Felipe worked on another drink, Cecile spun her mineral water and looked around. She liked dark bars, at least she had when she was eighteen, a time when her vocation hadn't been entirely clear in her mind. She and Paul had particularly

38

liked the one three blocks from her room when she attended Columbia University. She shook her head to clear out malingering thoughts and even malingering doubts about who she was and what she was doing in a posh bar in South Florida with an aging spy. It didn't seem real. Maybe she shouldn't even be a nun.

Yes. She was a nun. They never left her alone; the devils were still there. And Bobby Ortez, the Dirt Man, was quite possibly a real one.

"Time's up," Felipe said.

The bill had already been paid so they rose together, went out the front door, and proceeded past the Testarossa. They went behind the restaurant where a modest dumpster and a number of air-conditioning units filled up a large area. Heat rose from the alley. They were surrounded by the smell of fried food, the whirr of fans, the low cries of birds. A distant street lamp barely pierced the shadows, and the bulb over the back door flickered dismally.

Dirty Bobby came out.

He stopped, looking from Felipe to the nun and back. "No woman," he said.

"She's the one you have to deal with," Felipe grunted. "This is Cecile. She's looking for a friend. It was her friend that disappeared."

"I'm Bobby," Dirty Bobby said. "Okay, miss, you come in that red car?"

"Of course," she said, deciding instantly to play rich.

"Okay, what you wanna know?" Bobby looked as though he were swelling.

"I need to know what happened to my friend, Bradley Locke, who was last seen here."

"Why?" Dirty Bobby asked.

Cecile's eyes widened as she looked at him, the tomato sauce on his cheek, a flattened tomato wedge stuck in his apron, a lettuce leaf emerging from a pocket. He resembled a very ominous salad.

"I'm a friend from home." Cecile managed a smile.

"What you going to pay me if I got some ideas about this *tipo* you want to find?" Bobby asked.

Cecile looked at Felipe but he just shrugged and rocked from foot to foot. No help.

"A hundred dollars?" she finally said, waffling.

"*Qué putada!* Peanuts to me."

"*Boca de gusano!* Don't talk to me like that!" Cecile retorted.

"So, I need more money. You want a investigation, that costs real money." Dirty Bobby looked slightly abashed at Cecile's mispronounced Spanish words. "Maggot mouth," she had called him.

"Well, how much?"

"Five hundred I find out something for you. Then we go from there."

"Two hundred. That's it. What are my guarantees you don't take my money and run?" Cecile asked. "You could be lying. I'll give you a hundred now, a hundred when you get back to me. That way I'll be sure you don't forget. It's very important."

"My name is good. I got friends all over this town. Ask anybody. They tell you, Dirty Bobby, he's smart, works hard, knows a lot. You need anything, Dirty Bobby, that's me, he can get it. You can trust me. Know what I mean? I take a hundred now."

"Dirty Bobby?" She mumbled the name to herself. "Drugs and all that?" Cecile asked.

"I find you anything. I don't deal, see, I don't never do nothing wrong. Okay, hundred later." Dirty Bobby jumped up and down like a walrus waiting for a fish, his new sneakers making little puffs of dust rise on the dirt. "See, I wouldn't touch drugs. Not me."

Cecile knew he was lying.

Felipe was watching the conversation with growing interest. His hobby was extorting from drug dealers. He started a slow smile as his eyes took in Dirty Bobby's expensive shoes and diamond earring.

Cecile saw Felipe's change of expression. It made her

40

apprehensive, but she would confront that emotion later. She patted her purse. "Deal. Two hundred dollars cash total. I'll expect an answer from you by tomorrow. A very valuable answer."

"Tomorrow? I don't got no time. I need three days. You're talking to a working man here. I got responsibilities. Three days," Dirty Bobby said. "I gotta reach these people that I'm thinking about. These things take time. How about Monday night right here, same time same place? Bring the other hundred, maybe more. You gotta get ready to make a big deal with these ones I'm talking to."

Cecile looked down at her watch. It was ten forty-five. This was Friday. It didn't feel right, waiting. Bradley Locke could be dead in three days. But she had no choice. "All right. I'll be here then. Monday night. Three days. I'm giving you this cash now, Bobby. I expect full value for my money. Understand?"

She delved into her purse and found the envelope of cash that Damien had given her for expenses. She pulled out a hundred dollar bill and handed it over. "Could I have a receipt, please?"

"Receipt?" he laughed. "My word, eh? *Basta.*"

"Oh yes, *basta.*" Cecile stepped back and Dirty Bobby stuffed the bill in his pocket, then he turned and vanished into the bowels of the hotel.

She turned to Felipe. "Think I'll find anything out?"

"Can't say. That little creep's into everything. He stinks of drugs. I'll give you a call tomorrow, maybe I can find something out around town. We'll see his game."

"Thanks, Felipe. I could use some help on this."

"Sure, why not. Listen, instead of a call, let's get together. I'll meet you tomorrow night, my place. I live in Kendall. You come by about eight and we'll have a talk."

He pulled a scrap of paper and pencil out of his sports coat pocket and scribbled his address on it. "Just head out

41

Kendall Drive. Easy. Eight, tomorrow night. Saturday. You go on home, now. I think I'll hang here a little, maybe get another drink, maybe go follow up a lead I have with something else. I can get home by myself."

"You're sure? I could drop you off at your home."

"I'm set," Felipe smiled. "I'll catch a cab."

"Fine. See you tomorrow, Felipe. Take care."

Sister Cecile left in a hurry. Felipe watched as the red Ferrari spun out. He saw her turn back and give him a last look, then a wave. Damn nice car, he thought. This lovely lady was really a nun, his contacts had told him, and it made him wonder if he should have been a priest like his mama always wanted. He shrugged. It was too late now.

# 8

CECILE slipped into the Testarossa easily, looking back as she raced away. Felipe was a gray shadow, moving back in the night. He was gone. She didn't feel quite right about leaving him there alone.

She shrugged. It was his choice.

The condo was almost dark when she came in a half an hour later. Raphael had left a small desk lamp burning beside Paul's computer and a note beside it. "Paul is on the internet and I latched on to a real estate listing service. Several good leads to follow this weekend. Raphael."

That was good, Cecile thought. She settled into one of Paul's more comfortable chairs, pulled out her prayer book, and began to say her evening prayers.

Felipe Klondacki took a walk down a dark street in Coral Gables. Not much was going on. The streets were almost bare of traffic. An infrequent couple strolled by. Flashy cars going fast. Maybe he should just grab a cab and go home. He didn't need any extra money now. His kids were settled, his wife gone. He was getting old, tired, he should quit the games he played, but the years of scrounging for his kids had turned into a habit. He felt edgy. He'd never sleep if he went home this early. Besides, some of his best Agency scoops had come through his games. One never knew. Certainly the Agency didn't.

Felipe returned to the Hotel Place St. Michel. He found a waiting place back in the area behind the building and sat beside a metal post on a small loading platform. From there he was high enough to have a perfect view of everyone who came and went out the hotel's back door. He leaned back against the post and settled in, lit up a cigarette and inhaled deeply. Once in a while the kitchen door would open and someone would come out to have a smoke. Frequently the familiar scent that came across the hot night air was sweet, sweeter than tobacco. Felipe took a deep breath of drifting marijuana clouds and knew he was in the right place at the right time.

Eventually Dirty Bobby came out and began to walk away, finished for the night. A gym bag was swinging from his arm.

"Bobby," Felipe whispered loudly.

"Eh? Who that?"

"Me, Felipe. I've been waiting for you." Felipe jumped down off the loading platform, thudding on the dry earth like an overweight cat.

"What the hell you want?"

"I know you deal. I want some inside stuff, I want a cut or I'll see to it you're all finished." Felipe came up close as he spoke. He was a good six inches taller than the Panamanian but tonight he had no weapon. Felipe hadn't thought he'd need one traveling with the nun, and he still didn't. He was certain that his height and weight and experience would set him way above this thick little man. What he didn't know was that not too many years ago Dirty Bobby had been a prime mover in Noriega's *sapos*, the government secret police of Panama. Dirty Bobby could stop a man with one fast clip of those insignificant, chubby hands, then come up with tortures so subtle that even Felipe had never heard of them. He also carried a six-inch knife in his belt.

"I tell you what, *amigo, Estas loco*," Dirty Bobby said quietly. "You're crazy."

"Cut it out, creep. Tell me where you get your drugs or I turn you in."

"You got *nada* on me." Dirty Bobby's eyes popped

44

down to the gym bag he was carrying. It was a dead give-away. Felipe didn't miss it.

"I think I do, *amigo*."

"Eh? Like what?"

"Like, what's in the bag?"

Dirty Bobby shifted his feet and looked up at the big agent. His eyes moved back and forth. The area was empty.

"I take the bag, or I get a cut. Take your pick, Ortez." Felipe's fingers made a knot in his pocket as though he had a concealed weapon. Everyone carried a weapon in Miami. He knew Dirty Bobby Ortez would take that as fact.

The gesture worked.

"So maybe I show you some big time. Come on, I take you," Dirty Bobby murmured, apparently docile. "Look, I got a car, come on, we go for a ride, I show you where I'm selling my stuff. You want to get in on things, you make a deal with the boys I work with. Make yourself some money. We always need a few good men." Dirty Bobby beamed.

"I don't want to go anywhere," Felipe said. "I just want a cut. Finder's fee."

"Hey, I don't deliver all this I'm dead," Dirty Bobby said. "You want a finder fee, all you gonna find is my dead body. How 'bout you come along. I gotta collect the money before you get your cut. That's cool."

Felipe looked at Dirty Bobby. Felipe read all the signs that Bobby wanted him to see; the Latino was clearly scared to death. The CIA agent suppressed a chuckle. Easy money, he thought. All he had to do was ride along and collect it. He'd done this before.

Unfortunately, Felipe realized he had to break rule number one: always go in your own car. He had left his behind when he had come out here in the Testarossa. But this chubby little jerk was going to make a connection and give him half the profits. For nothing.

He was breaking rule number two as well: always

carry a weapon into unfamiliar situations. But this was Dade County, and Felipe knew it like the palm of his hand. He'd lived here unmolested for years. Maybe he'd just been lucky, but familiarity breeds arrogance. He'd handled a lot.

"Okay, take me to the money."

Dirty Bobby led the way to his gray Thunderbird, not a car bought on a salad maker's wages. Dirty Bobby unlocked the car, first disarming an alarm system with a device on his key chain. "I take you there. Enjoy the ride."

They made very good time. Dirty Bobby was a skillful driver, making use of every shortcut in the city as he wound his way south, all to the tune of a soulful CD that repeated the Spanish words, *"No siento nada,"* or, "I don't feel a thing," over and over.

Felipe knew Spanish. His mother had been born in Mexico, his father came from San Francisco. To his mother's great embarrassment and sorrow, for most of his life her son had looked at the Spanish culture and music of his maternal side as something to be barely tolerated at first and later only to be used in his career. Only now was Felipe giving his Spanish heritage the respect it deserved, and he found himself tapping the rhythm out with his hands. His Mexican mother would never know that the worm had finally turned. María García Klondacki had been dead for twelve years.

*"No siento nada,"* Felipe sang along, and he understood exactly what he was hearing. Unfortunately he didn't listen to what he was singing. He should have.

Felipe wasn't suspicious when Dirty Bobby pulled up by a pile of rubble, one of the few areas that hadn't been rebuilt since Hurricane Andrew had devastated South Dade. There were no lights for blocks and only the crickets and night sounds for company. He followed Dirty Bobby out, through a gap in a fence, into a former back yard of a roofless, gutted house.

Dirty Bobby glanced down at his watch, squinting in the dark. "My friends, they be along soon. We wait."

"Hell of a spot, Bobby."

"Sure. We do our business good and private. Have a seat. I let you in on this, we get new connections, right? New connections. New money. You got good connections?"

"Sure. I know plenty." Felipe sat down on a fallen wall, kicking some old roofing materials aside. Damn shame about the hurricane, he thought. It was taking years to put places like this back together. But it was happening.

Silence crept darkly into the spot, crickets stopped, and a black bird flew overhead emitting strange laugh-like shrieks. Felipe shuddered and shifted on the wall. Suddenly there were no stars.

Dirty Bobby walked behind Felipe and pulled out his knife, balancing it in the palm of his hand for a second before he executed a ballet-like turn and plunged it into Felipe's upper back. It was a perfect strike, but Felipe's instincts were working overtime. He turned and the blade twisted, wrenching out of his back, still held in Dirty Bobby's hand. Felipe felt the damage, a sharp pain, then an odd sense of numbness. He was a fighter. It didn't stop him from grappling for the knife, his greater height and old, but experienced muscles carrying him around and over onto Dirty Bobby. The thick-bodied Panamanian squirmed and writhed under the weight. Dirty Bobby fought to maintain control of the knife when suddenly it turned in his hand. Felipe wrenched the short man's wrist and the knife sliced into Dirty Bobby's cheek.

"Son a bitch," Bobby gasped and twisted desperately to get away. He was being flattened by Felipe's greater weight. Felipe was bleeding and alive.

Felipe tasted blood in his mouth. He became breathless. He had to kill this guy, kill him. It was his only chance. He knew he'd nicked Dirty Bobby from the sticky feel of his hand where he'd been able to knock the knife around. Felipe was on top; the shorter man was wriggling like a crazy bitch under him. But Felipe was dying. With that initial strike, the knife had slipped between the first and second ribs and sliced into the aorta. Dirty Bobby knew it. All he had to do was hang on and keep the knife away until Felipe checked out.

They struggled. Dirty Bobby was agile. He shifted his weight under the older man while he kept control of the knife. Felipe's greater strength ebbed in spurts as his life drained away. He fought in a hazy, desperately delirious attempt to live. The song the agent had just heard played over and over in his head. His struggling weakened. Clouds rolled into his mind. There was no pain.

They clutched and clung, rolling, tossing. Felipe suddenly relaxed, and he cried out in a foam of blood. "I don't feel nothing, I don't feel nothing." Then he said it in Spanish. Then he died.

His mother would have been proud. His last words were in her language. *"No siento nada."*

# 9

THE next day was Saturday. By noon it was eighty-nine degrees in West Perrine where Felipe had died. The turkey vultures were gathering, gliding in slowly shrinking circles above his ripening body. A police car that made regular tours of the neighborhood finally stopped. The buzzards were always assembling in South Florida. They hung in the air currents over downtown skyscrapers; they traveled in black troops across blue skies, but today they were definitely eyeing carrion.

The two cops sat for a minute, looking at the birds. Neither wanted to go investigate.

"Toss for it," the driver said. He pulled out a quarter. "Heads, I stay."

He won.

"Go ahead."

"Be right back," the other cop said and pulled out his service revolver. "Maybe you better cover me. Never know, out here."

He found the hole in the fence. He walked through, aiming to go directly under where the vultures were looping in the scalding sky. Moments later he found the body. It stunk already.

"Gotta call this one in," he muttered, taking a shallow breath. The carcass was bad. The heat worked fast. He looked around carefully just in case there was someone in the area who was still alive and in trouble.

Ten minutes later more police cars arrived with the medical examiner, forensic investigator, and technicians.

It had been a light day for murders and everyone was available. A new technician puked immediately. All the rest put on face masks and got to work.

The dead Caucasian male carried no identification, no wallet, no keys. The big birds had already started to pick at the face. Fingerprints were taken and whisked off to be faxed to the FBI in Washington. A police photographer took pictures. An undertaker arrived and the body was removed.

The police were very careful because this man could be anyone. He was well dressed, lots of expensive gold dental work, possible Spanish descent, no identification whatsoever. If the FBI had anything on him, the police would know about it. Quick.

When FBI Agent Beaver, in Washington, D.C., realized he had been handed the fingerprints of an undercover agent from CIA, he began to push all the buttons. He knew he would need a secure line. It was close to impossible in this technical age to get one, so he connected with personnel at CIA. "This is Agent Beaver, FBI. I got a body of yours to discuss. I better come over."

"Right." The personnel woman knew what that meant. She gave a room number and started making calls on the inside line.

"Forty-five minutes, the way traffic is," the FBI agent muttered to his secretary before he left.

An hour later the Miami police department had been told to put a lid on their investigation of the dead man, identified as Felipe Klondacki. The murder would be investigated by several FBI agents and some associates from an unnamed agency. They were to expect a man named Damien Drail to take an active part in the investigation.

Damien was informed almost immediately of Felipe's demise. "I'll fly out first thing in the morning," he said moments later to a worried Daniel Quickwater. "I'll check Klondacki's in-house files, then pack the bags. I'll take care of it."

"Do it," Quickwater said. "All hell's blowing up with this case. We need a man on it."

Damien nodded. No woman could handle this. Particularly that woman. A nun. Shit, it was all going to reflect on him.

Damien left early for home, a small house on Katherine Drive in Silver Spring, Maryland. He had already made travel plans. He would arrive in Miami the next morning. Everything was cleared. Now he had to deal with the domestic front.

He arrived at his house and opened the door softly, surprised that it was unlocked. He could hear his daughter, Leonie, and the housekeeper. They were in the front room and the television was on. He didn't stop, going directly up to his room. He didn't pause to wonder why his daughter wasn't in school at this early hour.

He was throwing some clothes into a bag when the housekeeper knocked on his bedroom door.

"Have you seen Leonie this morning?" she asked. Her old eyes were red rimmed as though she had been crying.

"No. I've been called away for a few days. Can I count on you?" He smiled expectantly. The housekeeper never let him down. She frequently spent long weekends with his daughter, and in fact was more like a grandmother to Leonie than a hired domestic.

"Poor Leonie was sent home from school early today with the chicken pox," she said. "One thing on top of another."

"Is it serious?"

"No, but they don't want her in school for a while. A week or two, until the scabs fall off," she said apologetically. "And I can't stay with her. I'm so sorry, Mr. Drail. My sister died. I'd love to stay, the child being so sick and all, Mr. Drail, but Betty died this morning and I've got to leave for the funeral tomorrow morning. In

51

Buffalo." The housekeeper sniffed. "I really should leave today."

"Damn. You're sure?"

"My sister's dead, Mr. Drail. I'm very sure."

"I'm sorry. Really. Very sorry. You have to go. I understand." Damien didn't know what to do. In the past she had spent up to a week with his daughter when he had been called for emergencies like this. "I'll think of something," he worried. "I'm really sorry about your sister. You'll be here tonight?"

"Until noon tomorrow. I'm flying out tomorrow afternoon. I have to be gone a week." The housekeeper rubbed her eyes and took a deep breath.

"I'll work out something," he muttered, hoping she wouldn't burst into tears. The germ of an idea had begun to form in his mind. "How sick is she, anyway? Leonie?"

"Not bad. Small fever but highly contagious until the blisters stop appearing. She can't return to school until there are no new blisters, they said. Until they clear up."

"Blisters. Right. Okay, I'll take care of it."

Somehow he would have to deal with that complication, but not until tomorrow, so he began to pack for an early Sunday morning flight to Miami International Airport. And send a funeral wreath to Buffalo. Too bad about Felipe Klondacki, Damien thought. Too bad about his housekeeper's sister. Too bad about Leonie and the chicken pox. Everything was going wrong at once. He'd have to take over for the nun, and he didn't particularly want to do that. Maybe he wouldn't have to. Legally he wasn't supposed to be on a domestic murder case, or a disappearance. It was going to be a tough call doing this right. "Give me the address of the funeral parlor," he said sympathetically. "I want to send something."

"Oh, you don't have to, Mr. Drail."

"I must." He patted her shoulder. "It's your sister."

The housekeeper mopped her eyes. "Such a kind man," she murmured.

But at least he was going to see that nun again. The

52

nun had been in his mind ever since they had met. Was she really that beautiful? Or was it beauty at all? He had dreamed a recurring dream about her, once last night, twice the night before, and he had awoken sweating. Railroad ties swishing past, the nun, the nun, over and over again. Running. He could never catch her. And somewhere in the dream was his twelve-year-old daughter standing in a haze, crying. It was only a dream, but he didn't like it.

He wrote down the address of the funeral parlor.

# 10

"I'VE got to get going on the case," Cecile fretted. It was Saturday. The nuns were traveling around Miami taking in the real estate situation. "I don't have a handle on anything yet. It's like air. Felipe covered everything. We had a productive discussion last night and I'm meeting with that salad maker on Monday, but there's nothing to do. I don't know why they hired me, Raphael. I don't get it."

"Leave the real estate to me," Raphael advised. "I'm not senile, Cecile. Recheck everything. You're smarter than this Felipe person. You'll find something."

Cecile nodded as they pulled up before another rambling, overpriced home in South Miami. "After today, the real estate problem is all yours, Raphael."

"I like the motel," Cecile said, two hours later. "If they drop the price we can't afford not to take it." She wiped her brow, totally exhausted. "Let's go home."

Nothing had been done about Bradley Locke.

It was late afternoon. Sister Raphael was asleep on the couch, pretending to be reading the *Miami Herald*. The paper was spread out over her face and she was snoring.

Sister Cecile prepared to meet with Felipe by taking a quick shower and dressing in her most severe northern habit: a dark polyester skirt and white blouse. She pulled out her biggest veil and she tucked it down around her ears, then she gave her gold cross an extra polish. She regretted her decision to go and chat with the agent.

Felipe was thorough but uninspired. This would be a waste of time.

The condo was clean, the dishes done, she checked the door locks and tiptoed out, leaving Raphael still asleep on the couch.

"Kendall," Cecile said, looking down at the slip of paper that held Felipe's address. Then she reached for a map. The Testarossa was equipped with maps although there was no place to put them and they had ended up all over the passenger side floor. The car was starting to resemble her desk back in Boston, she thought as she located her destination. It would be a quick drive.

Twenty-five minutes later she was in Kendall, a flat suburban area much like other flat suburban areas in Miami. Town houses lined Kendall Drive, one group after another, set back by tree-lined drives resembling Spanish villas, Mediterranean castles, or decorated with Nantucket gingerbread. It occurred to Cecile that each development was a theme park, attractively designed and set behind walls; communities by the dozen. Eventually she found Felipe's and pulled into a driveway lined with speed bumps, beside a series of other identical town houses. His was a pleasing gray with wide window drapes pulled against the late Florida sun. The design was early eighties modern, no grand Spanish structures or New England village, but there was a small white egret tiptoeing through the parking lot and attractive clumps of tall Alexander palms. It was early, still daylight and there were children playing nearby. Chameleons skittered into the grass as she passed.

There was absolutely nothing disturbing about the complex. Nothing at all, Cecile told herself.

She rang the doorbell and waited.

A minute expired before she heard someone come to the door. A strange, well-dressed man.

"Sorry, I'm looking for 812B." She shook her head and began to turn.

"Wait. Who do you want?"

55

"Felipe Klondacki." She started to move backwards.

Suddenly the man leaped out the door. He grabbed her by the arm and began to pull her back. "Who are you?"

Her arm hurt. She considered a hard chop to the right. She could break his arm. "Please get your hand off me." She wasn't worried. Yet.

He looked down where his hand was wrapped around her arm.

"I'm looking for Mr. Klondacki," she said. "I seem to be at the wrong place."

"Mr. Klondacki is out. Could I have your name?"

"Let me go before I scream." Or break your arm. This was nasty.

The man looked up and down the street. The children were still playing, traffic was coming along in the distance. The sun had almost set, sending bright evening streams across the flat landscape. His eyes traveled around her face, took in the veil, the gray eyes, the firm, lovely mouth. Was this a nun? She didn't look like a nun. Not with that face.

He let Cecile loose. "Could you tell me your business with Mr. Klondacki?" he asked, almost apologetically.

"Why?"

His eyes were still moving around. The man saw the Testarossa she had parked in the driveway. A strange look crossed his eyes. It happened, Cecile noticed, when anyone saw the car. She was beginning to call it the Ferrari syndrome.

"I'm afraid I can't say. Please come in," he said and stepped back.

"Something happened to him?"

"Please come in. I'm with the authorities."

She noticed he didn't say what authorities. He could be lying. "I'd like to see some identification," she said.

He pulled out a card and a badge and held it before her face, about an inch too close so she had to tilt to read the words. It put her at a definite psychological disadvantage. "John J. Walker, FBI," she read aloud. "All right."

56

She walked into the front room, Walker behind her. Walker was a domestic agent, not CIA, and that was bad. And there was another man, ten yards beyond, in the shadow of the room. She was surrounded by the opposition.

Instead of stepping back, she stepped forward and put on her most confident air.

"Mr. Walker, I have an appointment to meet Mr. Klondacki this evening. Has something happened to him?" She turned a fraction of an inch to send a slanted sunbeam of light reflecting off her gold cross and into Mr. Walker's eyes. He blinked.

"Yes, well, you're right. Something has happened to the man. Please, have a seat." He stepped back further and she followed him into Felipe's living room. She saw a set of wicker furniture covered with flowered cushions and a wicker table with a glass top. Wilted flowers in a blue vase and an ashtray filled with Camel cigarette butts lay on the table. Dismal. Dead objects. It looked as if the owner had left in a hurry. She looked for Felipe's body.

The second man stood in an open space between the living area and a hall-like dining area where a small table still held a drinking glass with Key Lime Hopper remnants floating in a quarter inch of water. Cecile's eyes focused on the section of wilted lime and she drew in a deep breath. "Where is he?"

The second man stayed where he was. Sister Cecile sat in the wicker chair as he began to speak. "We're investigating the situation. What is your concern? Are you a friend? Relative?" She was obviously a nun. Cecile saw his eyes straying to her veil. He looked skeptical. "You're a nun?" He finally asked the question.

"I'm a nun. Mr. Klondacki was helping me find a missing person, and apparently he had some information that he wanted to give me. My business with him doesn't have anything to do with you people, but please tell me what happened." She frowned at the coffee table. She understood too well the considerable jealousy between CIA and FBI, particularly when they worked at close quarters. That was why she was here, Cecile reminded herself. She would have to be very discreet about her CIA affiliation and call Damien as soon as possible.

"Do you work for someone?" Agent Walker asked. "I'd like to see your identification."

Sister Cecile dipped into her black purse and pulled out a small card with a photograph that identified her as a member of the Order of Our Lady of Good Counsel. She pulled out a second card: a plasticized copy of her Massachusetts private detective license.

Agent Walker looked at the material, ran a finger over the plastic, then handed it back. "Private Dick? Nun? What are you doing here?" He cleared his throat.

"Looking for a friend, as I said. Where is Mr. Klondacki?"

"Mr. Klondacki had an accident."

"Dead?"

"Yes."

"How?"

The agents looked at each other then shrugged simultaneously. Mr. Walker spoke. "Knifed. We think it happened Friday night. Last night. Unless you have other information." The agent was babbling. Cecile could see it was contrived blabber so that she would talk.

"Friday night?" She felt an icy tingle run through her body. Of course she had been with Felipe on Friday night. She had left him alive and standing on the sidewalk in front of the hotel, and he had told her he was going to have another drink. From there he could have gone anywhere. Dirty Bobby? Maybe. Yes. Poor Felipe. This was terrible!

"Where was he killed?" she asked, keeping her voice steady with difficulty.

"South. Toward Homestead."

"How did he get there?"

The agent shrugged. "His car's been found in another

58

part of town. He apparently was involved in a fight. It was a cheap death. Nothing gained."

"And a lot lost." Sister Cecile sighed. She blessed herself and looked down at the floor for a minute while she said a silent prayer. Agent Walker looked across the room at his partner and grimaced. His partner was still frowning. Sister Cecile saw the expressions. These men obviously thought nuns were stupid and ineffectual. Good. Her cover was in place. That thought helped her get a grip on herself.

"Poor man," she said. Cecile was thinking fast. It might not have been Dirty Bobby who had done the killing, but it probably was. She would have to tell these people something to make them happy, then leave.

"I was supposed to be getting information from Felipe Klondacki about my search for a missing friend," she said. "He was recommended to me by a friend, and we'd had an initial conversation, Felipe and I, on Friday night. We had dinner at Louie's, then we went out to the Hotel Place St. Michel. During the course of that evening conversation he suggested I stop by tonight, that he might have some further information. Now I'll just never know what he was going to tell me. I feel just terrible about this. You boys really must find his assailant quickly. You seem to have moved right in on the case." She heard a quiver start in her words. She struggled to maintain control. She had to get out of here before she broke down entirely and started crying for poor, dead Felipe. "I'll leave you my name and the number where I can be reached. I believe there's an answering machine, so if I'm out, leave a number and I'll get back to you."

She sounded like an answering machine herself except for the quivering undertone. She paused and reached into her black Boston-nun purse and pulled out a scrap of paper. She scribbled down Paul's address and the telephone number at the condo, grateful she had taken a moment to memorize all the numbers. She handed Agent Walker the paper with a deliberate thrust so he wouldn't notice that her hand was shaking. Bad enough he could hear her voice shivering because Felipe Klondacki was dead and she wasn't telling these people why. It was all she could do to keep from bursting into tears.

Agent Walker didn't suspect a thing. This was only a nun, a peculiar nun because of that car, but the car probably belonged to the local bishop. And from the sound of things she had been having an affair with Klondacki. They had actually been bar hopping? At the Place St. Michel? That meant money. Modern nuns were very strange.

Walker took the paper with Cecile's information on it and gave it a look long enough to realize that she was staying in an expensive area of Miami Beach. But again, that didn't mean a thing, knowing those Catholics. On the other hand, Agent Walker was thorough and as Cecile began to leave he fielded one more attempt. "You say you were working on something with him?"

"Not exactly. He thought he might be able to find out about my missing friend's associates. It was a slim possibility." The smile faded and reality showed on her face. "This is terrible, just terrible. Poor Mr. Klondacki."

"I see," he said, certain that he really did. This so-called nun was beautiful and she had probably been having an affair with Klondacki. Yes. An affair. "Thank you for your time. We may be in touch." He wanted her to leave fast before she started asking them for prayers. Or money.

After Cecile had left, John Walker turned to his partner. He lit up one of Felipe Klondacki's Camels. "What do you think?"

"Too good-looking, but a nun," his companion said. "We've been here seven hours and all we've seen is a nun. I never knew any nuns. You?"

"No. None." Walker chuckled at his pun. "Wonder what the nun was after."

"She's probably sneaking Haitians onto South Beach. Looking for a lost soul."

"Exactly," the other agent agreed. "Or trying to save Klondacki."

"Hey, hey, hey, nun, come save me!" Walker yodeled. Then he settled down on a flower print chair and continued to wait.

Dirty Bobby Ortez had taken Felipe's wallet after he had killed the agent. He had Felipe's address, and had been hanging out in the Kendall neighborhood all day, waiting to see if there was any follow-up. It had been a clean kill as far as he could figure, but it was always smart to know a little about the victim, just in case something came up later. A study of Klondacki's wallet hadn't revealed much. It held an ID for the agent's cover job and a few credit cards. Dirty Bobby had tossed them all as soon as he had filled up his car with premium grade Mobil gas using Klondacki's gas card and bought a new CD player and a few good discs at Circuit City with the Visa card.

Dirty Bobby had seen the two FBI agents and was not impressed. He had been dozing in a nearby mall when Cecile had arrived, then he stopped at the Circle-K for a forty-four-ounce "Thirst Buster" before one more drive-by. Inconspicuous in his Thunderbird, he arrived back at Felipe's for his final check just as Sister Cecile pulled out, the Ferrari engine whining.

He decided to follow her. Something about the car, something about the woman. He was dealing with her and he better know what was what. Besides, he *liked* that car. The nun, maybe, he would have to kill. She bothered him.

Cecile drove immediately back to the condo, parked in the underground garage, went through the evening security checks, and tiptoed into the living room. She didn't want to worry Raphael, so she resolved not to say a word. Felipe's death was difficult to comprehend. Dirty Bobby had killed him, Cecile figured. Or had he? Felipe had implied that he was involved with other things, more important things. The search for Bradley Locke was nothing to him. Not important. Nor was Dirty Bobby Ortez one of the principals in her own problem. He wasn't important either. He was a salad maker who just might know somebody who knew somebody.

Not important.

But he might be a murderer.

He might have kidnapped Bradley Locke.

Cecile flopped down on the couch beside the telephone and called the number Damien had given her to use in an emergency. It was late evening, but he told her the number was always tended. "Damien Drail, please."

"I'm sorry, he's not available, may I take a message?"

"Tell him Felipe is dead. Ask him to call me at once, please." She gave her number even though Damien already had it. She noticed her voice shaking. The call was probably being recorded. Her wimpy voice would be recorded for posterity forever.

"Control yourself, Sister," she said out loud after hanging up.

"What's wrong?" Sister Raphael asked from the kitchen where she had been all along, pouring ice water and rummaging silently, preparing a late snack.

"Somebody's dead. The man I saw Friday night. Just like that. Dead." That took care of her resolve not to tell Raphael.

"Lord have mercy on his eternal soul," Sister Raphael said as she walked into the room. "Was he a good man?" She had no problem combining praying for the dead and eating a slice of whole wheat bread covered with peanut butter. Her words sounded sympathetic, but stuck together.

"Good? Probably. He liked lime drinks, he was an agent. Now he's dead. I hope it's not my fault," Cecile said. "I feel terrible about it. I'm so afraid it's Dirty Bobby." She had tears in her eyes and her face started turning purple. It was a sure sign she was going to cry.

"Who?"

"The Dirt Man. He's a salad maker," she sniffed.

Raphael nodded and chewed. "Dirty Bobby," she repeated. "I don't think I would want to eat any of his salads. I hope they make him wash."

Tears were running down Cecile's face by now. "Felipe's dead," she said. "I can't help it."

Raphael came over and hugged the younger nun, patting her shoulder. "Now, now. Have a good cry. Tomorrow we can find the killer."

"Yes," blubbered Cecile. "Tomorrow."

# 11

BRADLEY Locke was going crazy from the heat. He could be dead tomorrow, or later today, even. Somewhere in the back of his mind he almost welcomed the possibility as he waited for the unknown. Even the palmetto bug he had left alive seemed to be wearing a death head.

This was not a life worth living. Only the hope of seeing his cat Bismarck again gave him something good to think about. Bismarck was out there waiting. Because of Bismarck, Bradley Locke hoped, and in hoping, he planned.

His planning took place flat out on the cot. He had taken to wearing only the pair of red plaid boxer shorts he had worn under his long pants. The long pants lay unused, neatly hanging on a small nail in the wall. The shirt he had arrived in was draped over the bucket that he euphemistically referred to in his mind as the chamber pot. The suit jacket had become a pillow. A small crumb of last night's supper lay on the floor beside the cot, his offering to the palmetto bug whom he had taken to calling George.

He lay in the heat, waiting for a rare breeze, and he tried to think. Already he had memorized every single flaw on the old plaster ceiling, he had finished reading the entire six month's worth of old *Miami Heralds*, and he had an itchy rash under his arms. He had considered writing a novel but the edges of the newspaper didn't present enough writing space and his ballpoint pen wore out during the first week, doing crossword puzzles.

Bradley had reached some fairly accurate conclusions about his captors because, among other things, he had trained as an analyst at CIA and knew how to think logically, or at least analytically. For example, he had guessed correctly that Olimpo was Panamanian because of his accent. In actual fact, he had decided Olimpo might be a fairly decent sort, except he was caught up in his own schemes. Bradley had also concluded that the man with the high voice, Bajito, was an educated Napoleonic type on a power trip. He recognized Bajito's fast Cuban twang as typical of that country. He assumed rightly that Bajito was the brains of the two and therefore, more dangerous. Bradley's prime objective, then, was to present himself as someone worth keeping alive. He would do this for Bismarck, if for no one else. Luckily, Bradley Locke had not yet been exposed to Dirty Bobby.

"I'm in here," he said quietly. "I want to get out. I mean, hey, you guys. Let's talk."

Nothing happened. He tried louder. "Hey, out there! Let's make a deal! Let's talk. I'm waiting. I got lots of things to tell you guys!" Then he tried the same thing in Spanish, because unbeknown even to friends in the Agency, Bradley Locke had learned Spanish quite well.

It was all in vain. Olimpo had gone out to get some more food from Taco Bell and some more chocolate cookies from the Farm Store.

"You stupid jerks lemme outta here I'll kick your *cojones* off!" Bradley finally bellowed. Nobody heard him but it made him feel better. Eventually he heard Olimpo's return, marked by a squeal of breaks and the slam of the outer screen door.

"Shit," Bradley said, softly.

He lay down on his floor, propped his cat-hole door open with a roll of newspapers, and called out, "Hey, *muchacho*!"

"Ey, *chico*!" Olimpo yelled from the next room. Olimpo had been bored stiff. Not even the trip out had helped. Bradley Locke had made his overture at the right time because Bajito was in town arranging to sell a *paca* of marijuana to some people from South Carolina, leaving Olimpo to deal with things alone.

"Hey, tell me what you want. Maybe I can help you get it better," Bradley croaked through the cat door. His voice was scratchy from lack of use. It was also hard to speak on his stomach with his mouth aimed at the cat hole. "I can tell you stuff, but money? I don't have money. I'll tell you information."

Olimpo walked into the room next to Bradley's and looked down at the opened cat-hole door. His voice was soft. "Ey, friend, you know a lot of stuff, we figure you got good connections. Money is out there."

"The car was a rental," Bradley protested.

"Sure. You won a fucking contest," Olimpo said. "We know more about you than you think."

"Like what?"

"Like you know a lot, like maybe you work for the man. Like someone's gonna pay real big to get you out. Like we're gonna sell you to Cuba himself."

"I don't know anything," Bradley squeaked through the door. "Look, all I do is read the newspapers. Where the hell you think all the governments get their intelligence? They read the newspapers. You know how to read, you know everything I know. I'm just a regular guy with a cat. It's too damn hot in here." He was whining.

"Sure thing, *chico*, I tell you what. We have a little conference, my friends and me, and then we get you out and talk. We have a little party tonight. You get ready for that."

Olimpo stomped his way out of the room and slammed the outer door hard.

Bradley pounded the floor in frustration. There went his chance. Olimpo was the soft one, he was sure, soft in the head from too much grass. Bradley could smell it every time Olimpo lit up another joint. The sweet-smelling smoke drifted through on a regular basis.

Bradley backed away from the cat hole and let it swing shut. All he had been able to see through it had been Olimpo's two hundred fifty dollar cowboy boots and the opposite wall of the room, a store room where Olimpo's boxes of marijuana lay. The dried green weed poked out of the cartons with a few loose chunks scattered on the floor. Bradley had spied on it for days; he knew whenever Olimpo came in to pick some out, and Bradley was beginning to want some for his own use, although he knew it was bad stuff. He'd even worked out a plan. There wasn't much else to do in his little closet of a room. After years of straight living, getting stoned sounded like an excellent alternative to dazed, overheated thoughts. It just might help him forget that he was baking like a roasting chicken in this tiny room with its one window.

Every day, Bradley had been saving the straws included with the drink in the Taco Bell food that Olimpo pushed in. He had worked out a method of twisting the straws together and had created a long device that could almost reach the marijuana bale. All he needed was one more day's straw and he could attach the little metal paper clip he had found to the end of the straws. Then he could hook himself a smoke.

As he worked at bending his paper clip perfectly, Bradley heard a car drive up. Probably the short guy, Bradley thought, the one with brains. There went his escape chance for the day. He went back to work contemplating his potential marijuana supply.

It was not Bajito this time. It was Dirty Bobby.

Dirty Bobby swaggered into the front room, sweat dripping off his chin. His nostrils flared in and out as he sniffed the air. "Weeds, again, Olimpo?" he asked. "Crapping up your mind with scummy drugs?" He laughed hoarsely. Dirty Bobby didn't like Olimpo on drugs. His hero was showing feet of clay. Olimpo, for all his charisma and all of Bajito's great ideas, was showing weakness. Or maybe it was necessary for his great mind, Dirty

Bobby thought as he stared at his idol. Olimpo was a gorgeous man, and maybe he needed the drug.

"Listen, man, I think you better cool it," Dirty Bobby said, "what with the chocolate, you know what I mean? Hashish taking you over, man."

"Sure, the chocolate," Olimpo nodded. "I got some good stuff. Got to check the quality. So? What's with you? You got fleas or something, getting in here like you running the cops in Dade County?"

Dirty Bobby blanched as much as his skin could blanch. Olimpo always got to him like that, the big voice, looking down at him like some god up there. It made Dirty Bobby melt all over inside and it also made Dirty Bobby want to kill Olimpo sometimes. Emotions were tough.

"Listen, Olimpo," Dirty Bobby began, trying to send his voice down a notch so it sounded better. "I got some news. Big news." He waited for Olimpo to turn and look at him, before he went on. "First thing you gotta know, I had to kill that guy come looking for our frien' in there." Dirty Bobby tipped his head at the back room. "He got on my case, see, started wanting to do with my drug sale. So I got rid of him. I keep in good practice with my blade. Cut a little here, a little there. The dude is dead."

Dirty Bobby pulled his knife out of his boot and began wiping it suggestively across his arm. "Left him dead out in Perrine. Butthead name of Felipe. I don't think he was no good to us anyway. I got a better connection."

"So," Olimpo said. "You got a cut," he said, pointing to a big Band-Aid on Dirty Bobby's cheek. "So? What's the connection?" He sounded big, deep, thoughtful. Olimpo always sounded great, even stoned.

Dirty Bobby spoke, his story coming out in soft little jerks while he picked his teeth with his knife.

". . . so, the dead guy got me meeting some nun-lady with a very fancy car. I mean, now we got some real dollars in sight because I can tell you that this lady has dollars. Looks like you got someone there in our back room

68

worth some money after all. I want to talk to him a minute, 'cause I gotta deal with this lady frien' who come looking for him. I want to talk to the dude. I don't think we need to sell him to Castro after all. We sell him local."

"I want to sell him to *El Señor*," Olimpo said stubbornly.

"You find anyone wants to go to Cuba yet?"

"No."

"You wanna go to Cuba?"

"You think I'm fucking crazy?"

"So we sell him to the nun-lady, like I said."

"Nun-lady? What lady?"

"Lady in the fancy car, who's looking for that jerk," Dirty Bobby said. His emphasis was on the word car, so he was hard to understand. "Lady in a Testarossa with fuckin' money is looking for Butthead there." He spoke very slowly as though he were speaking to an idiot. "Understand?"

Olimpo appeared to think a minute. "Listen, Dirty Bobby, I don't want you to see him. You see him, that means he gonna see you, and he never seen you. You want he should pick you out of a line-up someday?"

Dirty Bobby started shaving the edge of the wooden table with his knife. He just killed some dude, so that meant he was in the mood to do damage. Dirty Bobby got off on blood, and he knew it. He loved blood. Maybe Olimpo was right. He might lose control and cut the man, just for fun. "Might be okay," he said. "I kill him later."

"No. I don't want you talking to him just yet," Olimpo said. "I don't want him seeing so many dudes. You let me talk to him for you. He already seen me."

That made sense, although that meant Dirty Bobby would have to feed the words to Olimpo. He hated that. "Okay," Dirty Bobby said. "I want that you ask him about the lady in the red Ferrari. You ask him how come she's looking for him. You got that?"

"Lady in the red Ferrari? Nice-looking?"

"That car's always nice-looking."

"The lady."

"I looked at the car, see." Dirty Bobby stopped for a minute to think. He was not a lady's man, he was into cars, killing, blood, voodoo. Women, fine. He liked a good tough woman now and then, but men had so much more, he always thought. Like Noriega. He'd been really crazy about Noriega. "Okay, she was nice looking. Like a nun."

That was better. Olimpo nodded. "Come on, I go talk to him." Olimpo got up and walked into the back room where he kicked on the cat door. "Hey *gringo*, you in there?"

"Yeah. Let me the fuck outta here."

"Tomorrow, maybe, we talk about that. Listen, *chico*, you know some lady in a Ferrari?"

"Red," Dirty Bobby whispered behind him. "Red car."

"Red," Olimpo repeated carefully. "Red, Ferrari, Testarossa." He let the words roll out, slipping them around his velvet tongue, making Dirty Bobby writhe inside. But the words did nothing for Bradley Locke and the intelligence agent merely gave a large grunt as he stood up and went over to the door.

"Let me out, I'll tell you," Bradley said.

"Oh, no, *chico*. You tell me or you don't get no Taco Bell tonight."

"Oh, shit," Bradley muttered. "Okay, I don't know anyone in a red Ferrari Testarossa. Wish I did. Listen, we have to talk. Let me out and we can talk."

"How come you got some rich lady in a fancy car looking for you? A nun, maybe?"

"How should I know?" Bradley kicked at the door, catching his naked foot in the cat hole, scraping his ankle painfully. "Listen, I gotta get out of here. I got business at home. I got a cat, see." There was panic in his voice. It had been hotter than usual.

"Oh, sure, *chico*. You still got business with me, understand? Tell me about the fancy nun-lady."

70

"I don't know any fancy nun." Bradley took his two fists and pummelled them on the wall. "I don't, dammit. I don't know anything! It's too hot in here!"

Olimpo turned to Dirty Bobby and spoke in a whisper. "He don't know this lady."

"Think he means he really don't or he's just saying he don't?" Dirty Bobby whispered back. "I know how to make a man talk. Let me do that, we find out anything we want."

"I told you, I don't want him to see you," Olimpo whispered, then he shrugged. "Okay, *gringo*, you think about it. We be back."

Olimpo nudged Dirty Bobby and they walked out of the room outside of Bradley's hearing. They let the door slam behind them with a bang.

"I'll check the nun," Dirty Bobby said. "I followed her a little already. Maybe I keep an eye on her. See who she talks to. Then I'll tell you all about her."

"Follow the nun. Good idea, Dirty Bobby. See if she means it. Then we get the money. Either that or you gotta go to Cuba."

"The fuck I'll go to Cuba," Dirty Bobby murmured. But Olimpo didn't hear him.

"Yeah, sure, I go see *El Señor*," he said louder.

Outside the shack an egret took off from somewhere in the tall grasses and swished by Bradley's high, barred window, sending a long shadow across the room like some evil portent. It was so hot in the little room that Bradley's boxer shorts were completely stuck to him and his hands were slippery with sweat. He stepped back and sank to his cot, where he drew up his knees, tucked his face in his hands and cried.

# 12

SISTER Cecile and Sister Raphael went to Sunday Mass at St. Patrick's Church in Miami Beach. They sat up front and prayed for the repose of the soul of Felipe Klondacki.

"Do you think it was my fault?" Cecile asked Raphael as they stepped out from the cool church into the Florida heat.

"The dead agent?" Raphael shook her head. "No. He was probably meddling. Government people do that. It's more than likely he ran into trouble with that Omega Seven group of anti-revolutionaries I read about last week. He did say that he had very little to do with your case. His own business probably brought about his murder."

"Possibly," Cecile said. They were walking slowly to where Sister Cecile had parked the car. "I feel like someone's watching us," she said suddenly. "Stumble, Raphael. I'll catch you, then I can look back."

Raphael seemed to trip. Her arms went up. Sister Cecile made a grab, turned, and caught the old nun by the arm. They stood a moment, swaying while Cecile's eyes swept the scene. A few people near them looked concerned, but everything was fine.

Cecile's eyes went from the people to the street and she saw the Thunderbird slowly driving by. She saw the face through the open driver's window, round, dark eyes staring at the church door, puffy cheeks, thick hair. Cecile moved around to Raphael's other side, clutching an arm. "All right, Raphael, it's him."

72

Raphael began to step firmly. "You're squeezing my arm, Cecile. Let go."

Cecile let go.

"Much better. Who is it?"

"Him," Cecile said solemnly. "It's him. Don't talk now. He may be watching."

A ten-year-old boy was staring at the tiny horse on the front hood of the red Ferrari. The nuns nodded to him and ducked into the car, both caught for a moment in the stifling heat built up inside. Cecile started the engine and flipped on the air-conditioning. "It was Dirty Bobby."

She stepped hard on the accelerator and the car jumped into Sunday traffic. Normal cars seemed to fade out. "I think I can leave him in the dust, take a trip around Ocean Drive, duck down a few back streets. Did I ever tell you I rode with a driver on the Fiorano Test Track in Italy?"

"Fiorano? No. Is he still behind us?"

"Fourteen curves." Cecile ripped by a slow van. "We can lose him, then head back to the condo. I don't want him to know where I live. Lucky thing I ordered a cheap little rental for us to pick up tomorrow. I thought it would be nice to be inconspicuous, and now I have a second reason. Anonymity."

"Describe him to me carefully," Raphael insisted, her fluffy white hair standing on end as her head bobbed up and down. Cecile was driving like a maniac down Alton Road, bounding over potholes, passing cars recklessly. She made a quick turn on Española Way and then off again at the next street.

"Safe. We can go home now." Cecile slowed down, driving sedately.

"I need to know everything about him. And his real name, please."

"Dirty Bobby Ortez," Cecile began and continued talking as she dove back to Paul's condo in the Art Deco district of Miami Beach.

73

By the time they were back at Paul's condo, the Ferrari was going fast again. It seemed to have a mind of its own, Cecile thought as she jammed on the brakes and turned into the condo parking garage. "Raphael, look! In front of the building. Damien. He must have gotten my message."

"Good," Raphael said. "Maybe he can help straighten this all out. If it's true that Bobby killed Felipe, you may be next. Maybe we need a man."

"I'm not certain about that at all," Cecile said. "Men, you know, don't have a clue about subtlety. Personally, I don't think I'll ever need a man." She slipped into a parking space. "Except Paul, sometimes. But Paul is different. And the other problem, of course, is that Damien *is* a man. He *was* Helene's husband, but he's a widower now. When I met him, he had that look in his eye that men sometimes get. You know the look?"

Sister Raphael chuckled. "Well, it's been a while. But Damien is a respectable agent, isn't he? You think he could be dangerous?"

"No, actually. Men are used to women in the business world by now, aren't they? All the harassment cases, everybody is totally aware."

"Men have always been totally aware of women," Raphael pointed out. "That's the problem. I'll go on up, Cecile. You should meet him down front."

"Yes. I must, I suppose."

# 13

CECILE left Raphael off in the parking garage, by the elevator. She parked and walked around to the front of the building to meet Damien. Damien spotted her and came up, white shirt stuck to his chest, already dark with sweat. He looked too pleased with himself for a man come to save her from potential murder.

"Sister Cecile. I've been waiting."

She held out her hand for a quick shake, avoiding his lunge forward to offer a kiss on the cheek. His palm was wet.

"You should have gone into the lobby. It's very cool inside."

Damien shrugged. "I just arrived and no one answered your buzzer so I came outside to look around. The doorman gave me an evil eye, and there was a woman with blue hair in the lobby, and she started asking questions." He laughed.

"You got my message, then. About Felipe." She looked stern, shocked. He was being flippant. "Come this way."

He followed her. "Actually I heard about Felipe through sources even before that. I left in a rush. What's going on?" He looked around the lobby, brown eyes glinting as they roamed over the gleaming Brescia Oniciata marble walls and the gold-covered railings. There was the doorman looking attentive and another couple having a conversation at the base of the elevator. It was a rich place, a busy place.

"Let's talk about this upstairs."

"My friend will be upstairs already, but don't worry about that," Cecile said.

"Friend?" He made it sound suggestive as his eyebrows rose a fraction.

Cecile didn't answer right away. He watched as she poked buttons and the elevator began to rise. Elevator music was playing something surprisingly decent for an elevator, but then, the elevator was extraordinarily nice, too. "Whose place is this, did you say?"

She had already said. She distinctly remembered telling him she would be at her lawyer's condo. "My lawyer. Really, Damien, there is no need to know."

"He's staying here too? Maybe I should stay as well. I don't like the idea of Felipe Klondacki's death. There could be a connection."

"I don't like that idea myself," Cecile said, not liking either possibility that he mentioned. She led the way out and up to the condo door. Raphael had propped it open with a small marble sculpture in anticipation of their imminent arrival. Cecile pushed the sculpture aside and they walked in. Raphael was waiting.

"Sister Raphael, this is Damien Drail."

"Damien. How nice. I've heard about you." Raphael put out a wrinkled hand.

Damien had expected Paul to be here, not an old nun, and Cecile was pleased to watch his jaw drop. He took Raphael's hand and shook it, however.

"Nice to meet you," he murmured.

Sister Raphael simpered. She was acting old. Cecile knew it was one of Raphael's tricks to convince people she was inconsequential. Damien would never guess the old nun was her assistant in the case.

Raphael went on. "I put some ice in glasses, so you can make some cool drinks. We have bottled water here. Imported from a local spring. And we have some bagels. The neighborhood is full of wonderful bagels."

"Iced tea, a drink?" Cecile asked.

"Just water, please. May we speak privately?" He made a small chin movement at Sister Raphael as though he didn't want an old, babbling nun listening.

"We can talk on the porch," Cecile said, pausing to fill the glasses from Paul's cooler. She handed a glass to Damien. "Follow me."

The porch overhung Miami Beach. It was very private. Not a soul could hear them. That would make Damien happy, and they could be shielded from the sun by a half roof. They pulled wooden lounge chairs into the shadowy side. Damien made himself comfortable and took a long drink.

"What exactly is the situation?" he asked. He was serious at last.

Cecile talked. She told him everything about her meeting with Felipe. She could think of no reason to hide anything about it except the fact that she was meeting with Dirty Bobby himself on Monday night. She didn't want Damien to come along, and he would if she mentioned it. She was certain of that. Part of it was pure selfishness. She wanted to do this job by herself, but there was the other side of the coin. She had a bad feeling about Dirty Bobby. The last man she had been with when she had met Dirty Bobby was dead. She was not superstitious, but she was also not stupid. There were *no* coincidences in this game.

"The situation," she began, "isn't good. Felipe Klondacki told me that he was going to see some other people after he left me Friday night. He didn't say who. I left him at the hotel bar. Do you have any ideas?" Cecile asked.

"I have his reports," Damien said. "His final ones were in transit, but he was clearly involved with some local groups."

"So you know what he was doing."

"I plan to do a follow up," Damien said. "That's why I'm here. Felipe's death could be connected with the Locke case. Or maybe not."

77

"Felipe was into a lot of things. My guess is that his death was connected to his other spy games. Felipe told me he had discovered almost nothing about Locke." Cecile spoke evenly. Damien sipped water and scowled as he listened. Cecile saw glimmers of intelligence in his face; he must have something in his head, she thought. Helene had married him. He couldn't be a total washout.

But she didn't want him on her case. She preferred to work alone.

"I plan to go over the same trail he made and see if I can come up with anything he might have missed," she continued, swishing her water. "I've started at the beginning. Gumshoe work. And there's a small convent in town I plan to visit. The sisters there know a lot about local problems. The friend that I mentioned to you before is there, Sister Rita, and she may have heard of Felipe. I'll check for you."

"Thanks," Damien nodded. "Nice of you."

He was being sarcastic. Cecile ignored it. "What was the cause of his death?" Cecile asked. "The exact cause?"

Damien spoke tersely. "I have the FBI report. Felipe Klondacki was found in West Perrine in one of the housing developments that hasn't been cleaned up since the hurricane. He fought with whoever killed him. There was a lot of blood and it wasn't all Felipe's. Felipe was knifed in the back through the ribs and into the heart. Severed the aorta. The weapon was probably one of those Ka-bar knives the Marines like, but it wasn't left in the body. The doc who did the autopsy was familiar with the type of damage inflicted. He bled a lot internally. He didn't stand a chance. It was a good man with the blade, whoever did it. Very professional."

His dark eyes jumped back to Cecile from the horizon.

"Frightening," Cecile said. "Miami's full of professionals." Casual words, but she felt cold in all that heat. She set her glass down on the table in order to wrap her arms around herself. "Poor man," she murmured. "It could have been anybody."

78

·"Not exactly anybody," Damien said dryly.

"People kill for little reason these days."

"Maybe," Damien grunted.

Cecile could see he wasn't going to admit to anything, even to a nun who was in his game.

"I'll be here in Miami until this is cleared up," he said. "I'm reviewing all of Klondacki's associates, and so on. Meanwhile you can report to me directly about your business with Locke. Perhaps we can clear it up together."

"Fine," Cecile said, but she didn't like it. "Damien, is there anyone else but me on the Bradley Locke case? I mean, aside from maybe you now?"

"You and maybe me," he said. "I already told you that. Felipe was not an inconsequential agent. Getting old, but still the best and he came up with nothing. We need to find Locke, Sister Cecile. We still need to do it with an outside agent. That's you, not the FBI. I thought I made that clear. You haven't done much so far, and our best man is dead. I don't particularly want to take over this case. The FBI wouldn't be happy to find one of us in their territory. You know the score on that."

He was laying the guilt trip on her. It wasn't fair. "I'm working on it. It's only been a few days. Hardly that. I've made connections."

"Sure." Damien looked at his watch, then at Cecile's face. Still beautiful. Then he looked around speculatively, from the ocean view back through the glassy walls to the interior of the condo. "Nice place," he said.

"Thank you."

"I have another problem." He smiled.

"What's that?" She didn't like the smile.

"I thought you could help me with something. It's good that you have a companion living here with you."

Cecile waited. Something very bad was coming. "Yes?"

"My daughter has chicken pox."

"I'm sorry," Cecile murmured politely.

"Her school doesn't want her for a couple of weeks.

79

Probably two. I need to have her at home, but I'm here. The housekeeper had a death in the family and had to go away."

He paused while it sank in. "How many rooms do you have here?"

"I don't have any. The condo belongs to my lawyer."

"I did some checking on this lawyer."

"I did mention before where I'd be. It was no secret."

"Neither is what goes on between you and this lawyer."

It sounded like bribery or blackmail, but there were only two people in the world who knew what went on between herself and Paul, and of course that was herself and Paul. On the other hand, he was talking about a child who was also Helene's daughter. And she really had cared deeply for her friend, Helene. Sister Cecile waited to hear what would come next.

"Leonie is arriving at five o'clock at Homestead Air Force Base. I was hoping she could stay here. She isn't terribly sick. Just contagious and her school is very clear about these things. They want her to stay out of school until the scabs fall off."

"How did you ever dare put her on an airplane? The poor child!"

"It's a government plane. No big deal, but I want to have her somewhere comfortable."

"And you presume upon me."

"Who presumes upon that lawyer."

Cecile didn't like the way he said, "that lawyer." She was very fond of Paul. If she weren't a nun, she might marry him. Everyone knew that. But a little girl was arriving and it would be a crime to dump her in a hotel somewhere with nobody except Damien, even if he was her father. Besides, he would probably be out most of the time. That would be no situation for a sick little girl. It would be cruel. But was this child her responsibility?

"Raphael has work to do. She won't be here a lot of the

time, nor will I. Neither of us will be here to babysit. We can't possibly take care of a sick child."

She was weakening. It was in her voice.

"Leonie is twelve, well used to being alone."

"I can believe that."

"And you've already had chicken pox?"

Cecile nodded, fingering a tiny round scar on her forehead. "There's Sister Raphael. She's old. If she were to become sick it could be serious. She could develop shingles."

"Ask her."

"I should also ask Paul."

"Sure, ask Paul."

She didn't like the look in his eye, sneaky somehow. Of course Paul would say yes to a little girl. She didn't even need to ask him and she didn't plan to. She had already been in touch with Paul since her arrival, just telling him things were wonderful here. He wouldn't care about a little girl staying with them. Twelve *was* little, wasn't it? But she didn't want Damien staying here. That was probably the next scheme in the man's devious mind. "All right, Damien. Leonie, yes. You, no. That's the deal, providing that Raphael has already had chicken pox."

"I wasn't planning on staying here," he said, but there was enough of a twitch to his lips when he said it to make Cecile know she had guessed right. He had definitely wanted to slip into the condo along with his child.

"Where will you be staying?" she asked.

Damien didn't answer for a minute. "Down the beach, I guess. I'll let you know my number as soon as I check in." He rubbed his neck, thoughtfully. "Thanks. She'll be more comfortable here. Leonie is a sweet kid. Meanwhile, I'll be busy. I'm going to run a trace on Felipe's Miami business and see what he was into. If I find any connection with your thing, I'll join you in the search for Bradley Locke. Does that make sense to you?"

Cecile felt considerable relief. It was still her case.

"Fine. Meanwhile, I'll continue on the few leads that I have. I have ideas. Some possibilities. I expect I'll turn up something."

"Like what?"

"It's still my case, isn't it?" She smiled.

"True. I'm offering you support. Don't be touchy. You're being hostile. You report to me, remember?"

Cecile blinked. He was absolutely right. It wasn't his fault that he was rubbing her the wrong way. He really wasn't so bad, in fact he was quite good looking as men go, and quite intelligent. He really *didn't* want to take over her case. She would try to do better.

She forced a smile. "I'm sorry, Damien. I *am* being touchy. It's the heat, maybe, and of course I'm terribly upset about Felipe. I saw him that night, and he didn't deserve to die. One can only hope he made his peace with God." She stopped speaking for a moment. "I guess that about covers the business, then. Shall we go in and see about Raphael and the chicken pox?"

"Please."

# 14

SISTER Raphael had experienced chicken pox when she was eight years old and was thrilled with the idea of a small visitor.

"Damien's daughter. How fascinating. Such an interesting man," Raphael said after the man himself had left to check into his motel. "The girl must be quite lovely."

"Why?"

"He's nice looking," Raphael said. "You don't like him, of course. It's obvious."

"It is? I was trying hard to be nice. The man annoys me, but I'm getting used to him. I'll do better next time."

Raphael grinned. "There's the indisputable fact that he's a man. You're probably jealous because he married your best friend. I like him. You shouldn't be jealous, you know. You could have married and had a man and half dozen children by now. Plus all that money. You did have too much money, Cecile, and it drives some people absolutely wild to think you turned it all down to be a nun. *You* have no cause for jealousy."

"Me, jealous?" Cecile looked inward for a moment. She sighed and looked out through the glass wall that faced the ocean. "Maybe I am. It's hard to climb the mountain, isn't it? Pride always gets in the way. Meanwhile, I'll do my best with this little girl. It's occurred to me that I know nothing about children. I don't have a clue."

Raphael smiled. "You will."

"I'll need your help."

"I never had children either, don't forget."

"But you have nieces and nephews," Cecile said firmly. Raphael knew everything, Cecile had always been sure of that. "Besides, you're kind. Sometimes the most simple things are hard for me. Being civil, for example. It's easy for me to deal with the weak and the suffering, but I have trouble with the rich and powerful. I just don't like them all that much. And I simply don't *know* about children." She paused. "I have to go out now, Raphael. Work. Damien accused me of doing nothing, in so many words, but I just didn't tell him everything I have planned. He'd interfere."

"Where are you going?"

"Out."

"Out," Raphael said. "Good luck. On your way, could you drop me by that row of shops nearby? I need to get a few things."

They left five minutes later, still wearing the dark skirt and white blouse habits they had worn to church. Cecile could have worn her civilian clothes; it was too hot to wear the navy skirt but she wore it like a penance, offering the discomfort of sticky clothing for the repose of Felipe's soul and for her own shortcomings.

Suddenly Sister Cecile missed Boston. The case was getting to her, so was the heat. She was out of sorts from Damien's visit and the fact that he would be returning with a twelve-year-old to disorder her life. Being a babysitter was no way to be a detective. Leaving the child with her was such a typically male thing of Damien to do. Such a *male* thing to assume she knew about children just because she was a woman. Cecile realized she didn't have a clue about young people, but she would never have admitted that to Damien. Maybe she should have. Then maybe he wouldn't be bringing the child here, although there was no place for a twelve-year-old with him in a motel either. On the other hand, she had Sister Raphael, and Sister Raphael, as usual, always had the answer. Why couldn't she, herself, have the answer?

And was she really jealous? Jealousy, on top of everything else? "Sorry, God," she murmured inaudibly. "I'll work on this one."

Some days it was very hard to be a nun.

She dropped Raphael off at the Lincoln Road Mall, handing her a piece of gold plastic. "Use the credit card," she advised. "It's all part of our cover. Anything you buy for our survival here is okay. And take a taxi home. It's too hot to walk."

From Lincoln Road it took Cecile less than ten minutes to drive to Bradley Locke's former hotel. Cecile had all the information in her purse as to what room Bradley had stayed in, what car he had driven, how many meals per day went with the travel package (two) as well as a few places Bradley was thought to have visited. It was all in Felipe Klondacki's report that she had received back in Boston. Contrary to what Damien had said, that Felipe was one of their best agents, it wasn't a very good report and it wasn't very complete. The papers Felipe had filed were a sad reflection on a tired agent, Cecile thought. A dead agent. Now it was up to her.

Cecile found a parking space in front of the Bella Vista Hotel and parked the Testarossa where it would be visible through the glass front of the small, Art Deco building. Pink and green. She glanced left and right, up and down Collins Avenue looking for surveillance. There was nothing in sight but old men in sunglasses, women with hair green from chlorinated pools, and air-conditioned cars with heavily tinted windows going by too fast. There was no Thunderbird. No Dirty Bobby.

She walked slowly into Bradley Locke's former hotel. The Bella Vista was borderline seedy, with a steady clientele of Germans getting a budget price and Americans who had discovered one of the Beach's best bargains. There was a small dining and lounge area with a bar, and a front desk tended by a man in a panama hat. The man was smoking a pipe.

Everyone inside the Bella Vista had seen the Testarossa pull up and the nun slide out. A few eyes raked her curiously as Cecile came in and approached the desk. A veil of dense, freshly puffed pipe smoke surrounded the desk clerk like a volcanic spume. His name plate read "Ken Newly."

"Help you?"

"I'm hoping you can give me some information about one of your former occupants," Cecile began. She pulled back to let the cloud of smoke shift away.

"Yeah," he said. "Who's that?"

"Bradley Locke. He was registered here for a week and left unexpectedly." She smiled, then took a quick breath from a pocket of clean air.

Ken Newly scratched an ear. "I know Locke. Everybody comes here asking about that guy. I tell everybody what he did. He gets here, he eats his complimentary breakfast, he hits the beach, he comes back, writes a couple postcards, dresses up, and goes out some place in town. Five days of that. I seen his room. The man's been to Parrot Jungle, he's been on the air boats in the glades, he's been to the SoBe bars. He left all the matchbooks in a drawer and the detective took them."

"SoBe?" She pronounced it "so-be" as he had.

"South Beach," he said.

"Oh. Is there anything that Bradley may have said or done that might indicate where he could have gone that last night?" She was fishing. Of course she knew where he had last been seen, but maybe there was more.

"Not a damn thing. He always come back for his free dinner, part of the travel package. All but that last night. Sorry."

"No people he talked with? People who might have talked with him? Even a service person?"

"Nobody." Ken Newly stared at the nun. She looked good. Her cheeks were flushed from the heat and her eyes had turned from pale to dark gray. Some of her curls were stuck to the side of her cheeks by sweat. To Ken

86

Newly, the veil meant next to nothing. Nuns were women, that was all.

"Well, thank you, anyway. May I take a look around? Would that be all right with you?"

"Feel free."

Cecile stepped away from the pipe-smoke cloud and looked. The lobby was very Florida with industrial strength art deco furniture made from heavy metal pipes and pink plastic cushions. There was a scattering of small potted palms. The dining area appeared to be clean and cozy. The scent of garlic drifted out the swinging glass doors, garlic and tomatoes to be exact. The smell reminded Sister Cecile that it was lunch time. This was a golden opportunity.

She went through the glass doors and slid into a pink booth. Plastic coated menus stood upright between catsup bottles and napkin holders. A chalkboard advertised the day's specials, starting with Jambalaya and Cajun rice.

A few moments later Cecile decided on split pea bisque and the Jambalaya. She asked for mineral water to drink. After her order was taken, Cecile continued to read the menu like a novel. It was enough to make her contemplate moving out of Paul's condo and into a suite at the Bella Vista. She wondered where the chef had trained.

She flipped to the dessert page. "Maybe they have take-outs," she said out loud. She looked around to see if anyone had heard her. Nobody. There were only a few couples at random tables, heavily involved in eating. None of them looked like hangers-on, and that was a disappointment. What she had in mind was someone who spent a lot of time here. Maybe the cook? The wait staff? She would be lucky if they spoke English.

Then Cecile looked up as someone walked to the door and pushed it open. Interesting, she thought, as the newcomer—a woman—looked around, and then met Cecile's eyes with a knowing gleam.

Cecile felt a bell ring somewhere in the back of her mind. It was reminiscent of a chapel bell, or the bell rung at the Consecration. Something important was about to happen.

# 15

THE woman hesitated for a moment, then walked directly to Cecile's table. She sat down on the other side of Cecile's booth.

"My name's Violet," the stranger said. "I heard you talking to Ken. I was in the back."

The woman's red tank top clung to a thin, pale figure, her short skirt rose high. She wore white stacked heels and huge, gold hoop earrings topped by another pair of earrings, these diamond studs. "I heard you," she repeated.

"I was looking for information," Cecile said. "My name is Sister Cecile."

"About Bradley?" Violet asked. "You telling me you're a nun?"

"Yes." The pea soup arrived. "Would you like some? I missed lunch earlier."

"Sure. Tell Armand I want a bowl," Violet said to the waiter. "And some ham soufflé."

"You know Bradley Locke?" Cecile asked.

"I seen him 'round." She had a soft drawl, Central Florida Cracker.

"You know where he is?" Sister Cecile studied the woman in front of her. Violet had an attractive but pale face, a native avoiding skin cancer. There was something angelic about her pretty looks; light blond hair pulled up high on her head, a beginning of crinkles at the edges of her eyes. "He's missing."

"I heard. People been around, looking." Violet paused,

smiling slightly. "I got an idea about his friends. I mean, Ken could have told you stuff, like who else was checking up on Bradley. But Ken's funny. *El Chulo*, you know?"

Cecile didn't know. "Maybe you can help me?"

"Maybe."

The second bowl of pea soup arrived and both women began to eat. Violet made soft slurping sounds, like a little cat anxious to finish every drop before a bigger cat came along. Cecile decided to let her be the next to speak and worked on her own soup. The woman seemed touchy, slightly vague, as though she might drift away if she heard things she didn't like.

Violet didn't talk again until her bowl was empty and the second courses had appeared.

"So why are you a nun?" Her light eyes were curious, then they dropped to look carefully at her ham soufflé. She pulled off a bite with her fingers.

"That's what I do."

"That's cool." Violet thought a minute. "I hear a lot of people come in here looking for Bradley. I saw him a little. He's here, I'm here. We do some business."

"Business?"

Violet shrugged. "My business. Okay? Why do you want him?" She picked up her fork. Apparently she was not going to eat the entire soufflé with her hands.

Cecile didn't answer for a moment. She took a large scoop of Jambalaya instead. It had occurred to her at first that Violet was a prostitute. Yes, definitely, that's what she was, and she must have known Bradley like that. This could be another golden opportunity. "Maybe you can help me? I think he's in danger. I'm here in Miami for my convent, but Bradley's a friend of a friend. The friend wanted me to find him. I'm really afraid he's been kidnapped because I don't think he would have just vanished all by himself."

"Maybe, maybe. He wasn't rich, was he?" Violet began using the fork to eat.

"No."

"But he *looked* rich, didn't he? Fat rental car, nice face. I can always tell *real* rich. Maybe someone grabbed him," Violet said, chewing thoughtfully. "He was all right. I know everyone in town's been by here looking for him. I'll tell you what I know for two hundred bucks."

Cecile nodded faintly, feeling sick. Her golden opportunity was turning into Violet's golden opportunity. That was why Violet had come over. Money. She had known the Testarossa was going to cause trouble. She should have picked up the Omni first. "That's a lot of information, two hundred dollars' worth."

"Worth every penny, believe me, Sister. I want to drive that car, too. Let's go for a ride, then I'll talk."

"Money and a chance to drive the car," Cecile hedged. "The car's a rental. Not mine. Very tough to drive."

"I'm an excellent driver. I drove one last month. But first we eat," Violet said. "First things first."

Violet looked down at her ham soufflé and Cecile looked at her Jambalaya. They began to eat simultaneously.

"Great stuff," Cecile said when they were done.

"It's cool. I got a nice life here. *El Chulo* isn't so bad. Maybe I'll retire here."

"You live here?"

"No way. I got a place in the Grove. I'm a working woman."

Cecile was tired, suddenly. Goodness and evil were so close. She slid her credit card out for the waiter who came over and took it. Then Cecile pulled out two hundred dollar bills from her envelope and handed them to Violet, not without reservation. "I hope it's worth it," she muttered.

"Every penny, like I said," Violet nodded and stuffed the cash in her pocket.

Moments later the check was paid and they were out

91

on the sidewalk, climbing into the car. Violet took the driver's side, as agreed.

They left with a roar. Violet wove the beast in and out around cars, down a side street, then up and down Ocean Drive, along Miami Beach, honking and waving at a few people. At first she drove slowly so that everyone could see them. Then she sped up. "Too early," she muttered. "Nobody's out yet." She turned the car back and headed for the causeway.

"Now we'll do a little slumming," Violet announced as they passed by lines of elegant palms, with turquoise water gleaming on both sides of the road.

She hummed all the way into Miami proper and drove into a questionable neighborhood, looping in and around some heavily populated streets. She stomped on the brakes at a red light, then waved her hand to the left, pointing at a street sign. "Check that Fish Street, number seventy. Punk little man named Dirty Bobby Ortez lives down there. Dirty Bobby Ortez," she smirked. "Get that name, girl. He comes in last week and starts shaking up the joint trying to find out how much this Bradley buck is worth. I seen him around. Dirty Bobby sells, see. He works a group here in town, runs the voodoo show right here on Fish Street every Wednesday night. Eleven P.M."

"Eleven at night. Right there. You think I should go?"

"Voodoo? Sure. Maybe they'll toss your Bradley up on the table for dinner, cut out his heart. I'm telling you, this is good, clean fun. This is what you paid for, so make a note." She talked in spurts, the same way she was driving the car. Cecile's head began banging. Dirty Bobby.

The red light changed and Violet gunned the car, heading back to the Bella Vista. "Dirty Bobby, he knows something about your friend of a friend. Talk to him, you find out, but don't dress like a fucking nun. I mean, like a nun." She grinned. "Sorry," she said.

"Good advice," Cecile said in a soft voice.

Dirty Bobby. At least Violet's information confirmed

what she already had on that man. Now she had an address. Fish Street. And voodoo?

She heard distant drums in her imagination.

"Anyone else looking for Bradley?" she asked Violet.

"Couple of people. Some older guy with a gold tooth looked like a cop, and someone else, little Cuban guy comes in sniffing around right after Dirty Bobby, name of Bajito. Means 'shorty' in Spanish. He sure fit the part!" Violet laughed. "Bajito hangs with Dirty Bobby. I don't know why they're both asking about him. Ken didn't tell him nothing either. I seen Bajito around, though. He hangs out some place west. I done a job there with a friend once."

"Really? West? In the Everglades? Do you think they'll be back? I'll pay for any information you can get me. You say they work together, this Bajito and Dirty Bobby?"

"They work together, and they don't, if you know what I mean. They don't got a lotta trust. Dirty Bobby's one mean son of a bitch. You don't want to get close. Nobody does."

They were at the hotel again and the car wasn't even panting from the exertion. Both occupants jerked forward as Violet put on the brakes.

"That's it."

"Thank you, Violet. You've been very helpful. Two hundred dollars' worth."

"How much more if I find out something really good for you?" Violet asked.

"Another two hundred," Cecile said. "It's important. Bradley's life may depend on it."

"Bradley was okay," Violet said thoughtfully. "No reason to kill that man. He was definitely a gentleman. What did he do?"

"He has some important information. And I don't want him to die." Cecile added, "It's beginning to look like a kidnapping."

"Umm, yeah. Okay, you give a call for me here in a

day or so. Meanwhile, I'll start looking around and see what I can scrape up," Violet said. "You call back here at the hotel, talk to Ken. Violet Packard, that's me. Ken, he knows how to get in touch with me in a hurry," she grinned. "Ken's *El Chulo*."

"I will," Cecile nodded, not quite ready to ask what *El Chulo* was.

"I'll keep looking," Violet muttered to herself, and continued talking as she hopped out of the car and swayed away on her white stacked heels. She was walking with a bounce and looked happy. It sounded as though what she was saying was, "That's a cool nun," but it didn't seem likely.

Cecile got out and went around to the driver's side. She sat in the car and put her head back against the perfectly shaped leather backrest and breathed out a long, deep sigh. Then she headed back to the condo, one eye on the rearview mirror.

# 16

AFTER fourteen tries, Bradley Locke finally hooked a shoot of marijuana on the bent paper clip. Dry and green with too many of the little leaves falling off the thin branches, it came slowly across the floor. The weed was almost weightless. Bradley held his breath and dragged it tenderly until it finally reached his cat hole. It was his first success after days of saving straws, sticking them together, breaking them as he tried and tried again to make his device.

Victory was sweet and so was the air twenty minutes later when Bradley had finished constructing the first joint in a thin newspaper wrapper. He hid the extra grass in the pile of newspapers. Not that anyone ever came in. He hadn't seen a human face in weeks.

He lit the joint with his Mickey Mouse cigarette lighter. He didn't smoke these days, but he'd carried a lighter ever since he was a teenager when he'd smoked to be "with it." Cigarette lighters were handy in a thousand ways; today's a case in point. And this lighter was a lucky piece. They hadn't taken it from him. In fact they hadn't taken anything but the money from his wallet. Life, maybe, wasn't a total bummer, he thought as he puffed away. It was amazing how it all came together with a good joint. Not that he had ever really done anything with drugs. It hadn't been his thing. Drugs were strictly for medicinal use. They were bad.

This, he thought carefully, as he puffed and puffed on the joint, is an anesthetic. He wouldn't smoke grass anymore once he was out of here. But he sure could use a few extra tacos for supper. He was suddenly starving.

He looked around for some leftover scraps to eat but there was nothing but the small crumb he had made a habit of leaving out for the palmetto bug. Briefly he considered picking up the crumb and eating it. There was the bug himself, nibbling at a puddle of spilled taco sauce. Some people ate bugs, Bradley knew. He would never eat George. And he wouldn't eat the scrap either.

"Not good to eat bugs," Bradley murmured. "Not you, George." He inhaled smoke from the joint and let out a long silver stream onto the bug. "Have a blast, George," he murmured.

George began to wobble about on the floor.

Packages covered Sister Cecile's bed. "Raphael, what on earth have you bought?"

Sister Raphael emerged from her own room when she heard the younger nun calling her name and came into Sister Cecile's room.

"I went shopping," Raphael announced, taking a slow turn on her flat black shoes, "for our Florida habits." She wore an off-white skirt and blouse with her cross taking center stage, hanging from her withered neck. "All in that new wrinkle-free cotton. One hundred percent cotton is the only thing that's comfortable here. I used that credit card, and the store people didn't even question it. Do you like it? Do you think the credit card will work on all these nun clothes? I mean, ethically?"

"It's all part of the operation. We need them to survive here. They're our cover." Cecile laughed suddenly. "Get it? Cover?"

"I do," Raphael sighed.

"That looks very comfortable, and don't worry, Paul will verify the expenses as part of my operation. Although, I suppose that means I'll have to tell him there actually *is* an operation. What's all this stuff on my bed?"

"Hot weather clothes for you. Some skirts and blouses. A few things I thought you might need."

"Good." Sister Cecile began dumping out the bags. Two off-white cotton skirts, one long, one short, and an off-white cotton suit of some sort, and several blouses. They were attractive and considerably more wearable than the heavy navy skirt and blouse she had on. And Raphael had gotten everything in the right size.

Raphael continued, "The real estate person called twenty minutes ago and the owners of the motel are willing to drop the price twenty thousand. I said we'd go ahead if they went down another ten because we simply must make that swimming pool operational and it does need serious work. I could move right in, you know, and start supervising the workmen. The utilities are on."

Sister Cecile nodded. "If they drop it another ten, we can't refuse, can we? Unfortunately, I don't believe we can buy the motel with the credit card even though buying the home is our cover story for being here. That's taking ethics a little too far. I'll have to start making telephone calls north and lining up the money."

"I already have. The motel's a perfect place. I've been talking to the Archdiocesan people here in town. I have a friend in the Miami chancellery. They think it's a good idea. And I have a call in to Mère Sulpicia in Paris."

Cecile was amazed. "How did you get all this done?"

Raphael looked out at the kitchen. "It's the microwave."

"Oh."

"Well, it's very fast. Also, I'm thawing a steak for us for Sunday dinner. And we're going to have to get some chips and things on hand for that teenager who's coming. Damien is bringing her right here, isn't he?"

Cecile felt a shudder of apprehension as she glanced at her watch. "Very soon. But she's only twelve. She's not a teenager."

Raphael smiled at that bit of erroneous thinking. "Teenage starts at age ten and frequently lasts until the

97

age of twenty-five. Wait and see. It's six o'clock right now. They'll be here soon. I found some frozen taco mix for the girl, and there's ice cream. I'll buy groceries tomorrow if you give me cash."

"Fine. I called the rental agency earlier and we can pick up the other rental car in the morning. You can use it," Cecile agreed, noticing, suddenly, that once again her life was being ordered by the older nun. "I'm your superior, you know."

"I know," Raphael said. "I'll check that steak."

Violet Packard had really been impressed with the Testarossa. Driving that sweet car had been a nice break in her life. Sister Cecile had been okay, too, even though she was a nun.

Violet arrived back at the Bella Vista feeling important but slightly uneasy. She'd made two hundred dollars for doing nothing and she felt vaguely guilty because she hadn't told the nun everything she could have. Violet had plenty of guilt, but she didn't usually notice it. This time she did because she was well aware that Dirty Bobby was closely connected with Olimpo Olarte-Rodríguez, and that the little creep, Bajito, was another associate of Olimpo's. Two of Olimpo's cronies doing the same thing meant that Olimpo himself was involved.

Violet was drawing a little picture of a triangle on the paper napkin in the hotel restaurant. She drew letters in each corner: an "O," a "B," and a "DB" for Olimpo, Bajito, and Dirty Bobby. Olimpo was key, and she had liked Olimpo. He had been almost kind, and he had a real way with words. Not the other two. Dirty Bobby was a sadist and Bajito was just an ambitious little twerp, too smart for his own good.

Violet finished her triangle and sat back against the booth's sticky plastic and closed her eyes. She was having a late afternoon beer; business wouldn't start moving for another hour or two. She felt she should do something. Maybe she should go see Olimpo himself. He was pretty cool, but running a bad group. And he always had hashish, she recalled. For a prostitute, Violet wasn't much of a doper, but she never looked a gift horse in the mouth and Olimpo had been generous. She'd been to his shack one night for a party and was certain it wouldn't be too hard for her to find the place again. "Maybe I'll take a little ride out," she said out loud, pushing the beer in a circle to make a wet pattern across the table. Then she yawned. "Maybe later."

"How about right now, Baby," came a voice and Violet looked up. Sure thing, lover, she thought. Maybe she'd go to the shack tomorrow. There was always tomorrow. Time now to make a few bucks.

Damien and his daughter Leonie arrived at the condo at six-thirty, just about the time Sister Raphael put the instant taco mixture into the microwave.

"We can turn it on as soon as they get here. She'll probably be hungry."

"She's sick, Raphael. She has the chicken pox. Maybe some ginger ale would be good."

That was when the buzzer sounded and Raphael bustled to the door to let them in. Moments later they were all together: Leonie Drail, a thin, light-haired child covered with red spots, and Damien looking ineffectual, perhaps because of his change in roles. Introductions were quick.

"I'm fine," Leonie said when Raphael asked if she'd like to lie down. "I could use a Coke. Or maybe a coffee. And a bathroom."

"Coffee?" Cecile recalled that coffee was supposed to stunt one's growth. However, Leonie was already about five foot three. "Tacos," she said firmly. She had read somewhere that one should be strict with children at first, then smile later. "But, first, your room, Leonie, and the bathroom. Damien, if you would be so kind as to bring in Leonie's luggage, we can see to all the settling in."

Damien obliged with a grunt and soon Cecile and Leonie were alone in Paul's third bedroom; a room complete with private bath and extension telephone. "Cool," Leonie said and flopped on the bed. "Dad's been really crapped up about this, me getting sick and everything. He said you knew my mother?" She looked tired and feverish, but restless as she got up again from the bed and began walking around the room touching things.

"Yes." Cecile popped open Leonie's suitcase latch and began pulling out a rumpled wad of wool slacks, thick sweaters, and heavy socks. Everything had been stuffed in. Leonie must have packed this herself, Cecile thought.

Cecile looked over at the girl, who had crossed the room and was looking out a glass wall. Cecile eyed the suitcase and the winter clothes and felt itchy. No one could wear those woolies here. Right now the child was dressed in blue jeans and a sweatshirt and it was eighty-five degrees out. Her blond hair was a sticky mess, not to mention her face, a pretty face under all the chicken pox, but a very sad face. There was a lot of work to be done here. Helene's daughter had problems worse than chicken pox. For Helene she would do her best, Cecile determined, and she squashed the frantic urge to call Sister Raphael in for help.

"This room is all yours," Cecile explained and suddenly she smiled quite unintentionally. "The television has a remote, the bathroom is private, and of course we have a full refrigerator and freezer in the kitchen. Do you know how to use a microwave?"

"You gotta be kidding," Leonie said.

"Okay. You're contagious until the pox stop forming those little dewdrop blisters, so I'm afraid you have to stay indoors. Sister Raphael put a box of baking soda in your bathroom. A soaking bath with half a cup of baking soda in it is recommended when those things start to itch unbearably. And you'll have your father's number. He'll be on a case. I suppose you know."

Leonie looked at the nun. The twelve-year-old had

100

moved to a defiant stance, her skinny legs spread in Clint Eastwood position. "Daddy has a thing for you."

"Well, I'm sure he can handle it."

Leonie laughed, sounding like her mother, years ago. "You're cool." She looked unendurably sad in spite of her laugh.

"Thanks, Leonie. Now we have to get some supper."

Sister Cecile looked at the girl, and then something inside her gave way. The nun came up to Leonie and gave her a big hug, letting Leonie bury her face in Cecile's new cotton blouse for a moment. Cecile patted her gently. "You'll be fine. Really, you will."

Silent, Leonie jerked away and stomped over to the window. She looked very small.

"You're so much like your mother," Cecile began tentatively. "She was pretty, like you."

Leonie didn't turn.

"She was adventurous," Cecile added. "Always investigating things, inventing new names for things. Are you like that?"

Leonie's stiff shoulders popped up in a bumpy shrug.

"She was a lot of fun, Leonie." Cecile stopped. Maybe this wasn't the time to talk about such things. "I'll call you when supper's ready."

# 17

DAMIEN left an hour later, fed with steak and the knowledge that his daughter was in safe hands. Cecile had told him briefly about her trip to the Bella Vista and how she had met a prostitute named Violet who claimed to have known Bradley. It probably didn't mean a thing, Cecile had declared.

Damien wasn't sure he agreed. It might be important.

The only help Damien had been able to give Cecile was to tell her what *El Chulo* meant. That, he had informed Cecile with an evil grin, was Spanish for pimp. "Where did you meet one of those?" he had asked.

"Violet mentioned the word. I was just curious."

Damien left reluctantly because he *did* have a thing for Cecile. It was more than a thing; he wasn't at all certain he could handle it. His normally surly daughter had actually spoken to the younger nun, and he had heard Leonie chatting to Raphael in the kitchen. Being a single father had not been in the cards when Leonie arrived twelve years ago. His wife's death had been hard; it had turned Damien hard too. He still tried to be a good father, but Leonie looked so much like Helene that it was impossible to be around her for long without hurting. He was always hurting.

His usual justification for leaving Leonie was his work. He would habitually immerse himself in the case at hand, review all the facts, and do something. Something dangerous, usually, because Helene was dead. Death seemed like an answer sometimes.

Damien drove directly to the Bella Vista.

Violet had finished with her customer and gone for a stroll down the beach. It was a slow night and Ken didn't have any more hot tips. Ken was her pimp, but unlike many in that profession, he was an easygoing sort who only took a percentage from the profits he himself generated. Violet's private customers were her own. Ken always kept his eye out for likely prospects so he could get his cut.

Meanwhile, Violet walked. She carried her shoes and felt the sand between her toes. Walking in sand was good for you, and she loved the sand. Exercise kept her in shape, and being in shape meant money. The day would come when she would be too old for this business, she thought as she kicked sand. But she would probably be dead by then. She wiped the sweat off her chin and turned around to go back to work.

When Ken spotted Damien he could smell a profit. He set his sleepy eyes at half-mast and began studying the old-fashioned, hand-written register, making invisible calculations with his finger in order to appear busy. He wasn't at all surprised when Damien came up to him with that sideways movement common to men looking for action.

"Girl named Violet around?" Damien asked.

Ken's face was impassive. "Violet? What's she look like?" He looked down at the register as if to see whether there were any Violets listed.

"Pretty. Nice-looking woman." Damien guessed.

"Who's looking?" He looked up again and met Damien's eyes. Dark, deadly serious. No fun in this man. Ken didn't like what he saw.

"Name's Mike," Damien improvised. "Friend of mine told me she hung around here. Said to look her up."

"You into anything mean, Mike?" Ken asked. He didn't like Damien's looks. Damien looked too smart to be a hired hand. He was the boss type, and he could be into something nasty. Ken felt a very faint obligation to

103

protect Violet from the worst of possibilities, although it didn't always work out that way.

"I am one extremely considerate gentleman," Damien smiled.

Ken wasn't sure about Damien at all, but business was business. This one he'd leave up to Violet. "She's around. Get yourself a drink at the bar, I'll tell her you're waiting when she turns up."

Damien nodded abruptly and went, going into the same dining room where Sister Cecile had been earlier that day. The bar was to the rear and he settled onto one of the tall stools, ordered a beer, and took a long drink when it arrived moments later.

He was on his second beer when Violet came up beside him and pulled a stool so close that their legs brushed. She moved her leg again, just enough to let him know it was on purpose. He was shocked to find himself reacting to the old familiar routine much too quickly. Violet was attractive; he liked her moves, and he felt a warm heat inside him. Damn, he thought. Get control.

"You Violet?"

"Who's asking?"

"Me." Damien smiled.

"Sure, I'm Violet."

"You got some place we can talk?" he asked. He watched her eyes slide down his shirt to his pants. He was a professional, he was beyond this stuff. Really. But it was sex and it had hit him like a stomach punch because he wasn't prepared. There was nothing in the agenda about this. Violet, in the tank top, huge heels, and shimmering thighs, had gotten to him in seconds.

"I got some business I want to talk over," he said again, embarrassed when she didn't answer right away. "Important stuff, see."

"Important stuff," Violet repeated. "What's your name?" she asked.

"Uh, Bill," Damien answered, forgetting he had been Mike a few minutes ago. It was Violet's doing and she was good at it; the contrast between her profession and the way she looked was making Damien unravel. For all her experience, she still had something of the child about her and it really worked on him. It was as though she had never quite grown up.

She nodded. "Up front they said your name was Mike. Okay, now, tell me the truth, Billy-Mike, you tell me who sent you along or we got no business at all. Who put you on to me, Billy-Mike?"

Violet licked her lips long and slowly, grinning at him from her seat on the bar stool, looking directly up into his eyes. Then she looked down to his chest as though she could see right through to the pink skin hiding behind a sweat dampened white shirt. She grabbed for the stomach and nuzzled him, right there. "Speak up," she ordered, rubbing her face into his soft flesh.

He couldn't stand this. She was coming at him right in the bar. His heart started thumping and he knew they had to get somewhere else. "Damn nun. Sister Cecile," he mumbled. "She told me about you."

"That nun?" She laughed again, licking him right through his shirt. "Let's go, sweetmeat. You got a nice reference. Just make sure you give the sister a great big cut next time you see her."

She steered him past Ken, giving the desk man a big wink, then on to a first floor room way in the back, down a corridor, out of sight.

"Money," she said when they were alone in the room. She held out her hand and mentioned the going rate.

Damien produced the bills and handed them over. She placed them on the dresser and gave them a pat.

"Too damn hot," she said and started stripping down fast until she had nothing on but the heels. "Cheap air-conditioning around here." Then she turned to see what Damien was doing. He had gotten as far as unbuttoning his shirt and then he stopped as though paralyzed while fear of AIDS and other social diseases coursed through his veins.

Fear wasn't enough. He'd better think a minute.

He didn't ordinarily do prostitutes but he had become intoxicated, physically and mentally, with what was happening to him. Nice-looking woman, clean-looking, really. "You sure you haven't got AIDS?" he croaked. Leonie needed a father.

"Not yet." She paused. "Maybe. No." Then she shook her head. "I take precautions. See, I got this bag here full of all sizes."

"So I'll be all right?" He knew it sounded dumb. This was not just dumb. It was unprofessional. "I got a kid."

"You'll be just fine."

He hoped so. Really he did.

Why was he doing this?

# 18

WHEN it was over, Damien lay back on the pillow; he was covered with a fine sweat. It was startling to discover how exciting it was, the danger of it, the threat, the almost disembodied sensation of the sex act with a stranger. He liked this woman, Violet, so that made it all right. Almost moral. He laughed. "I don't do this, ordinarily."

"I reckoned you were someone who'd never done it before, but then when you said you had a kid, I figured, well, maybe you'd just done it once. Know what I mean?"

"Think you're funny," he said.

"Think you're too good for me," Violet retorted. She was already up, heading for the bathroom. She stopped and turned to him. "So, say you get AIDS," she said suddenly. "Your wife takes the kid. No big deal."

"Wife's dead," Damien said and turned away. Damn it.

"So, who keeps the kid if you die?"

He shrugged. "I made a will. She gets the money."

"Who's the guardian?" Violet was a businessperson, even stark naked except for the shoes. Besides, she had a big thing for kids.

"I haven't done that," Damien said, pulling on underwear that had somehow gotten down to the foot of the bed and was full of sand. Violet had kept her shoes on and the whole bed was full of sand that she had picked up on the beach.

"My God, what if a truck hits you. Your kid becomes a

ward of the courts. If she's rich, all the creeps on the family tree will claim her."

"Not likely," Damien grunted, reaching for his socks. I don't even have any family. Then he thought a minute. "You're right."

Damien suddenly felt guilty for all the wrong reasons.

"So fuckin' write it out on a piece of paper, right now. Don't wait. Sign it and the kid's safe. Who's gonna be the guardian?"

Damien fell back on the bed again. He had come here to find out about Bradley Locke. Was that true, or wasn't it? And so far he hadn't even mentioned the missing agent's name. Instead he was being asked to make out a codicil to his will by a prostitute he had never seen before. He closed his eyes to shut out the cheaply furnished room. This really was nuts.

"Nobody," he muttered. "There's nobody who could handle Leonie and the money. So what? I'm not about to die." He sat up.

"You might. What about the nun? You know, the nun, your reference?" Violet chortled. "Hell of a guardian, a nun. Hey, you buy the farm, she's an unwed mother."

"Sister Cecile?" Damien's eyes glazed over. It was the nun's fault he was here. It was her fault in more ways than one because if Cecile hadn't gotten him all fired up he wouldn't have come here and, well, she was probably the best person in the world to make Leonie's guardian. Leonie needed a guardian. "The nun was a friend of my wife's," he said. "That's it."

"Couldn't be better. Do it."

Violet tottered over to the desk and pulled out some Bella Vista stationery. Her skin was pale all over, not a strap mark, not anything except for the shoes and a couple of purple bruises on her buttocks from a bad night last week. Damien could barely follow her words as she waved the paper at him, but he tried even as his eyes focused firmly on jiggling flesh.

"You're crazy," Damien said, but Violet was persistent, and sat down next to him, rubbing against him like a sweet, hairless kitten. It was reflex again. He didn't even know this woman, but it seemed as though she cared. She really must care. He started to nuzzle her neck.

"Write it out on this," Violet purred. "We'll take it out to the desk and Ken and I can witness it for you. Then he can run off a couple of copies and you'll be all set. Nice and tight. It's my good deed for the day, see. I don't do good deeds much, but that nun made me feel like I should do something good today. I owe her one."

Damien Drail shook his head. He was too hot inside and didn't want to do this. He had something else in mind. This was ultimately the most pointless thing that had ever happened to him, next to coming here in the first place, but Violet wouldn't let up. He could humor her, maybe. It didn't matter.

He sat down at the cheap plastic desk, dressed only in his underwear, and wrote exactly what Violet Packard said. He wrote the date at the top, then again at the bottom.

"I shouldn't be doing this here," he muttered. "It's ridiculous. It's obscene. It probably isn't even legal. I'm not even dressed."

"Damn to hell it's legal. You think I'm some non-person?" Violet said. She was busy pulling on her clothes. Business hours were over. "You should have done this a long time ago. Shit, I mean, if I had a kid, I'd have US Savings Bonds, guardians set up, the works. Then when I kick off, O.D. or something, it's okay. Kids are things you don't mess around with, you know what I mean?"

"Sure, you're right. See? It's done. We go out and sign the thing. Are you happy now?"

"Fine." Violet bobbed her head up and down, ending in a flip that tossed her hair back and up where she caught it at the top of her head and wound it around into a twist. She started jabbing hairpins into the golden mass. "See, when I fall in love, I'll have a kid, quit work, maybe, and live pretty good. No drugs, no guys. I've got money put away for myself. No sense retiring alone. You probably think I don't have plans for myself, just live day to day going through money like fuckin' water. Not true, see. I got fuckin' plans for my whole life."

"Right." The paper was done. Now she would shut up and let him leave. He put his trousers on, found his shirt on the other side of the bed and pulled it on, all the while staring at Violet who was sitting before the mirrored desk, applying makeup while keeping an eye on Damien through the mirror. She had stuffed the money in her bag, mentally figuring that Ken's percent wouldn't be quite as big as it should be because she'd just given this man important legal advice for free. "How do you know the nun?" she asked.

"Friend of my wife's, like I said. They were in school together a long time ago."

"You got it on for her?" Violet asked.

"She's something, you know," Damien said.

"It's the car. How the hell does a nun get off in a car like that?"

Damien shrugged. "Her father was rich. She decided to be a nun and left the money behind, but I guess it's still there, somewhere. She's down here setting up a retirement home for old nuns," he added, throwing Cecile's cover into place, just in case. He was dressed and not anxious to talk about Sister Cecile. He should be asking about Bradley Locke, but now if he asked Violet, and Cecile had asked Violet already, it would blow Cecile's cover. It was dumb of him to have come here. He hadn't even thought of that aspect of the situation. Maybe he was losing it. His eyes traveled around the room then back to the desk where the codicil to his will lay in wait. This was crazy. He was definitely losing it.

# 19

DAMIEN left shortly after the codicil was signed and witnessed. Ken Newly was happy to make several copies on the hotel copier. He charged fifteen cents a copy. Three copies for Damien and one for his own records. "Sort of like a death certificate," he confided to Violet later as she passed him ten dollars for his cut of the trick.

"Sure," Violet agreed. "You got yourself a will, Ken? It's real important, you know?"

"Yeah, sure. I'm doing it one of these days."

Violet nodded. "Listen, I'm taking the rest of the night off. Not many guys out tonight. I need some sleep. See you later."

"Later," Ken said as Violet turned and walked out the door.

Violet didn't go far. Her little five-year-old Honda was parked nearby and she had her own plans for the rest of the night. Plans that didn't include sleep at all.

Six or seven months ago, she couldn't quite remember when, she had gone to a party at a place down south near Homestead. Dirty Bobby, that little creep, had been there, and so had Olimpo Olarte-Rodríguez. And Bajito. Violet was positive that Olimpo's little group must have had something to do with the disappearance of the man Cecile was looking for.

And then there was Damien. Damien had something to do with the nun, but Violet couldn't quite figure that one out. Whatever, Violet was bored with her life as a prostitute and curious about the man, Bradley Locke, that she had been hearing so much about lately. She had liked him when they had done a little business together, and that was more than she could say for most men. And now Bradley Locke had vanished and everyone in town was looking for him. Maybe he really *was* rich. Probably that Damien had been looking for him too but hadn't gotten around to asking.

"Funny thing about Bradley Locke," Violet said aloud as she pulled out into the dark street. She invariably talked to her car. "Funny thing. He kept talking about his cat. He's got a good heart, I guess. A man with a heart of gold. And there aren't many of them left."

Then she drove steadily and silently, leaving Miami's South Beach behind. She hit the causeway and crossed Biscayne Bay, humming to herself as she drove through the city. It was hard to remember exactly where Olimpo's place was. She had been more than a little stoned at the time, so her recollections were hazy. The idea was to let her car go west on the Tamiami Trail and it would take her there. That usually worked.

It was dark along the trail with the horizon line a touch lighter where the Everglades stretched out flat. Narrow side roads spread out and vanished beyond waving grasses until she saw Indian signs and huge pictures of air boats. Rotting vegetation and the sweet scent of the tropics blew in her open window, bringing Violet memories of her dismal childhood.

She had been raised in a flat, blistering house in central Florida. She had grown up in a town with dusty streets and dying trees whose name she had left behind with her father and her alcoholic mother. She had liked her father until he'd noticed she'd grown up one day when she was eleven. After that life had become too hard to remember. She had locked her mind into compartments: one for reality and one for dreams. Drugs helped. It was still like that, and she still had her dreams. Lately, she had been trying to get off the drugs.

112

As she drove, Bradley Locke's face became superimposed on her dream world, a strange mix of the real and unreal. Mosquito bodies accumulated on her windshield while she drove, forming a hazy film of the reality ahead of her. In her mind she built a picture of a man she barely knew. He had been tall, brown hair, eyes the color of amber. She liked that. Amber eyes.

She remembered Bradley's mouth, warm, sensitive, unlike the gaping maws most men had for mouths. He had made little meowing noises, she remembered, and he'd talked about his cat. What a crazy guy. She laughed at the memory. Her heart felt so light that she almost missed the turn onto a side road, but there was a sign for Duke's Restaurant before it, and that was how she remembered. A left at Duke's Restaurant.

It had gotten dark with the abruptness that startles people who first come to Miami. Violet sometimes thought she could even hear a thud when the sun set so fast. The sudden thud of darkness had always seemed to her just like the sudden ending of a life.

She drove slowly on the narrow road then, because her car was old and the road was rough. It was next to impossible to see the potholes that could kill her frail muffler.

Before Violet went too far she switched her car headlights off and began to creep along in the dark, barely able to keep on the tracks of the road. Directly in front of her a bird took off into velvet air, then another, their massive silent wings carrying them into the night. Finally she spotted lights ahead. Olimpo's place.

Carefully she maneuvered the car around to be facing back the way she had come, backing it into a tiny dirt space off the road where it could not be seen from the house, or even from the road itself. She left the keys under the floor mat on the driver's side, shut the door soundlessly, and stepped out into the night.

Violet walked quietly, although the animal sounds of the Florida night would have covered any but the noisiest approach. Grunts, snorts, squawks. She stepped

113

on something soft, something that moved and hissed. "Fuckin' alligators," she whispered.

The house was a dismal shack, with only three small rooms. Presumably, once upon a time, a family had lived there. An abandoned garden lay to the right. Tiny Seminole pumpkin vines were growing up a tree. From the vines the small, heavy fruit hung down like children's playthings, round balls black against a night sky. She began to look carefully at the ground in front of her, swatting at the invisible mosquitoes with noiseless, ineffective swipes.

She started to hum again, then stopped herself. There were two cars parked outside the shack, Olimpo's gray Mazda and Bajito's rusty blue Chevy, bought cheap from a retiree out of Buffalo. Violet remembered the gray Mazda. She had come out here in it with Olimpo that night with one of her girlfriends, swayed by his sweet-talk promise of good money for a full night's work. From what she could recall of the evening, Olimpo had been all mouth, Bajito had been sexy but kinky, and Dirty Bobby had been a sicko. There had been others and all in all she had come back with a purse full of money and a feeling that in spite of the financial rewards she just might be in the wrong business. She really hoped Dirty Bobby was not around.

She listened to the low rumble of voices from within, voices rising out of the screened front window like night frogs. From the sounds she deduced that there were two men in the first room. She discovered that she could see into the second room by climbing up on a trash can, tightly lidded against raccoons. The window was open but screened against bugs and she pressed her nose tightly against it to see in.

The light was dim, shining from the front room through a half closed door, but she was able to detect a strange thing snake out across the floor, a line, she finally realized, that was composed of red and white straws with some kind of hook on the end. "What the fuck," she murmured. As her eyes grew used to the light she saw the bale of marijuana. Fascinated, Violet watched the line come and go as if there was a fisherman fly casting at the other end. Finally she saw the hook snag a piece of marijuana from the bale. She watched the gentle tugging begin, then she saw the branch come loose and begin its slow creep across the floor where it disappeared, cut off from her vision by a jag in the wall. Someone was there, snagging a good smoke. A prisoner, she thought triumphantly. Maybe Bradley Locke was here!

Violet climbed down off the trash can, and started to shake. Reality began moving in with its familiar terror. Fear jagged through her body. She was a prostitute who had been abused by her father. Her sense of self worth was close to zero. All the grand plans of marriage, financial security, having a kid, all the things that real people had, the things she had told Damien about earlier that evening, were a dream that had no foothold in reality. It was all talk, like winning the lottery. More likely she would end up dead, just as she deserved. And she knew it.

So it didn't much matter what she did. But somehow, there in the dark, ominous night, she made a serious resolution that she, Violet Packard, was going to save Bradley Locke.

# 20

"SHE'S impossible," Cecile said, late that Sunday night. "She barely speaks to me. I tried so hard to be nice."

"She's perfectly normal," Raphael said. "Very lonesome for her mother."

"Helene's been dead for a long time. She barely remembers her."

"Leonie remembers. The myth if not the reality."

"Well, I'm just grateful she's not *my* daughter. Imagine sleeping in that disgusting tee shirt. It's filthy. We're going to have to remove it forcibly and wash it. That and the stuffed octopus. It has ten-year-old jelly on it. But she is a sweet child, I'm sure. She'll appreciate a clean octopus."

"No she won't. Don't forget, Cecile, she's ill and thrust into a strange place in a strange town. With us. She's probably frightened. We have to be very gentle. I have six nieces and I remember little Susan, my sister Ellen's youngest, wore the same nightie for two years when she was young, not to mention the ragged blanket she carried around. Now Susan is a mother and does three loads of laundry a day. And there was Howard with that disgusting orange rabbit. He took it everywhere and today he's a CEO. He probably keeps the rabbit in his lower desk drawer."

"All right. I won't wash the octopus. At least for a few days."

116

"Good," Raphael said. "Now I can sleep easy. I was worried. See you tomorrow."

"Good night, Raphael."

"Good night, George."

Bradley Locke was crying. Being stoned with friends is one thing, being stoned with a palmetto bug named George while locked in a hot room out near the Everglades is a horse of a different color. If Bismarck were with him, Bradley was convinced, he wouldn't mind staying here forever. No one else had ever been faithful and true. His wife had left him for that creep station chief, his best friends in the Agency always got transferred somewhere else, but Bismarck would curl up in his lap every single night. Bismarck understood a man's insecurities and deep desires: friendship, loyalty, consistency. The things that mattered were instinctive to the cat. Bismarck was always there. But he wasn't here.

"Bradley! Bradley!"

Bradley heard the sound but barely registered the fact that it was his name floating in through the high window of his stuffy room. It was probably Bismarck's ghost calling him.

"Bradley, get the fuck over to the window."

This was clearly not Bismarck.

"What?" Bradley spoke softly, stood up, and started turning around in order to discover where the voice was coming from. Finally he settled on the screen. Barely visible in the dark outside was something resembling a face. "Who are you?" he asked cautiously.

"It's Violet Packard, from the Bella Vista."

"Who?"

"Well, you never knew my name. I did some business with you a couple of nights. Pink garters, meow meow. Remember?"

Bradley's head swam in the overheated air. It was the damn prostitute. What the hell was she doing here? "Yeah. I remember."

"I'm gonna get you outta here. Look, when do those guys leave you alone?"

"They don't. Olimpo's always around." This was a drug induced hallucination. It had to be. He barely heard her next words.

"Okay, I gotta work on that. I'll try a little diversion. Stay cool."

Violet dropped down off the trash can to the ground with a soft thump. She'd found her Dulcinea, or maybe she was Dulcinea and he was Don Quixote. It wasn't a very good analogy because she didn't think of herself as Don Quixote—she was a whore and she knew it—but on the other hand, Bradley Locke was no Don Quixote either. Nevertheless, she remembered the story because she had been forced to listen to the music of *Man of La Mancha* for the hellish years she had spent at home after her father had noticed her. Her mother had gotten drunk to music every night, weeping with each song as she poured down one beer after another. When Violet Packard's mother would pass out on the couch, Violet's father would come onto Violet, and the music would end. When she had run away at age sixteen, the idea that there was a quest out there somewhere had been ingrained permanently on Violet's psyche. As long as the music kept playing, everything was all right.

She was humming again as she made her way back down the road to where Olimpo's car was parked. Maybe if she could blow it up, or something, the people in there would come out and she could sneak in and get Bradley. Maybe there were some explosives in the trunk. This was Miami, after all.

Violet tiptoed around the gray Mazda, frowning at the dents and the dull finish. It was a disgusting car. Olimpo should really upgrade. She would be doing Olimpo a favor if she blew his car up.

First she popped the hood and disconnected the wire from the coil to the distributor and tossed the cap on the ground. The wire was easy to see in the hazy moonlight

118

so it was a quick job. Then she made a big mistake. She dropped the hood.

Smash!

"Holy shit," Violet muttered and took a dive for the shrubs, some unfortunately thin Florida shifferia, where she flattened out as she heard the screen door bang open and Olimpo's voice roar out. "Who in hell's out there! I gotta big gun. You better start coming out!" Then Olimpo let off a shot because he wasn't kidding, and this really *was* Miami. He was sufficiently stoned to shoot wild, but still had enough wits left to look as well as shoot. His eyes began roaming around the area; Violet could see their whites in the dark.

Violet knew she was in trouble and she started to shake hard. This was not going as she planned. The tune in her head was gone and she could almost feel the pain coming. Nothing new. She was resigned to it, deserved it somehow. It was Daddy all over again.

"Don't shoot, Olimpo. Don't. It's me, Violet, I was out here with the boys a while back. Remember me?" She stood up, lips trembling, sweat rolling down her chest, absorbing into the tank top until it was soggy. She knew what was coming next.

"Look, I was out with these *fulanos*, see, they dumped me off along the Tamiami and I didn't know what the fuck to do, so I came to your place, see." She stepped forward, holding out her hands to show she didn't have any weapons. Her fingers began flapping.

"Don't you believe her, Olimpo," Bajito squeaked from behind. He had just come out, armed with a semi-automatic. "She's from the same hotel our *chico* comes outta. See, don't be so dumb you don't see a connection."

"You think that, Bajito, eh?"

"Sure. Get up here, you. You!" He was yelling in a soprano warble. The gun swept the area.

Violet almost laughed, almost wet her pants, almost cried, but she stepped forward another step. "I'm right here. No gun, no nothing."

119

"In the house," Bajito commanded.

Violet began walking toward the house, her head down, long blond hair falling out of the bun she had wrapped around the top of her head back in the Bella Vista. This was going to be very, very bad.

It was a little different this time. Bajito jammed his gun in her ribs when they got inside, Olimpo was behind them waving his gun ineffectively because he didn't need a gun now that Bajito was in control.

"Look, I just got stuck on the road, believe me," Violet was saying in a monotone; it was a line of defense she didn't expect to be accepted.

"We gotta get rid of her," Bajito said. "How much you know, *chica*, you know anything?"

"I don't know nothin'."

"Hey, Bajito, she don't know nothing," Olimpo said. He was mesmerized by her golden hair and long legs. "Let's have some fun."

"I don't believe it," Bajito poked the gun into Violet's ribs harder. "Tell me!" he demanded.

"Nothin'," Violet said. "Really." She thought she was going to puke.

This was just the beginning.

"We're gonna keep her, maybe get rid of her later. Right now we gotta talk, Olimpo," Bajito said. "We keep her in the back room with the *chico*. No trouble. He won't mind." Bajito laughed.

Olimpo didn't like that much. He'd rather keep Violet in with him. It didn't seem fair, but Bajito was the smart one, so Olimpo just nodded and figured he could work out something later when there was nobody else around. "Okay, sure, toss her in the back."

Violet barely knew what was happening, pushed through a room, dragged past the bale of marijuana, and stuffed through the door to Bradley Locke's private room. The door slammed behind her with a crash. She fell down on her knees before a startled Bradley Locke who was just finishing a long drag on a joint. He stopped and stared as Violet raised her eyes and focused on him, the man she had only recently set up in her mind as a great hero of some sort, a knight of old. Lochinvar. He was dressed in red plaid boxer shorts and he was stoned, but, yes, the man was handsome even through tear stains and unshaven features and a thick smell of body odor. She smiled happily.

As for Bradley, he had never seen anyone more beautiful in his life. Not even Bismarck.

# 21

LEONIE Drail almost listened to the two nuns. Normally she didn't have much to say, and there was very little she wanted to hear. She had learned to keep her mouth shut and hear only the blah, blah, blah of other people's words, keeping an ear cocked for an important sound or phrase, at which point she would tune in. She had her own interior life. When her mother had died, her father had provided her with a British Nanny who did everything. Now there was a pleasant housekeeper. And Leonie read a lot.

Leonie Drail's private school was filled with rich girls who traveled to expensive dumping grounds where the children of the rich were stashed. The other girls wore miniature mink coats and Hermes scarves. From the beginning, Leonie hadn't been as attracted to them and the rich lifestyles around her as much as to the *Case of the Nervous Newsboy* and similar stories. More recently her heroes were Nancy Drew, Beth, and George, girl detectives. Only last week she had read her first teen romance, but she still preferred intrigue.

Of course she knew her father worked for the government, and she knew Sister Cecile was a private detective because she heard Sister Raphael say something about it and then go on to talk about how they were really in Florida to establish a retirement home for old nuns. Ha, Leonie thought, some story. So she continued to listen for key words. And she always eavesdropped on telephone conversations.

When she saw Sister Cecile head for the telephone early that next morning, Leonie excused herself, went to her room, and closed the door. Then she picked up her extension telephone.

"Convent of the Little Sisters," Leonie heard a soft voice. Then she heard Cecile. "Hello, this is Sister Cecile of Our Lady of Good Counsel in Boston. Is Sister Rita still there?"

"One moment please."

Dullsville, Leonie thought. Nun stuff. She almost hung up. Then she listened.

"Cecile? How *are* you?"

"Rita, you're there! I never expected to find you still in the convent. I'm so glad. After all that liberation theology, you aren't still digging water wells in Nicaragua?"

"It was good, but I'd forgotten about God," Sister Rita whispered. "Then I remembered. Listen, Cecile, this is great! Are you freezing to death in Boston? Tell me!"

"I'm in Miami. And Rita we must get together. There's a lot to talk about."

"You're here! Great. Can you make it for dinner?"

"Maybe. Maybe a late lunch? But I have a big favor. There's a man named Felipe Klondacki who was murdered Friday night. Knifed. He worked with underground stuff, this and that. I need information. Can you help me?"

Sister Rita laughed. "Same old Cecile. Of course. Omega Seven stuff? Haitian stuff? Alpha eleven? I'm the source. What was the name? Klondacki? Tell me everything you know and I'll check it out. There's a place we can meet later, downtown, about a block from the Miami River. It's called *La Cocina Buena*. We can get together this afternoon and grab a bite to eat. How about four-thirty? That will give me time to make a quick check. It will be great to see you. Are you still rich?"

"Unfortunately. I keep trying to give the money to soup kitchens but Mère Sulpicia in Paris tells me to use some of it in my work. It's good for traveling," Cecile said. "And people tend to give money when they see money for some reason. Now, this Felipe, it's important that you go deep," she said. "He was murdered, and I feel somewhat responsible. I need to know who did it."

She continued talking for some time, filling in Sister Rita about what she wanted to find out.

Leonie heard everything. She hung up a moment after Cecile did, her mind spinning. Sister Cecile was involved in a murder! "Convent of the Little Sisters," she repeated. Sister Rita, and *La Cocina Buena*, the restaurant where they were meeting. What she wouldn't give to be there! Maybe she could solve the murder of this Felipe person herself. That would really surprise these people. She would like to do that.

"I have to go pick up the other rental car," Cecile was saying after a breakfast of frozen waffles popped in the toaster. "I'll give you the new rental, Raphael, and I'll use the red car."

"I should think you might want to be less obvious," Raphael said. "Perhaps I should take the Ferrari."

Cecile frowned. "The gears are much too powerful."

Sister Raphael raised her chin an inch. "I do aerobics *and* walk two miles a day. That's more than you can say."

"I jog. However, I suppose it might be wise, just this once. I have some places to check out this morning, and I really don't want to be noticed. You could drop me off at the rental office and do the shopping with the Ferrari. And we have real estate appointments. You can handle those yourself. We need things like fresh vegetables. Do you like broccoli, Leonie?" Cecile asked.

"No."

"Get some broccoli, Raphael, and how about carrots, Leonie?"

The girl shrugged. "I itch," she said.

"I'll pick up some more baking soda, some root beer, and maybe some Mexican stuff for lunch," Raphael said.

"And lettuce. I think we all prefer salads. Then I have an appointment with the motel people at two. I won't leave the Testarossa in sight. I think they're going to meet our offer for the motel."

"Good. Leonie, is there anything we can get for you? Raphael will be back for lunch," Cecile said. "I'll be a little later because I'm seeing an old friend this afternoon."

"I'm fine," Leonie said. Old friend, she thought with an interior grin. Ha.

"You don't mind being alone for a while?" Cecile asked. "You won't be frightened?"

"No, really. I'll watch television and drink ginger ale. You guys have fun."

Ten minutes later the nuns were gone. Leonie stood by the huge glassy wall and watched until she saw the red car pulling out, jerkily merging into a light flow of traffic before it sped down the road. The old nun was driving the fast car. Leonie liked that. Then she turned and went to Sister Cecile's bedroom and began pulling out all the drawers. Nuns seemed to wear the same things anybody wore. She studied the bras for a minute. Leonie had some but they were nothing like these.

She found Sister Cecile's notebook in a small drawer in the bedstand. She pulled it out and discovered quite a few hundred dollar bills and the report Felipe Klondacki had made on the disappearance of Bradley Locke. Leonie read the report.

"Felipe Klondacki," she said firmly, pronouncing the agent's first name with a Spanish accent. "Bradley Locke. The Bella Vista Hotel," she muttered over and over along with the address. The Bella Vista actually didn't seem to be too far from here, somewhere down the beach in the less trendy section. Leonie already knew the general area from her father's travelogue as they had come in from the airport. Damien loved to explain things to his daughter. He was her hero in many respects, not a bad father at all, just a father who wasn't there a lot.

She found another scrap of paper with an address and a

word scribbled on it that looked like "voodoo." Under that it read, "Wednesday night, eleven o'clock."

Leonie memorized the address under "voodoo." It might be fun to be there. Some kids at her school really freaked out on voodoo. "Cool," she said to her octopus, who had accompanied her on the foray through Cecile's drawers. She had plenty of things to investigate now. Sister Rita, Felipe, voodoo. Then she tucked all the papers back, leaving things exactly as she had found them. She had learned how to do that with her father's possessions. He never knew that she read everything he ever brought into the house.

Back in her bedroom, Leonie removed her heavy dungarees and sweater and put on the faded, oversized tee shirt that she used for a nightie. Then she went back to bed, cuddled in a ball, her octopus hugged tightly to her chest. She had almost stopped developing new chicken pox; the little pearly blisters had appeared on nearly every part of her body, but she was still running a slight fever. Maybe tomorrow she would feel better and could get something done.

Leonie was asleep in minutes.

# 22

THE car rental agency was near the airport, on LeJeune Road. The Monday morning traffic was light and it took less than twenty minutes to get there, something to do with the way Sister Raphael was driving. She was grinning by the time they arrived. "I don't know if animals go to heaven," she said to Cecile, "but maybe cars?"

"Maybe cars," Cecile agreed. Her knuckles were white from clenching her hands together in a silent attempt to remain calm. It was a credit to Sister Raphael's guardian angel that they had arrived in one piece, but the older nun had gotten the hang of driving the powerful car quickly and would probably survive the morning. Cecile had kept turning around as Raphael drove and hadn't seen a sign of Dirty Bobby in that Thunderbird. Maybe it had only been a fluke at church. Maybe it hadn't been Dirty Bobby after all.

"I'll see you back at the condo," Cecile said before she got out. "You be careful."

Raphael barely turned her head. "Don't worry about a thing."

It took Cecile half an hour to get the small rental car. Definitely not as nice as the Ferrari, but it was practically invisible, air-conditioned, and dull. That was all that mattered.

Cecile pulled the car out into the traffic with her list of objectives in mind. Number one was some decent clothes for Leonie. The poor child had looked miserable in those sticky dungarees and that heavy sweater. Then she would swing by Fish Street where Dirty Bobby's voodoo show was going down on Wednesday night and check out the neighborhood. After that she would meet Rita. Later tonight was the meeting with Dirty Bobby at the Place St. Michel. That was the tough one.

It was going to be a full day.

Sister Raphael went back to the beach and did some errands. It was still early, and the car was such fun to drive that she decided to go for a ride across the Julia Tuttle Causeway. The sandy area bordering the major road connection from the island to the mainland had recently been converted into a tropical rain forest, utilizing hundreds of huge palm trees, native and exotic, sixty-year-old sago palms, and tropical hardwoods. It was a project designed to enhance the approach to the beach as well as clean up the rough edges of the causeway where there had been countless muggings over the years. Fishermen still managed to make their way through brilliant flowering hedges to the long stretches of beach. It was too good a place to fish to leave alone and fishermen were still seen hauling in a good meal.

Raphael loved the palms and brilliant flowers. The windows of the Ferrari were heavily tinted so that it was almost impossible to see her inside, but the bright Florida sunshine made the whole world outside the car glow like a piece of heaven. She was even more delighted with the car, although it seemed to have a mind of its own when it came to going fast.

Before she knew it, Raphael was off Route 195 and moving slowly in an area of downtown Miami that she recalled hearing was not safe. She felt a moment of panic as she realized she was on Miami Avenue heading by the Florida East Coast Railroad Yards. Derelicts hung out on the corners eyeing the car hungrily. She took the first left, determined to turn around and go back the way she had come as fast as possible. Unfortunately Miami's incredible lack of proper road signs threw her again. Route signs for

I-195 clearly pointed in three directions at once. She wandered for ten minutes, driving the car fast, sweating even in the deep air-conditioned interior. "Help, St. Anthony," she repeated several times. "Please find a way out of here!"

Dirty Bobby spotted the red Ferrari driving up and down and around his neighborhood and couldn't believe his eyes. He had been on his way to a local botanica to pick up some material for the next meeting of his voodoo guild as the car zipped right by him. It had to be the same one, he thought as he spotted the license. QEV something, he read, and frowned. That was it. He had already decided he had to kill the nun in the red car. She was almost a witness to his killing Felipe. It was only a matter of time before she connected him to Felipe's death. Meanwhile, they would get their ransom money some other way. Maybe through a Canadian like Olimpo had first suggested. Canadians were good for international intrigue.

But the nun had to die. He couldn't afford to leave her alive. That was the trouble with people in this country. They couldn't just let a killing go. Always questioning, always trying to find out who did it. Who cared!

He gunned the Thunderbird and started to follow Raphael in her quest to get back on the causeway and go home. Finally he saw the car pull over. A veiled head popped out to ask a pedestrian for directions. It was a good way to get killed in this part of town, Dirty Bobby knew, but he didn't hesitate to pull over by the same pedestrian and roll down his window. "What did the nun want?" he asked.

"Uh, how to get to the beach."

"You tell her? Tuttle Causeway?"

"Yeah."

Dirty Bobby pulled away. He would get there first, shoot a tire out of the Ferrari, and get rid of the nun. One shot. Maybe it wouldn't kill her and he could finish her at his leisure. It would be fun to watch the Testarossa crack up, though. Maybe it would burst into flames like on TV. Good idea. He pulled ahead and drove like a maniac, taking a short cut to the causeway entrance. Like the big bad wolf, he was going to get there before she did.

Dirty Bobby drove like crazy and pulled off the causeway beside a grove of Washington palms to wait, his rusty old SID-Saur 220 aimed discreetly out the window.

The bright red of the car moved into his view.

He let off a shot. Dead hit.

A terrific bang erupted from the Ferrari tire blowing out. The Testarossa began to career wildly, nearly smashing into half a dozen cars. Sister Raphael struggled with the wheel to maintain control. She knew she had been driving too fast. But not that fast!

"Stop!" she cried. Her old muscles began to react with antique reflexes formed fifty years ago. Darkness threatened to engulf her as too much blood rushed to her brain. Arteries strained, expanded, and worked! A rush of adrenaline pumped through the venerable nun. She controlled!

The car's low-slung suspension was what saved her, giving Raphael a tight feel of the road even as the blown wheel forced the car to veer right, barely swiping an oversized palm before it finally swerved into a section between palm trees, rocks, and fishermen. Miraculously, Raphael stopped the car and sat, her old heart rapping against her chest, her face flushed with the thrill.

Well, it was a thrill, she told herself. She drew a deep breath. It was the first real breath she could remember taking since the tire blew.

"This is what race car driving is all about," Sister Raphael said out loud as she unstrapped the seat belt and emerged shakily from the car, not sure she should be emerging at all.

Three fishermen stood by the car door as she struggled out, one angler holding a huge tarpon. Raphael stood there for a moment, smoothing her veil and staring at the fish. She looked very much like an elderly nun but inside, her mind was whirling, trembling, and riding on a dangerous high. "Well?" she asked.

"Heck of a car, Sister," the fisherman said, eyeing her rumpled veil. "Not a scratch on it."

"And that is one nice fish," she returned. "Now, I believe my tire blew. I'd like to call the car rental office and see if they might come by and fix it. It's got to be their fault."

Sister Raphael was shaking all over, her knees visibly knocking, but she leaned back and the fabulous car held her up as she talked to the lean, dark fishermen. Her old hands rested flat against the hot sides of the automobile, grasping for support. It was a good car. Definitely this was a car that deserved to go to heaven.

"I got my cellular phone," one of the men said. "You can call from here."

Somewhere down the road, Dirty Bobby watched the scene in dawning horror that a miracle had occurred before his very eyes. No. Not a miracle. There was no such thing. Just a fluke. His eyes narrowed as he watched Sister Raphael and the fishermen. It wasn't even the right nun, he realized. What the hell was going on here?

He turned away and started up the Thunderbird, unaware that God was clearly not on his side.


Leonie was sound asleep when Raphael walked into the condo at exactly one o'clock in the afternoon. Raphael was balancing a gigantic tarpon and a collection of frozen Mexican food. The girl didn't wake up until Raphael's second trip up from the parking garage with another load of groceries.

It was the singing that finally woke her up.

Raphael was in the kitchen warbling, "O Sacrament Most Holy," very loudly because, thanks to the good Lord, the car's excellent breaking system, and her incredible driving expertise, the car had writhed to a stop without a scratch. It had gone from fifty miles an hour to zero in less than fifteen seconds. That was worth singing about.

The Ferrari rental people had arrived sixteen minutes after Raphael had called them from the cellular telephone, appalled and apologetic. They had changed the tire. "I can't believe one of our tires would go," the manager had said, a small man who had come along to check on the expensive rental. He had stared at the blown tire suspiciously. "A round hole. Looks to me like a small bullet hole. I'll have this checked by our people."

Raphael was on her way in less than half an hour from blowout time. She was barely behind schedule.

Sister Raphael was slamming cabinets as she put things away, still euphoric. Leonie grinned when she heard the old nun making such a racket; the car must have been a wonderful experience.

That was the moment Leonie decided that Sister Raphael was really cool.

Leonie dressed slowly for the second time. It was hard pulling the dungarees over the pox on her legs. Even cotton underpants felt bad. The sweaters she had packed were ridiculous. No one had told her how hot it was here in Florida; even with air-conditioning it was purely tropical. It was going to be blistering and nasty when she sneaked out to visit the voodoo place she had read about in Cecile's notes. But nothing would stop her, not chicken pox, not anything.

Leonie took her time and studied herself critically in her dressing table mirror. "Ugh," she said. "Seriously disgusting." She wasn't going anywhere for a while, not wearing these things. She was held captive by a pair of nuns and her abominable northern clothes. "The return of Spiderwoman is going to take a little longer," she said to the image in the mirror. "But she will *return*!"

When Leonie came out to the living room ten minutes later, lunch was on the table. Burritos again. Frozen in

132

the middle, hot on the ends. Sister Raphael had mastered the microwave.

They had just finished eating when Sister Cecile walked in. She was back earlier than she had told them. "Too much stuff to carry around," she explained. "Besides, the ice cream would melt."

Cecile dumped the packages down on the couch except for the one she handed to Leonie. "This should make the wait bearable." She smiled at Leonie's expression.

Leonie was trying hard to give Cecile the "who needs you" look. Leonie didn't like Cecile. Too bossy, too proper, too trying to be nice. But the girl looked in the bag, anyway.

Leonie saw junk food: plain potato chips, garlic and onion flavored potato chips, vinegar and salt flavored potato chips, Corn Crumpet O'Doodles, nacho sauce dip, hot and spicy cheese dip, ten cans of various soft drinks, three candy bars, and a half gallon of Breyers butter pecan ice cream. There were also several fashion magazines dealing with teenagers and a number of comic books. Leonie's eyes widened as she looked inside the bag. "Dad will kill you," she said, slowly pulling out the vinegar and salt flavored potato chips, but she didn't feel a bit unhappy.

"I don't think we should tell him. I'm supposed to be responsible for you, but you have to live, too. And I expect you to join us for broccoli from time to time. Deal?" Sister Cecile held out her hand to shake.

Leonie wasn't sure about this, but she held out her hand and they shook, solemnly. Then they both spotted the giant fish on the counter.

"Fish?" Leonie asked. "I hate fish."

"Raphael, the fish," Cecile said. "A huge fish? Where did you get that fish? Did you pay money for that thing?"

"A friend gave it to me. I'll tell you later."

Raphael shut her lips firmly.

Cecile nodded as though fifty-pound tarpons frequently

appeared in her life. "Leonie, if you don't like fish, you don't have to eat it."

Leonie saw strange looks passing between the two nuns. They had some kind of secret language. Not the normal adult secret language that she could penetrate, but a nun secret language. She would have to learn it. And she would find out where the fish came from, too. She could find out anything. Meanwhile she would humor them. "No big fish. I like little fish."

Things were starting to look up after all, she thought. She didn't have to eat the fish. She pulled out the ice cream and went over to the freezer to put it away. Then she mumbled something to the nuns and went to her room to go through the other food, privately. It didn't take long for her to formulate a plan. She would eat all afternoon and watch MTV from her bed. She began with the first bag of potato chips and started flipping the television through its fifty-seven channels.

Sister Cecile poked her head into Leonie's room and threw some more bags onto the foot of her bed. "More stuff for you," the nun said. "I'll see you later tonight. Have fun."

"Thanks a lot," Leonie managed through her potato chips. She sent a spray of crumbs out with the words but Cecile didn't seem to notice. Cecile just smiled and left, closing the door gently behind her.

Leonie felt a strange feeling pass through her. Like she could cry, or something.

She frowned and pushed down into the bed, stuffing another handful of chips into her mouth. Something was going on here, and she wasn't sure she understood it. It seemed, like it or not, that these two peculiar people were conspiring together to see that she actually enjoyed herself. The situation was totally weird.

# 23

Olimpo and Bajito both spent Sunday night at the shack in the Everglades. The end result was that nothing happened between Olimpo and Violet. The captives remained captive in the back room. What they did together the two kidnappers did not know, nor did they even think about the back room. Bajito, in fact, stayed all night in order to prod Olimpo into doing something constructive about Bradley.

Monday morning, over cups of sour instant coffee, he tried again to make Olimpo see the light.

"I asked everyone I know about a trip to Cuba. Nobody wants to go back there, because who's to say they can get out again? I mean, you come to Miami in a rubber tire raft, damn Communists shooting out the rubber, sharks eating your mother-in-law, you don't want to go back again." Bajito pounded his small fist on the table for emphasis, spilling his coffee. He paused and lit a cigarette, blowing out a perfect smoke ring.

"Get a Canadian. They go there all the time."

"I don't know any Canadians. I went up to some the other night. Thought they were Canadian, turned out they were from South Miami."

"Ummm," Olimpo said. "Gotta be someone who knows Castro around this town."

"Sure, lots of people, but they admit it, they get shot by one of the Alpha groups. So, we got to get moving. Time don't wait for us, see. People forget. So we're gonna try for some ransom. Now. Today. No sense keeping this

Bradley Locke any more. Keep him back there forever? That don't make sense, so we go immediately after this nun Dirty Bobby met," Bajito said. "No delay." He waved the cigarette. "We don't know nothing about this nun. But Dirty Bobby said the nun is rich, and she's looking for our guy. There's our money. Forget Cuba." Bajito made his voice firm.

"Dirty Bobby says, Dirty Bobby says . . . The Dirt Man thinks he's God with all that voodoo. I don't like the way he looks at me. He's in love with me or something." Olimpo wiggled in his chair, scratching his shoulders on the chair back and looking up at the clock on the wall. It always said two o'clock, although the real time at the moment was closer to noon.

"So, who cares," Bajito said. "Don't knock the voodoo. It brings in money. Dirty Bobby's got the answer. I tell you, Olimpo, when he stops by with lunch today, you and me are gonna tell him to get the ransom from this nun. Then we're gonna collect. You got this *fulano* eating and shitting in a back room for weeks, now we get some *puta* there too. Next thing we'll have kids, babies, a whole damn family. Goo goo. I hate kids crying all the time. That's what's gonna happen next. We gotta deal with these people, get rid of them. It's a fuckin' freak show in our back room."

"I was gonna take care of the girl. Violet. She didn't know nothing. Now she knows everything." Olimpo looked sullen.

Bajito shrugged. "So? We kill 'em all. First we get some money for the *chico*. Where the hell is Dirty Bobby?"

Bajito stood up and began to pace the room. His shirt bulged slightly over beltless pants. Bajito Suárez had a small potbelly.

"Dirt Man's coming at noon," Olimpo said. "Bringing drugs, he picked up a couple of *pacas*. I told him to bring lunch too. Later I gotta go in town, do some business. I gotta make a living, you know? I gotta arrange a sale. You keep an eye on the *gringos* in the back room this afternoon. Meanwhile Dirty Bobby has to get in touch with the nun about our price. That make you happy?"

"That makes me real happy. How much we going to ask for?"

"Half a million? How about a million?" Olimpo beamed. "And a diamond watch. A real one. Three watches. One for each of us. The watches up front, the money at trading time." His deep voice made the deal sound even richer than it was. "A million bucks," he repeated. "And three diamond watches."

Olimpo had convinced himself. "Okay, Dirty Bobby's gonna ask the nun for a million bucks. And watches."

Bajito agreed. Olimpo was so convincing that there seemed no other possibility.

Dirty Bobby arrived shortly after, carrying a bag filled with Cuban sandwiches and some soft drinks. He watched Olimpo slip food through the cat hole to the prisoners, then he settled down to smoke while Olimpo and Bajito ate and drank Pepsis.

Finally they talked.

"We want you to get together with the nun and give her the price for our *chico* in there," Olimpo said.

"Tonight," Dirty Bobby agreed. Shit, it was a good thing he hadn't taken out the nun. "Tonight I'll set the deal." He was sitting back in the wooden chair; the back legs of the chair were bowing dangerously. "She's coming to the bar at my hotel."

"Good. We gotta get rid of these people."

"People?"

Bajito had been silent up to now. "Yeah," he said, his voice squeaky. "We got that *puta* in the back room now. She come sneaking around last night so we tossed her in. We can get rid of her later."

"Oh, sure, I'll take care of her. You wanna me to do that now?" Dirty Bobby asked. "Maybe tonight. We can have some fun first."

"You're meeting with the nun tonight," Olimpo pointed out.

"Oh, sure, I forgot. How much we asking for the *chico*?" Dirty Bobby asked. He had already put his attempt on Cecile's life out of his mind.

"A million bucks," Bajito said.

"You shittin' me, Bajito. A million?" Dirty Bobby spoke gruffly, trying to mimic Olimpo's voice, as usual.

"I thought you said the nun was loaded," Olimpo said.

Dirty Bobby rocked his chair back a little farther, knocking it against the mildewed paper peeling from the wall behind him. "Well, she got this car, worth maybe a hundred grand. So there's money. And she's looking for the man. Nun says he's an old friend that disappeared, and she wants to find him. You think she wants to find him *that* much? I mean, we're fucking talking a million bucks here."

"Maybe he's a lost brother," Bajito put in. "Why else we got a nun here?"

"Would you pay a million bucks for a lost brother?" Dirty Bobby laughed.

"So, maybe it's her boyfriend," Olimpo said.

"She's a nun," Dirty Bobby affirmed. "I know a nun. That one's a nun." Dirty Bobby spit on the floor.

"A million bucks," Olimpo said again. "Firm. A million bucks or Bradley Locke is alligator food, cut up into nice little pieces. And," he added with a mental drum roll, "three diamond watches. Man-sized watches. Big diamond watches. We want them right away just so we know she means it. Know what I mean? You tell her the watches up front. Or I chop him up myself. Tiny little bites." Olimpo smiled at the power of his words.

There was dead silence.

"A million bucks, three diamond watches," Dirty Bobby repeated finally, sweat beading up on his brow.

Dirty Bobby left soon after. "A million bucks, a million bucks," Dirty Bobby repeated as he drove away. He was going to get a million bucks for Bradley Locke. He would. Olimpo would be really pleased with him. Dirty Bobby flexed his stubby fingers around the steering wheel as he spun the Thunderbird out onto the Tamiami Trail, picturing a diamond watch on his wrist. And a million bucks. It was the American Dream. He almost believed it. Because Olimpo had said it.

# 24

LEONIE Drail began to watch television and eat junk food, methodically moving from one channel to another, from one bag of chips to another. She quit eating after she was well into the second bag. There was a limit to piggy behavior.

The white sacks Cecile had tossed in before she had left were still on the bed, unopened. It was a matter of pride not to look inside and see what was in them. Leonie was determined not to be sucked into liking Sister Cecile. Cecile had been very offhanded about the stuff anyway, whatever it was. Probably not important. More chips, comics, maybe schoolwork.

Leonie waited, eyeing the bags. Eventually Raphael knocked on her door to tell Leonie that both nuns would be gone for a while. "I have some real estate business," Raphael explained.

"Okay. See you later," Leonie said from the bed. She waited until she heard the front door close. She was alone.

She opened the bags.

"Check it out, Batman," Leonie said when she saw what was in the first bag. "Jumping Jehosiphat," she said when she inspected what was in the second bag, and finally, "Jeewhillikers, Spiderwoman, these are some rags," when she had spread out the contents of the third bag. Sister Cecile had been shopping in a big way that morning at several boutiques on Miami Beach and had bought everything she could imagine a twelve-year-old might want to wear in a warm climate. The stuff was really cool, Leonie realized. And it cost. The nun had good taste. Not that she liked the nun. She would definitely not be bought.

Leonie stripped off her dirty tee shirt and jeans. She put on the pale green pre-washed baggy shorts and the loose sleeveless top.

"Sheer comfort," Leonie muttered and posed before the full-length mirror on the bathroom door. Holding her octopus up beside her face, Leonie turned and strutted. At the moment she felt she resembled Dracula's daughter, but that wouldn't last forever, she hoped. She was feeling better already. In fact she could go for a glass of milk.

Five minutes later Leonie was in the kitchen going through the cabinets just in case she had missed something.

The telephone rang.

She picked it up in the living room.

"Hello."

"Sister Cecile, please?"

"She's not here now. Could I take a message?"

"Who's this?"

It was a man's voice, an unsettling, charming man's voice, but Leonie was used to men's voices on the telephone. "Leonie Drail," she said.

"Leonie Drail, are you a nun?"

Leonie started to chuckle. She still had a piece of cold burrito in her mouth and it fell out. "Darn," she muttered.

"Something wrong?"

"My burrito flew out," Leonie choked. "And I'm not a nun. Are you kidding? I just have the chicken pox."

"That's something like being a nun."

"Uhh-uh," Leonie agreed.

"Leonie, could you give Sister Cecile a message, please. Tell her Paul Dorys is in town for the Bamboo Society meeting. That's tomorrow. Then I'll be doing

141

some fishing. And tell her not to worry, that I won't show up at my condo unannounced."

Leonie was scribbling fast on a notepad beside the telephone. "Okay, I got that. Should she be in touch with you at your condo?"

"You're at my condo."

"I am?"

"Your condo is my condo. I'm staying on a friend's boat, tell her. And I'll be in touch. I'll be gone fishing for a few days. Toward Bimini."

"Gone fishing," Leonie mumbled and wrote the words down. "I'll see that she gets the message."

A few minutes later Leonie had hung up and was back delving in the refrigerator. Maybe after she got something more to eat she would leave, she thought. Now that she had Florida clothes she could find that nun, Sister Rita, and see what was happening.

The nuns had a revealing conversation in the parking garage before leaving the condo for the afternoon.

"You had a flat tire?" Cecile could hardly believe it. "On the causeway?"

"The man said it looked like a gunshot hole in the tire, Cecile. He was going to check. You should have seen my driving. I was great."

"Dirty Bobby must have shot at the Ferrari," Cecile murmured thoughtfully, looking at the red car for bumps and bruises. Everything looked fine, although the shiny red paint was getting a little dusty. She wiped a finger on the smooth surface. "You're lucky to be alive, Raphael. I think I'd better drive it from now on."

"Not a scratch," Raphael pointed out. "I handled that machine like a professional. Those fishermen were impressed."

"Evidently," Cecile agreed. "I'm glad the doorman likes fish. He told me he has a large family when I gave it to him."

"I could drive the Ferrari for the rest of the day if

142

you're worried about anything," Raphael said. "He must realize he failed to shoot me off the road. He probably won't try again."

"No. You're closing in on the motel deal, by yourself. You should take the cheap car," Cecile said. "It will keep the price down. Meanwhile, I think I'll go check up on the scene at Fish Street before I see Sister Rita. I didn't have time this morning. I got stuck in those shops buying things for Leonie with that credit card. At least the card is good for something."

"Be careful of the car, Cecile," Raphael warned. "It's a *machine*!"

Fish Street was a dismal street in the seedy area near where Raphael had been lost earlier that day. Cecile parked several blocks away from the address Violet had given her and walked, picking her way around small children scrabbling in dirt and dark men sitting in clumps. The possibility that her car might be stripped was in the back of her mind until Cecile saw two unemployed teenagers. "Watch my car, I'll give you a hundred bucks when I get back."

"A hundred? You're kidding!" They eyed the car down the street.

"One hundred dollars. Deal?"

"Deal." They nodded and settled in to admire the beast.

Cecile started to walk. There were tight rows of depressing homes. Some windows were settled over noisy air conditioners, wall bangers that whirred and dripped water. Other windows were open. Small, dry yards grew weeds and scraggly hibiscus. Number seventy was the last house on a block that melted into small industrial buildings exploding with old radiators and car parts. The street beyond oozed green and pink blood, radiator fluid, steering fluid, transmission fluid, brake fluid. An occasional distant hiss and emerging clouds of steam filled the air.

Cecile was dressed simply in one of her new white outfits and a small veil. Her cross gleamed brightly on the white blouse. She could always pull the old Parish Visitation Trick if her presence here was questioned. Nuns were always doing body counts for the church and could appear almost anywhere with impunity.

But if Dirty Bobby were there, he would recognize her, so with that in mind, Cecile went directly up to a group of men who were staring idly at a river of green radiator coolant flowing by. "I'm looking for the Ortez home. Do any of you know where that is?"

"Ortez?" They all looked blank.

"Dirty Bobby?"

"Over dere," someone pointed a cigar at a door.

"Is Mr. Ortez at home?"

He shrugged.

"I'll see." She smiled demurely. "Thank you very much." She walked to the building, not feeling a bit demure. She was frightened. The house was peeling stucco, a two-story town house with a filthy yard. She went to the rear to avoid the men's following eyes and knocked loudly. The door popped open an inch. She called in. "Hello! Anyone there?"

Nothing. Nobody. If she broke in and entered she could lose her license. Or he could kill her. Or she could find Bradley Locke. It was worth a chance. It was her job.

She walked in, letting the screen door bang behind her. It sounded like a gunshot. "Yoo, hoo!" she warbled.

Nobody answered.

She walked into a kitchen. Dirty pots and pans covered a filthy stove. A wooden table in the middle of the floor was cluttered with empty beer cans and half a bag of potato chips. The other half was spilled on the floor where lines of ants were busy carrying off crumbs. The sink was piled high with dishes and the room smelled like death. Cecile hoped it wasn't Bradley's death.

She started looking. First the closets. Bags of trash that smelled badly. That explained the smell. Then the living room, a stifling room cluttered with old furniture, beer bottles, and fast-food wrappers. Then a grimy bathroom.

Down a tiny hall she found what must be Bobby's bed, lumpy and almost alive. A fan in the window was spinning slowly, sending in a hot breeze. No body. No Bradley. There was another bedroom. Locked.

This was it. The last room. She began manipulating the lock with trembling fingers. She could smell something bad again. Worse than the kitchen. The lock wouldn't open. From her purse came the small metal tool, a professional lock pick Paul had given her for Christmas two years ago along with lessons for its use. She had mastered it in three hours.

"Pick, pick, pick," she muttered and inserted it, moving metal up and down, a quick turn and the lock snapped open. It was an easy one.

She put the pick back into her purse and waited. There was a strange sound, maybe a radio? Then she heard a loud cock-a-doodle-doo. She opened the door to the room and stared.

There was a rooster, a small, fluffy rooster.

No Bradley, no body, just the bird stuck in a cage, crowing gamely. It began to peck at her through the bars, a glazed look in its red eyes. She walked in and the bird attacked the cage violently.

"It's okay, bird," Cecile whispered. "I would never hurt you."

The rest of the room resembled a dump; piles of old clothes were strewn in one corner, a few bags of moldy bread in bags, an open window that let in almost no breeze. It was revoltingly hot. Cecile wiped a hand across her chin. She was dripping wet.

There was one last place to look, another door. She opened it up and found a small closet filled with clothes. She looked hard and discovered the clothes were all stained with dark splotches. She backed out.

The rooster let out a loud squawk.

"Well, sorry, bird, I was looking for Bradley."

145

She closed the closet door. Then she heard a sound like a gunshot. It was the bang of the screen door in the kitchen. Footsteps stomped in her direction.

Trapped. She looked around for an escape. Nothing. No way out.

She raced to the door and closed it, then ran back to the closet, closed the door behind her, and crouched down, covering herself with fetid, sour rags.

She heard Dirty Bobby's voice.

"Son of a bitch, who unlocked my door, damn bird! You been getting out? Someone after my secret weapon, eh, crazy bird? I forget to lock you in? Ain't nobody gonna steal you, bird. I got you some crazy food, get you ready to kill Pucho's *gallo*. Eat this, get crazy!"

Through a crack in the door Cecile watched Bobby take a handful of moldy bread and toss it into the cage. Just as the bird started pecking at the food she saw Bobby take a pointed stick and jab at the bird. "Get crazy, bird. Kill! Kill!" The man started to laugh a demented laugh. He walked to the door and left.

Cecile could hear the lock click shut. She heard clucking, pecking sounds as the bird ate. Then silence.

She waited for an hour in the stinking closet for some sign that Dirty Bobby had left the building. It was tough breathing. There was nothing to do but pray as she attempted to get comfortable, so she prayed, running through the entire fifteen decades of the rosary. Eventually she heard a strange, distant roaring. The rooster noises had settled into a deathly stillness, punctuated by an infrequent squawk.

She finally took a chance and opened the closet door.

One step at a time she crept out of the closet. The rooster remained silent. Tenderly, she shut the closet door behind her. With a quick glance at the killer rooster, she tiptoed to the locked door and pressed her ear against it, listening.

There was a strange sound, all right. It was not a roaring as she had first thought, but a dreadful noise as though someone were in dire pain. Bradley, she thought in horror. Dear God have mercy, the poor man's being tortured in the next room!

She kept listening and eventually realized the horrible groans and sputters were rhythmic, rising and falling as though someone were breathing.

Breathing. Snoring, she thought suddenly. Dirty Bobby is in that other bedroom, sound asleep. Snoring.

It was easy to unlock the room from the inside. All she had to do was turn the little locking knob, very, very slowly. She opened the door with wet palms, sure it would slip or bang and make some horrible sound. It didn't. She gave a last glance at the scraggly little bird, wishing she could take it along with her. Poor thing. It deserved a bird bath and some real chicken food.

She closed the door gingerly. If Bobby were lunatic enough to think the rooster was escaping from that cage and unlocking the door, it would mean instant death for the poor bird. She couldn't help that. Good luck, bird, she thought, and left the door unlocked. She didn't dare use the pick to relock it.

Cecile stepped into the hall. She looked around cautiously while the horrible snores pulsed. She took a few steps. She spotted Dirty Bobby spread naked on his bed, his bloated, hairless flesh covered with a fine sheen of sweat, the formidable snores rising and falling in cadence with the movement of a mountainous, tattooed chest. Fascinated, she squinted to make out the tattoo: a coiled snake wrapped around a unicorn. She tried not to look further, tried to repress the impulse to stare at all that steaming, snoring beef.

She looked.

"Dear Lord," she whispered and turned away.

Cecile left fast. Through the living room, out the kitchen door, she was careful not to bang the screen. Then she raced down the dry, dusty space between the house and the warehouse next door. She escaped the back way, wherever it took her, around and behind old buildings, through a few yards, between fences. Finally she found herself on a recognizable street. Gasping for decent air, she headed back to the Testarossa.

"Everything okay?" she asked the two teenagers who were sitting on the curb beside her car, smoking.

"Them guys wanted to touch it," the dark one said. "I told 'em I'd kill 'em."

"They didn't touch it?" she asked, reaching for her envelope of money and pulling out two fifties.

"No chance," the lighter boy said around a cloud of cigarette smoke.

"Good. Thanks." She handed them each a fifty. It was a lot of money, but Cecile had never been anything but a realist. The world was very mercenary. That was why she became a nun, she mused as she opened the car door.

The car started with a gratifying rumble and she was off and out of the decaying neighborhood. But her time there still lingered in her mind. The picture of Dirty Bobby, naked on his bed, was still ingrained, a clear picture in her memory, mocking her preconceived notion of just what a naked man should look like. On second thought, she considered, maybe *that* was why she had become a nun.

She glanced down at her watch. The day had gone by too fast, and that thought brought her back to reality. It was time to meet Sister Rita. Thoughts of her old friend Rita, who had been through such a struggle in her search for truth rose in Cecile's mind. The continuous labor for God's goodness had taken her friend half a lifetime. And that, she thought firmly, was really why she had become a nun.

# 25

LEONIE waited a few hours before her next move. First she had important things to do like take a nap and eat junk food, but by four o'clock she was awake and pacing the condo. She didn't like being cooped up.

The number for the Little Sisters of the Poor Convent was in the telephone book. She dialed the number and asked for Sister Rita.

It was just moments after Sister Rita had left to meet Sister Cecile that Leonie dialed the convent number.

"I'm sorry, Sister has just left for the afternoon."

Her quarry was gone. Speaking in her most sophisticated voice, Leonie said it was very important that she reach Sister Rita and that she would definitely call back. "When is Sister Rita expected to return?" she asked.

"Oh, five-thirty or so. She rarely misses a meal, and of course compline is at eight. She should be available for calls at five-forty-five."

"Thank you. I'll call back," Leonie said and hung up. It was only a little after four o'clock. Maybe she would head out and scout the restaurant where the two nuns were meeting instead of calling Sister Rita back.

Leonie grabbed a piece of paper from the pad by the telephone and scribbled a quick note: "Went for a walk. Be back soon. Don't worry." And signed her name. That would keep the nuns happy.

Leonie had some money of her own, close to sixty dollars that she had brought along for emergencies. It was enough to make her feel secure taking a taxi, so she strolled out the door of the condo, went down the elevator, and directly into a waiting taxi cab. "I want to go to *La Cocina Buena*, by the Miami River," she said. "It's a restaurant."

"Sure. Hang on kid."

Sister Rita had gone to Barnard with Sister Cecile back when they were both still civilians. Shortly after graduation Cecile had entered the Order of Our Lady of Good Counsel and gone to France, to Paris where the motherhouse of her order was located. Rita Morgan, who became Sister Rita, had entered the Maryknolls, an activist missionary group. As a Maryknoll Sister she had gone to Latin America where she had embarked on a heavy agenda of lifting the inhabitants from poverty to resistance. Eventually, she had switched horses in midstream and jumped religious orders to the more contemplative Little Sisters. Now she was a Little Sister of the Poor working with new immigrants in Miami.

The nuns met at four-thirty in the restaurant on Calle Ocho.

"They arrive with nothing, and they're usually all wet," Sister Rita was explaining ten minutes into their reunion. "Of course the Cuban policy is driving everyone crazy now. They let them in, keep them out. Who knows what's next. Everyone's confused. Immigration is a mess, and I love them all." Rita smiled, her freckles still evident. She was as attractive as ever, but getting plump and now avidly eating something that resembled dog food with green olives in it.

"This is America. People just keep coming," Cecile said. "Boston is filling up with Orientals." She was working on black bean soup, dipping in a chunk of Cuban bread and stirring, then slurping from the soggy ends.

"Over three thousand souls a year from Cuba until this last policy shift. I'm teaching them English at the church."

"That's why everyone has an accent here," Cecile said.

150

"The Haitians. Such a story. Our government tosses them back, they return. Haitians run across MacArthur Boulevard at midnight, swimming ashore from leaky old boats, rubber rafts, all half dead. I checked on your Felipe Klondacki, by the way," she abruptly changed the subject. "He's well known. He works for the CIA, reports on movements."

"I was told he was under deep cover."

Rita laughed. "Really? He takes bribes, but he's a good man. Took, I mean. Dead."

"Knifed."

Rita nodded. "So many in this business end up like that. Life is short. My friends tell me he was a fair person to deal with. They'll miss him. He was an honorable man, they say. Among thieves."

"What was he into that would kill him?" Cecile asked.

Rita scratched her ear. "Everything he was into would kill him. He connected with anti-Castro groups. There's folks stockpiling all kinds of stuff out there, planning one revolution after another. Klondacki watched the scenes in other countries, too. Corruption is all over the Caribbean. It comes with the financial aid." She gave a grim chuckle and speared an olive. "Olives," she said, waving her fork, "will make anything taste good. Try them in eggs sometime; you'll be amazed." She paused and ate the olive. "There's always an inequity or an injustice. Someone's always cheated. That's the realization that sent me back here to take care of people. I'd rather clean up the mess than make more of it."

Rita sighed and stirred some yellow rice. She uncovered another olive. "Louis Bojanis is the man for you to see. Tell him we're friends; he might tell you something. He lives in a houseboat on the Miami River. I have the location for you; he should be tied up there today. He moves out, moves around. Sometimes he's out at the Anchorage. That's where people moor out beyond the Grove. Don't worry about your car. Leave it here and walk. It's not a

151

long walk. He likes it if you bring presents. A good bottle of rum would go over big with Louis."

"Did you talk to him about me?"

"No, but the fellow who knew Felipe said he was the man to contact. And I already sent word around that you were coming about six o'clock with the expectation that you could be there. Can you handle that?"

"Sure."

"Great." Rita grinned. "Now, tell me what you've been doing. Tell me everything. It's been a long time. What do you think about the altar girls? Remember how we wanted to do that? And whatever happened to that luscious lawyer you didn't marry?"

"Paul Dorys? He's in Boston. Still there." Cecile dipped more bread into the soup and they talked. There was a lot to cover.

Half an hour later Cecile patted her lips clean of black bean soup. She hugged her old friend good-bye. "Good to see you. I'll be in touch."

"Sure," Sister Rita winked. "Maybe you can do *me* a favor next time."

Dirty Bobby had put the word out about the red Ferrari. Anyone who saw it was to call in to the Xerobia Botanica with a location, and Dirty Bobby would follow up. He couldn't kill the nun until the ransom was worked out. The first attempt had been a mistake, but sometimes those things happened. Sometimes the urge to kill was irresistible. It happened that way from time to time. In the meantime he had decided that if he wanted to stay healthy, he had to keep his eyes on her. She was dangerous. She was also foolish to be driving a car like that because she could be spotted anywhere. The Dirt Man put the word out.

Dirty Bobby had excellent cooperation among the locals. Unfortunately, by the time he heard the red car was in his own neighborhood, it was too late and the car had gone. But when the second call came in, that the

152

car had moved to a location not far from the Miami River, Dirty Bobby was there. He had a compulsion to keep an eye on this woman. The fact that she was a nun bothered him. She bothered him bad. And as soon as he collected the ransom, she was a dead woman.

At Sister Rita's advice, Cecile left the car exactly where it was, parked in a legal spot where there was enough activity to keep the Ferrari relatively safe from being stripped by passing vandals.

Sister Cecile set out on foot for the Miami River. She loved to walk, and Sister Rita's directions looked easy. On the way, she kept her eyes open for a liquor store where she could buy some good rum.

She noticed the people, the dark haired, attractive groups of Latins, the children. She noticed a young girl, who from the back looked like Leonie but couldn't be, and she saw dozens of unemployed young men milling this way and that. She didn't see Dirty Bobby, but he was clever enough to stay out of sight.

The Miami River is barely a river. Before they knew better, the engineers turned it into a long, straight canal that went in a continuous line all the way from Lake Okeechobee in central Florida to Biscayne Bay. By a fluke, or perhaps an engineering oversight, a few bends were left in the river for its last mile, before it merged with the bay. There the Miami River still resembles a river, and there one can find curious boats from all over the Caribbean, strange crafts filled with stolen bicycles ready for export, filled with tennis balls from Guatemala waiting to be unloaded, filled with fabrics, filled with people. The Miami River is an odd place, reminiscent of another time when the Native Americans dwelt there, or later when the first settlers built their homes and lived on the land. Even today, English is rarely heard there, and when it is, it's viewed with suspicion.

Sister Cecile spoke French. *"Où est Louis Bojanis?"*

153

she asked as she approached the boat where he was reputed to live. What she meant to say was, *"Dónde está Louis Bojanis?,"* but the six-foot-four Haitian whom she addressed was so intimidating that it came out in French by mistake. It was a fortuitous mistake. The Haitian wouldn't have understood Spanish.

"In the boat. What's in the bag?"

"Oh, uh, Cuban bread, something to drink. Coca Cola," she said, not daring to mention the expensive rum. Snatch and run was the lifestyle in parts of Miami, and she wasn't inclined to be a victim.

"Go ahead, he's there." The man smiled. He was incredibly tall, Cecile realized, with large teeth, eyes that glistened, and an Acadian manner. Very polite. She turned to view Louis Bojanis's boat.

It was a rectangle with a pointed nose, painted pea green, what paint there was. Old tires for fenders lined the craft's sides. The name of the boat was scribbled across its bow. The *Phagocyte*. It was a strange name for a very strange boat.

She looked into the bag to make sure the rum was still there. It was. She was ready.

# 26

CECILE hopped aboard the *Phagocyte*, jumping a fifteen-inch expanse of water between the crumbling edge of the river and the tattered houseboat. She pushed her way under laundry strung on ropes from assorted poles, then she saw a hammock suspended from the yardarms, and finally several eviscerated fish cooking slowly over a hibachi-type grill planted on the deck. Beyond that there was an open door to some steps leading down into the living quarters of the boat.

"Mr. Bojanis? Hello!" she called, wondering if he had a gun on her. "I'm the friend of Sister Rita's," she announced.

Nothing. Not a sound except the distant stutter of a motor somewhere else.

She stood calmly, wondering if she were going to be shot. Maybe she would die a martyr after all. At that thought he appeared.

"I'm Louis," he said. He had an East Indian accent, lilting words emerging from a grin that split a very dark face. He was about Cecile's age, and handsome. He had a sharp-looking knife jammed through his belt.

Cecile's eyes stuck on his face, then on the weapon that he pulled out and began spinning. "One second," he said, then he turned and deftly flipped the cooking fish with the blade.

She watched him wipe the knife on a finger, then carefully lick the finger off. "Dinner," he said. "You're the friend of Rita's? I got a call you were coming. How do

155

you do? And how do you know her?" The early grin was gone. The black eyes were serious.

"We were in school together in New York a long time ago. We both became nuns." Cecile held out the bag with the long bread and six-pack of Coca-Cola and rum inside. He took it, looked in, and nodded.

"We go inside. Fish be done in five minutes. Come, we have a drink."

The cabin was immaculate, two bunks covered with black cloth, a sink, a teak table, two decent chairs, a refrigerator running off a sputtering generator. Everything shipshape. He poured drinks in plastic cups, rum and Coke. No ice. One for her and one for him. He took a long drink, then watched her to make sure she drank too. Then he poured seconds.

"Channel cats cooking. You'll like them. Now tell me the truth about Rita the nun," he said. "You such a good friend, is it true she gunned down six American boys in Nicaragua?"

"I heard," Cecile began hesitantly, "I heard the truth of that story is that she hid them from the Sandinistas under a chicken coop, fed them, and put them on a boat going to Spain. They never came back."

"I heard that," he agreed and grinned.

Great grin, Cecile thought, and jumped into her reason for being there before she had too much rum and forgot it. "She said you knew about Felipe Klondacki. I want to know who killed him."

"Ah, yes. CIA fellow. I hear about that. I got one suspect. Then there are the others. Two groups want him dead, see. One is the party he took the guns from; he didn't pay enough. Other ones want him dead are the ones he sold the guns to!" Louis chuckled. "See, he played like that. Always asking for it. So he got it."

"Specifically, I want to know if someone named Bobby Ortez killed him. They call him Dirty Bobby."

"Dirt Man." Louis Bojanis made a long hooting noise

156

that sounded like a night bird. Cecile thought it was a laugh. Then he didn't answer. He drank.

He nodded at her plastic cup. "I don't drink alone."

She drank. Then he spoke. "I tell you all about the Dirt Man. You ready?"

"I'm ready."

Ashore, wandering about as though she were a native, Leonie Drail was thoroughly enjoying herself. She loved crowds and confusion. The color of the riverfront was exotic and noisy, and a child with a chicken-pocked face and new, neat clothing was almost invisible.

Leonie had spotted Dirty Bobby back on Calle Ocho when they had both begun to trail Sister Cecile from the restaurant. Leonie had noticed him, not because he was so unusual, but because he was following the nun. Her nun.

She had watched him slip behind a door when Cecile had looked back once. She had seen him waddle across the street, and finally she had seen him follow the nun here.

The three of them arrived at the Miami River at approximately the same time. Leonie and Dirty Bobby both watched Cecile go aboard the *Phagocyte* and talk to Louis. They both watched her disappear down below. They both decided to wait.

Leonie planted herself in front of a shop among a group of children. She was small for her age and fit in nicely.

Dirty Bobby settled in to wait, too. He lit a cigarette and propped himself up against a storefront. This was going to be a silent deal. The irresistible urge was rising again. Not really his style, no blood. But safer this way. He really wanted to kill her and clear things up for his future. But he wanted to please Olimpo and get the money. It was a very tough call. Get the ransom. Get the nun. He fingered the blackjack in his pocket. Maybe he should just soften her up, make her easier to deal with later. That

157

made a lot of sense to the Dirt Man. Besides, what was she doing in there talking to Bojanis? Maybe Bojanis needed to go too.

On the boat, the level of rum was going down fast. Louis liked company when he drank, and he wouldn't talk unless he was drinking, so Sister Cecile had to drink, too. "The fish is great," Cecile slurred, picking the last barbecued bite from the bone with a plastic fork. "What else can you tell me about Dirty Bobby?"

"He's a killer. Noriega's man. Executions. He likes to kill, see. He talks about it to his friends in Opa Locka who do a lot of business running guns, and they tell me he did a knifing Friday night some place. Like, he puts beads up on a window of the Xerobia Botanica downtown. A bead for a kill. He put up a new bead the other night. My people keep track. So I start looking around very hard for you because you be friend of Sister Rita. But nothing's free." Louis was very lucid, his words clear, rhythmic, like a drum beating.

Nothing's free. Cecile knew what that meant. "How much do you want?"

He topped her glass with rum. "Look. I got a friend needs a green card. They got him out at Krome Detention Center. You know that place? That's where they put the illegals they catch that got no family. Krome is very uncomfortable, you understand? You fix it for him, I start to look very hard and find who kill Felipe Klondacki. Maybe Dirt Man didn't do it. Who knows? I find out."

"I don't know about your friend in Krome," she said. "I don't know how to fix things like that."

Louis smiled softly. "Call up someone, talk with that nice voice. Get my friend out. Here's how. He's coming up at Immigration Court, there on Northwest 79th and Biscayne Boulevard. You get a hold of Deputy District Director of the I.N.S. That man is there. One word, he fix anything. I give you the name of the man. You get to him. I give you my friend's name, you get him out of

Krome. You get him a green card, I find out anything you want."

"Government people?" She thought of Damien, then. He was government. And suddenly, she thought of Paul. He was even better. Paul had friends in Miami, judges, government people, immigration lawyers. "Well, maybe I do," she said. "I'll try. Maybe I can."

"Sure you can." Louis wiped a bead of sweat from his forehead. The evening was hot. "I want my friend out. You come along like a saint to help. Like Rita. A saint." Louis scribbled something on a piece of paper and thrust it at Cecile. "My friend gets out, you get what you want."

She looked at the paper and saw a man's name. She stuffed it in her purse. "Okay, I'll do my best. Now, another thing, I'm looking for someone named Bradley Locke. Ever hear of him?"

The dark man looked inward. Maybe he was finally drunk, Cecile thought. He should be. She picked up a can of Coke and poured it into her glass, allowing it to overflow and dribble down on the table, diluting the rum. "Oops," she said.

"I clean later." He was still thinking, oblivious to the mess. "Now there's people who talk about coming into money," Louis muttered. "Some man they put on ice some place. I put out a feel for that. We be in touch. Soon as I hear my friend is out of Krome, I give you a call with all the news. Okay?"

"Okay," Cecile agreed. "I'll give you my telephone number."

Cecile left the boat with her head held high but slightly tilted. She was not rum-drunk, but the fifteen inches between boat and shore that she had gracefully managed when she arrived looked much more than fifteen inches now. Maybe the boat had shifted, she thought.

Louis appeared beside her and took her hand. "Okay, you take a hop, you won't fall in."

She hopped. "Thanks, Louis. I'll be in touch."

"Oh, sure."

Dirty Bobby saw the nun hop onto the bank. He took out a dingy handkerchief and wrapped it around his face, leaving only his eyes exposed, and he waited.

Cecile wasn't sure she had accomplished anything by all this. She stood on the bank for a moment and swayed, then started back along the riverside. She walked for a few moments trying to clear her head. She didn't see Bobby Ortez fall into step behind her; she didn't see the Dirt Man's pudgy arm take a swing with the blackjack and miss because she had just bent over, adjusting to the heavy mixture of rum and intense heat. She only saw the river, black and swirling, and she saw the long narrow barracuda that inhabited the area. She stopped to look.

Leonie watched, then ran. She came up fast behind Dirty Bobby, frantic as the man took the first swing at the nun and missed.

"Damn," Leonie cursed silently. "He's crazy." Then she saw the Dirt Man raise the blackjack for a second swing. This time it couldn't miss.

"Look out!" Leonie's scream was bloodcurdling. And it was just in time.

Cecile stopped, pivoted, and saw the upraised arm. She saw dark eyes above a filthy bandana. She ducked instantaneously. It wasn't quite enough. The blackjack dropped hard and smashed Cecile on the shoulder. The blow was immediate and painfully sobering.

Cecile began to move. She dipped, she swung, and she moved fast, diving for Dirty Bobby's legs as he took another swing. Four hefty shots of rum diluted with Coke and channel catfish had left Cecile lucid, not quite drunk. Now she was functioning at full speed. Dirty Bobby's legs flew out from under him and he flipped right over the embankment and into the river. The movement left Cecile on the ground eating dirt. She groped wildly, then rose, conscious of the ripping pain in her shoulder and wild splashes from the Miami River.

Tottering on the riverbank, Sister Cecile looked down and in the evening light saw chaos. A masked bandit was flailing wildly, barely swimming. From the back it could have been anyone. A mugger. A killer. Dirty Bobby. Cecile saw him finally reach a small boat tied nearby. She saw pudgy fingers grasping the painter and a huge barracuda swimming inches behind.

Then she ran.

Leonie had moved back right after her scream. There wasn't much she could do now. Even the Silent Avenger had limitations. Not silent, Leonie corrected in her mind as she watched the scene unfold. She withheld a gleeful squeal when Dirty Bobby pitched into the river, and she scurried back, further out of sight when she saw that Cecile was okay. Her work was done. "The Avenger rules," she crowed.

She watched Sister Cecile brush herself off, check her purse, and take a quick glance at the river before racing off in the direction of her car. It almost looked as though Sister Cecile were giggling, but that couldn't be. It didn't make sense. Maybe the poor nun was crying.

Leonie didn't know all the facts. Sister Cecile was still buzzed, but not quite drunk. She *was* giggling.

Leonie observed Dirty Bobby scramble out of the water and heave himself into a small boat just as a long, black fish leapt out of the water. Then Dirty Bobby made his way to shore, grunting and cursing.

Cecile was almost out of sight when Dirty Bobby spotted her and shook a fist. The nun was walking fast, already half a block from the incident. Sister Cecile was safe.

When all was clear, Leonie returned to the scene of the fiasco. She had seen something drop and she was curious. Her eyes swept this way and that over the ground until she spotted what she was looking for. She bent down and picked up the blackjack, holding it loosely the way she imagined a gangster would. "Cool," she whispered and stuffed it in her bag. Now the Avenger was armed and dangerous. But it was getting late.

161

Leonie had to find a taxi and head back to the condo before the nuns panicked. Time to resume her disguise as harmless, small girl, sick in bed.

# 27

LEONIE took a cab but it was still close to eight o'clock when she arrived back at the condo. She was starving and exhausted.

"Where on earth have you been, dear?" Sister Raphael asked as she let the girl in. Her words were quivering from anxiety. "I was so worried. Miami isn't safe! The way people drive in this city is a crime in itself. You could have been killed!"

"I went for a long walk," Leonie said. "I'm careful. Really." She didn't look well. Her face was flushed from the heat and a resurgence of fever. "What's for supper?"

"Good fish from the grocery and some cold cuts in case you hate the fish," Sister Raphael said, still anxious. "I picked up a little snapper. Cecile called and she's on her way home. Why don't you take a little rest, cool off in the shower maybe. I'll call you for supper. But get some ice water, first. One can't be too careful about heat exhaustion. Put your feet up for a while. It's easy to become dehydrated in this climate."

"Ice water," Leonie agreed and stopped by the cooler to fill a glass. She took it with her to her room and closed the door. She sat down on the edge of her bed to drink, patting her bag. The blackjack was still there. Moments later she lay back on the bed, feet up, just like Sister Raphael had suggested. Her hand was wrapped around the blackjack and her mind was busy dreaming up scenarios where she could use it.

* * *

By the time Cecile arrived, Raphael had almost forgotten how worried she had been about their charge. Leonie was home now. Safe and sound. The girl had only been for a long walk. There were other things to talk about.

"Cecile, I got the motel," Sister Raphael bubbled. "It looks like something out of *Key Largo* the movie, you know?"

"Great. I knew you could." Sister Cecile hiccuped. Her face was unusually red and her breath smelled odd. A clump of dirt was lodged in her skirt pocket and a dark smear ran across her face.

"Are you all right? Get a drink of water, Cecile. Leonie just did."

Cecile giggled. "Water. That might help. What's for dinner?"

Then she noticed the message Leonie had scribbled by the telephone earlier in the day. "Look, Raphael, Paul called. He's here in Miami!"

"I saw that. Isn't it wonderful! Maybe he can help."

"No. It says here he's at a Bimbo Convention and then he's gone fishing. Bimbo?"

Raphael came over to look at the note. Then she looked at Cecile. "It says Bamboo Convention." She smelled Cecile's breath up close. "Are you all right, dear? You're covered with dirt. What happened?"

"I'm wonderful. I needed to see Paul about something anyway. Isn't coincidence wonderful!"

"Wonderful, but don't believe it, Cecile. There are no coincidences."

"No? I wonder if Paul has a Bimbo."

"I think you need a nice cold shower, Cecile."

Somehow, later, they all did the dishes. Cecile was almost totally sober by that time, and food and rest had rejuvenated Leonie. Then Cecile excused herself. "I have to go out to that hotel bar," she said quietly to Raphael. "That man, Bobby, I told you about, is expecting me." She gave a shudder as she remembered the naked truth of

164

Dirty Bobby. She still wasn't sure if it had been he who had tried to kill her today. Thanks to her guardian angel, of course, he hadn't succeeded. She still needed to meet with the man.

It was not a prepossessing thought, and her shoulder ached abominably. Best not mention the attack to Sister Raphael.

Leonie was wiping the table and heard every word of the nuns' soft discussion. A bar? Bobby? She would remember that. Nobody knew how important she was to this business, but she knew better. She was going to crack this case yet, whatever it was. She had already saved the nun's life, for heaven's sake.

"Be careful," Raphael whispered. "Bobby probably murdered Felipe."

Leonie frowned at the words. Bobby definitely was a murderer. Unconditionally. After what had happened today, Leonie felt a real sense of mission. She was needed.

She began to plan.

Sister Cecile dressed slowly in a clean, new off-white skirt and blouse. Moving her shoulder was tough. A purple welt had appeared. She probed around it with gentle fingers. Nothing broken, but it would be difficult to arm wrestle for a while.

As soon as she was ready, she left. Quite sober and dead serious.

Cecile took the red car, surging over Biscayne Bay and on to Greater Miami. She turned off the air-conditioning and rolled down the windows. Real air. Dirty Bobby's house had stunk, and lingering rum fumes still blew roughly through her mind. She needed a clear head for what was coming.

"I wonder who yelled for me to watch out," Cecile mused aloud. "Probably an angel," she murmured. "Definitely an angel. Thank you, God."

The past week drifted through her mind. She recalled her last trip to the Hotel Place St. Michel. That first night in Miami, such a short time ago, had already receded into nostalgia territory. Felipe Klondacki had been alive, his tired, worn figure, the old stone building, the gentle feeling of ideas half formed and just begun. She thought fondly of her first meal in Miami at Taco Louis's place, and wished she had been adventurous enough to have tried those plantains. It had been a good night at the start, and now Felipe was dead. And now, she realized, she was afraid.

She considered her fears.

Dirty Bobby? What a pig. Probably he had killed Felipe. Probably he knew where Bradley was. And it must have been him today, trying to kill her. Those eyes could have belonged to no one else. Of course he wouldn't know that she had known it. Would he?

No. She was closing in for the kill. Or, at least on the killer. But where was Bradley Locke?

She walked in to the Hotel Place St. Michel, noticing different things this time: the hand-tiled floors, vaulted ceilings, well-placed antiques.

She entered the bar. She moved immediately to the rear where she took a small table and settled in. She ordered a seltzer, something she could drink fast. The day had left her thirsty, and some residual fear did too. Her mouth was dry.

Cecile glanced at her watch. Had they set a time for this rendezvous? Ten or ten-thirty. She couldn't remember. Probably when he could get off from the kitchen. It was already past nine-thirty.

She drank quickly and ordered another. Her hand was shaking when she took up the second glass.

Dirty Bobby looked through the back door and saw the nun. He had been going out the kitchen door and around to the bar door every ten minutes all night to check on her arrival. He didn't notice her hand trembling on the

166

glass. He just remembered how she had dumped him into the Miami River and there had been a fucking barracuda swimming around in the water, six inches from his skin. It still made his flesh crawl. Being close to danger was an aphrodisiac to him, though, and he felt the usual things happening to his body, just remembering it. Sexual thrills for the Dirt Man came at a big cost. The last time he had felt anything like this was when Noriega had whacked him over the head with a gun butt.

Sex and a million bucks? He saw the nun, apparently complacent, sipping a clear drink with a slice of lime stuck on the edge. Looked like a gin drink. Was she a nun or not a nun? He tore lettuce and considered the situation. Nuns weren't things he often dwelled upon. He had shot two nuns once in Panama and gone home to a dinner of rare lamb braised in garlic and wine. That had felt okay, but he remembered the meal better than he recalled those murdered nuns, their white veils splashed with blood, red on white like the tomatoes he now started arranging in circles on beds of cottage cheese. It meant nothing except the thrill he always felt when he killed somebody. Killing this one would be good. He could almost feel the bang in his gut already. Another bead in the Xerobia Botanica.

Cecile hadn't gotten halfway through the second seltzer when Dirty Bobby slithered up beside her. "Come through the back door and we can talk," he said, his thick lips pulled back in a smile.

"Fine. Right now?"

"Give me a minute," Dirty Bobby said and was gone.

She was expected to follow him? She looked around the mahogany bar where the man had vanished out a narrow door. The tall bartender she had heard called Joe was busy polishing glasses with a white towel. She took a last sip of her drink and put some change on the table for a tip. She slipped over to the bar. She forced a smile up at the bartender.

"Joe, I'm meeting Dirty Bobby," she whispered, "I have to use your door." She skirted behind the tall bartender and found herself in an alley-like room filled with freezers and refrigerators. She spotted the exit door and left.

The darkness of the Miami night was shocking. Dirty Bobby emerged from the gloom, balancing on the balls of his feet, smoking a cigarette. His eyes slid up her body.

Cecile took a shallow breath. "You thought you might have some information about Bradley Locke?"

"I heard things. Hard to track this down, understand?"

"I'm sure." Her voice was sounding better. No fear, she said to herself. None. She had seen this man naked, snoring. What was a dark alley meeting next to all that?

"It cost all that money you gave me," Dirty Bobby said.

"Yes?"

"I find out he is alive and well."

"That's wonderful." Was he lying?

"Some people have him safe. They want a deal."

Cecile nodded. "What's the deal?"

"Million bucks. And a couple other things."

"Too much." It was an automatic reflex. The government would never go for it. She knew the government.

"Million," he repeated. "It's what they tell me."

"I have to talk to these people. Maybe half a million?" She didn't sound scared anymore, but she was. Dirty Bobby wasn't likely to kill her, or Bradley, not until he had the money. Not that there would ever be any, she realized with sudden clarity. The government didn't pay for hostages.

She smiled brilliantly knowing, like Von Clausewitz, that when one's back was against the wall, one attacked.

"It's got to be a million." Dirty Bobby wrinkled his mouth. Bad teeth gleamed in the darkness. "No bargains."

"No bargains." Bradley Locke was alive, but he might as well be dead. This was not going to work. "Then I need time. A week to get all that money together."

"Long time."

"Lot of money," Cecile countered. This was hopeless.

"I tell you what, it's not me, you understand, who does this. I just got the message. And, see, I got this driver's license, proves they got him." He stuffed it in her face. Bradley Locke, clear as glass. "I gotta see about this week thing." He stopped, then. "They want three diamond watches too. Men's watches. They want them up front to prove you're gonna come through with this. Maybe you get them right away, then I can get you the week you want. Maybe."

"Three real diamond watches?" Very weird, she thought.

"Yes. Tomorrow you give me the watches, I'll know for you about the week. I call you."

"Tomorrow? How about I call you?"

"No. I call you. Give me the number. And the watches you leave off some place. I tell you tomorrow where. You have them ready. Real ones."

She didn't like it, the deal was impossible, but she could still buy time. She gave him the condo telephone number, scribbling it on a piece of paper. "Call me in the morning, please. Will you be here late tonight?"

"I work until midnight," he grunted.

"When will you call?" Cecile didn't want him calling when she was out. What if Leonie picked up the telephone?

Dirty Bobby shrugged.

"I need to know right away. I have to raise a million dollars. Remember?"

He looked at her. He looked incredibly stupid.

"I gotta get back to work. I call in the morning."

"Wait. Felipe. Remember *him*?"

"Don't know no Felipe."

"The man I was with when we met here before," she said patiently. "What happened after I left? Do you know where he is?"

"He's a nothing man. Nothing. *Nada*. Know what I mean?" Dirty Bobby's eyes were black, all pupil. "He

169

was all done. You know that? Like, you're a nice nun."
He laughed.

"Felipe was all right then. Have you seen him?"

There was just the barest twitch to Dirty Bobby's liberal lips, barely noticeable.

"You saw him later that night," she said. "Didn't you?"

Dirty Bobby grinned. "Sure. I see you later, too. Later."

He turned and was gone from the alley, going into a different door from the one she had come out. The door closed with a thud.

Later, she thought. He was planning to kill her later too. No. It couldn't end. She had too much to do.

Sister Cecile left, looking carefully in every direction before leaving the dark alley. Fear followed her, not fear of death, but of failure.

Maybe it was the same thing.

It was good to get back into the Ferrari. It started in an instant and Sister Cecile roared away. For the moment she was free of Dirty Bobby, but the impossibility of raising a million dollars rested like an elephant on her mind.

# 28

TUESDAY morning in the Redlands was very hot. Olimpo's place was borderline Everglades, not far from the endless acres of palm nurseries, not far for the sea of grass. A late night rain had left things damp and humming. Mosquitoes that usually attacked in droves at night were still waiting outside the screens long after first light. The tiny bugs sang diabolically like tiny sirens trying to lure the captives from their bed. It was a lost cause, though. The bugs couldn't get in; the prisoners couldn't get out. Bradley and Violet had checked the windows a hundred times and knew escape was impossible. The screens were left intact because the windows were too small for human bodies to push through. Mosquitoes were less intelligent and they kept trying to get in through the wire mesh. Occasionally one succeeded.

They were lying on the cot together, Bradley in his red plaid boxer shorts, Violet in her purple bikini undies and tank top. They were too hot, too sticky, but nevertheless caught up in a peculiar kind of bliss found between couples in love. Once in a while Bradley's hand would run along Violet's bare midriff. She would rub the back of her hand against his unshaved cheek.

After an initial orgy of marijuana and sex late Sunday night, they had both come to earth on Monday morning and decided that together they would escape, survive, and start over. They even mentioned marriage although neither was sure the other was serious. The euphoria continued all day Monday through a day-long conversation

171

between the two of them about their respective child-hoods. Maybe it was the drugs, maybe it was Bradley himself who regarded Violet with the same glowing care and concern he had previously lavished on Bismarck alone. Whatever it was, it happened. For the first time in her life Violet was able to speak of what she had endured from her father. It was not a pleasant tale.

As for Bradley, he talked to her about his lonely upbringing in the Midwest as an only child, how he had lost his best friend at the age of ten, his mother at seventeen, his wife when he was twenty-seven. He spoke fondly of Bismarck.

There was more.

"I can't believe you get banana cravings, too," Bradley sighed that Tuesday morning.

"And that you have a cat named Bismarck. I had a cat named Busy before Daddy kicked him too hard," Violet said.

"I'd like to kick your father, Violet. There's so much I'd like to make up to you."

"Daddy died of rabies three years ago," Violet reminisced. "A dog bit him and he never went to the doctor. I never had a chance to see him when he was sick."

"Thank God. He would have bitten you."

Violet giggled and sat up on the cot. "I hear a car."

"What else is new."

"I have a premonition, Brad. I think we're going to get out of here soon. Life is getting better. I mean, look at us. Look what we got together."

"Dead or alive," Bradley said sourly, then, "Listen at the cat hole. Once in a while I can hear what they're saying. You have to get down on the floor and practically stick your head out."

Violet lay down on the floor and poked the swinging door open. They both could hear the screen door slam as Dirty Bobby came in, then they heard Dirty Bobby bellow something.

Violet scrunched her eyes closed with the effort of

listening, gesturing behind her with her hand for Bradley to be silent. Bradley used the moment to study Violet's barely clad body spread out on the floor, buns up.

"Money," Violet finally muttered.

"What?"

"Shush." She kept listening then finally pulled herself away from the hole. She sat up and pulled up her tank top in one movement. She rose and went over to the cot and sat down beside Bradley. Her face split in a big grin.

"What'd I tell you," she said.

"What'd you tell me?"

"They want time to get the million bucks."

Bradley gulped. "What?"

"They want a million bucks for you, and the nun asked for a week."

"Or?"

Violet shrugged. "I heard Olimpo say, 'Three days.' "

"Then?"

"Nothing. Do you believe that? A million bucks. You're worth a million bucks."

Bradley stood up and walked around in a small circle. "Who the hell is this nun?" he asked finally. "You met her, right?"

"A fuckin' million fuckin' bucks, Brad. You're really something."

"Don't use that word. You want our kids to grow up saying fuck all the time? Who's this nun?" he asked again.

"The nun? Well, she shows up at the Bella Vista the other day looking for you. I hear her talking to Ken and so I come up to her later and say I might know about you." Violet laughed. "I said I'd give her some information if she'd give me a few bucks and let me drive her Ferrari. She's got this really bad red Testarossa, Bradley, like you won't believe. The car is very sweet. She says she's a nun, though. I mean, she really is a nun, I guess. I know a nun. We talked a little. She knows this other guy, Damien. You know him?"

173

"Damien Drail?"

"Yeah. Hey, you know him?"

"How do you know him?"

Violet began twisting her pale hair back up into its knot. "He came by the hotel." She looked very innocent.

"You know his last name just from stopping by?"

"Bradley, darling, I used to be a working girl. You know all that. Besides, this Damien needed some advice about his kid. He's got a kid, see, and he's not smart about taking care of her. Wanna have kids? Really?"

"Kids? Sure. Let's have kids. So we stop saying fuck, like I said. But, see, this Damien is big where I work. Very smart."

"Mr. Perfect? I'm telling you he didn't do so well arranging for his kid, but I straightened him out. I have this thing about kids. Sometimes I wish I was a kid, like before everything started happening, you know? Like, if it had never been that way, I'd be all grown up now. I'm still a kid. Somehow I got stuck back then. So whenever I see a kid with a problem I get this feeling. I want to fix things."

"Violet, you're a darling," Bradley said fondly and came over and sat down beside her on the cot. His hands started moving around on her damp skin.

Violet slipped into a sudden dream as she felt Bradley's hands on her. Bradley Locke, her Lochinvar, was going to fix everything in her life. He already had. "You're *my* marvel," she said as he began covering her shoulder with kisses.

They sank together to the hidden, swimming depths of a cot in a hot room somewhere in the steaming land by the Everglades.

# 29

YESTERDAY'S fear remained. Sister Cecile had seen Dirty Bobby up close. She had been certain the devil was in him; she had never seen the devil so near. It made her move slowly, carefully. She was walking on glass.

Sister Raphael knew something was different about her friend that next morning when Cecile returned from an early morning excursion bearing some very expensive-looking packages. Something about Cecile's face; her eyes were bleak, her skin pinched.

"Are you okay?" Raphael asked.

"Fine."

"What's wrong?"

"I just bought three Piaget diamond watches for a total of $36,700.00 charged to my account with the gold credit card. It's the least I can do for Bradley Locke."

"Money again," Raphael said. Maybe that was the trouble.

"It doesn't matter. Money. Any telephone calls?"

"No. Dirty Bobby didn't call." Raphael watched Cecile's face. "What happened, Cecile?"

"Nothing. He didn't call?" She tossed the boxes on the couch. "Well, it's still early, and I have the watches. I've got to reach Paul, too. He may not have left yet for the Bimbo Convention. Maybe if I can get his secretary in Boston, I can get the telephone number of the fishing boat he's on."

Sister Raphael nodded. Sometimes she knew enough to keep her mouth shut, although she mouthed "bamboo" very carefully. Maybe it was the thought of seeing Paul that was making Cecile so tense. It never occurred to Sister Raphael that it was the thought of death.

Cecile dialed the number of Paul's Boston law office. Five minutes later she hung up, grinning. "I got the number of the boat he's on, and it's a *bamboo* convention."

"I know," Raphael said. Cecile was starting to look better. Raphael was satisfied, and went back to the computer where she had been doing some figuring.

Cecile started dialing again, this time routing through the marine operator. Leonie, who had been hanging around the kitchen, suddenly vanished to her room.

The connection to the "Short Tort" was swift. "Captain Eager Legal here," came a voice.

"Is Paul Dorys on board?"

"On the main deck. Who's this?"

"Sister Cecile."

"Hold on."

There was the elusive sound of water and wind. Then Paul came on the line.

"Cecile, you found me. How are things?"

"Wonderful. You were at a bamboo convention?"

"Anything to be near you. When can we get together?"

"I don't know. We'll be closing on the retirement home soon."

"Who's the little girl I talked to?"

"Leonie Drail, an old friend's daughter. But Paul, I need you to do me a favor. Don't you have a friend here in Immigration Court? A higher up type?"

"Sure. Peter Gardner, otherwise known as Eager Legal."

"He wouldn't happen to be the Deputy District Director would he?"

Paul laughed. "Sure. If he weren't running a Mahi Mahi on the line you could talk to him."

"Great. I want him to give a permanent visa to somebody they have locked up in the detention center at

Krome. A man from Haiti. He shouldn't be in detention and he has good friends who will take care of him in Miami. They even have a job waiting if he gets a green card. He's a political exile. He meets all the criteria for being paroled."

"You're asking for the moon, Cecile. You're talking Haiti."

"No, I hear he's a good man. He has friends waiting; he even goes to church."

"Which church is that?"

"I didn't ask. Listen, his name is Jean-Claude Planier. You have to do this immediately, like today, life or death matter. Can your friend actually get him out? Jean-Claude Planier. I believe the word is 'paroled.' Get him paroled."

"In fact, the Deputy Director can do that with a phone call from the boat. Ultimate power. Does this have to do with the retirement home? Is there a connection?"

"No."

"If I do this will you marry me?"

"Paul, we have a bad connection. I can't hear you. Just get it done. Please? Can you hear me?"

"I hear you."

"Bye, Paul. Remember the name, Jean-Claude Planier." She spelled it. "Thanks. Call me when you come ashore."

"Bye, Cecile."

She didn't hang up for a moment; she listened to the sounds coming in from the Atlantic Ocean. She heard a long sigh on the line, coming from a great distance. It was either Paul, or it was the wind.

Leonie waited until both parties had hung up before she put down her receiver. Then she meandered casually out of her room, thumbing a comic book.

Cecile headed back to the kitchen to find Raphael. "Time is running out, Raphael. I have the watches ready, but no word from Dirty Bobby and I hate waiting for telephone calls. Maybe if I get into the hot tub, Bobby

177

will call. Will you get the telephone for me if it rings, and get me out of the tub if it's you-know-who?"

"Go ahead. It should relax you. How's Paul?"

Cecile looked worried. Not the look that had been there before, a different sort of worry. "He asked me to marry him again."

"He loves you."

"I love him, too. You know that. But *this* comes first." She fingered the gold cross around her neck. "It always will. It's hard, sometimes. Is it easier when you're old?"

"No. It's harder when you're old." Raphael's blue eyes were inscrutable. "But better. Richer. You're lucky to love. Paul is a good man. Now, go take your bath. It's sure to make Dirty Bobby call."

It did. He called just as Cecile had covered her hair with shampoo bubbles and the hot tub had worked up a good froth with Paul's bubble bath soap. Raphael picked up the telephone in the living room where she and Leonie had started a game of double solitaire together. "Sister Cecile? Yes, please wait, she'll be right with you."

Raphael lay the receiver on the table and shook her head, saying something that Leonie interpreted as "evil man."

Leonie was quick. "I gotta go to the bathroom," she murmured as Raphael left to get Cecile.

Both nuns had noticed that Leonie was looking better today. New pox had stopped appearing and she was dressed in a pair of pre-faded terry cloth baggy shorts and a matching blue cotton pullover. She headed straight to her bedroom, her step bouncy.

Leonie took the telephone off the hook and waited, listening. She picked up her stuffed octopus with her free hand and gave it a hug. Then she put it down and covered the mouthpiece with her hand. There was the sound of a man breathing, kind of thick and heavy, and then she heard Sister Cecile. "Hello."

"It's me." The man's voice.

178

"Yes. Will the week be all right?" Sister Cecile's voice was strained.

"No. Three days. We want the million bucks in three days or they tell me the fuckin' *hombre* is alligator meat. Three days. By Friday, two in the morning. I tell you the place to take the money later. And the watches you run by me in an hour. You got the diamond watches?"

"Yes, I have them." Cecile broke into a cold sweat.

"You deliver them right now to the front of the Flagler Memorial Library. I'll be there."

"Right now? And three days? That's pushing it, Bobby. Three days for a million dollars?" Sister Cecile's voice sounded cool again. "Did they say alligator meat?"

"Alligator," Dirty Bobby confirmed. "They kill Bradley Locke, toss what they got left to the alligators. No one ever see him again. That's what they tell me."

"Where do I bring the million dollars? What are the instructions for that?"

"I'll get back to you about it by Thursday noon. I find out by then. I gotta talk to these people some more. You get the money ready, bring the watches in an hour. You got the watches?"

"I do. I really do have the watches. Where is the library?"

He gave terse instructions.

"Fine, I'll be there. But three days, a million dollars? It's going to be hard."

"I'll call you again about that. Soon as I know."

There was a click as the man hung up. Leonie listened for a moment as Sister Cecile rattled the telephone, then the young girl hung up too. She flopped back on her bed with a tremulous gasp for air. Ransom money in only three days! No way her dad was going to get a million bucks ransom out of the agency he worked for. What was the nun going to do? Sister Cecile was doomed to failure and Leonie didn't like that at all. The nun was okay, she had decided. Well, maybe not exactly okay, very strange. Nuns were strange.

She would have to help again. "Yipes," she whispered softly. "My Batgirl sensors are warning me of *danger*!"

Leonie came out from her room a few minutes later. She tried hard to be casual. "What's for lunch?" she asked, sitting down by the solitaire game and lifting up a ten of diamonds. She placed it on the jack of clubs.

"Tuna sandwiches. Your father is coming. We have some business," Sister Cecile said. She was standing in a robe, her hair in a towel, bubbles dripping down her face. "I've got to finish my bath and take a quick ride downtown."

"Where?" Leonie asked, wondering what Cecile would say.

"Uh, the library."

Leonie nodded and turned her eyes back to the cards. She saw Raphael turn over an ace of spades. Wasn't that the card that meant death?

"Can't you wait until after lunch?" Leonie asked. Death? She didn't like that card at all.

"No, I have to do it now."

"You're coming right back?" Leonie asked.

"I promise."

"Good."

# 30

DAMIEN arrived at lunchtime to a scene of idyllic peace. Sister Raphael and Leonie were in the kitchen making salads, concocting a radical dressing made with peculiar condiments found in the cabinets. Sister Cecile was back from letting him in, sitting now next to the *Miami Herald* that lay open on the couch beside her. She was wearing another of her new white nun-outfits.

Damien stared, motionless, taking it all in, never suspecting that ten minutes before, Sister Cecile had returned from running three diamond watches to downtown Miami and passing them over to the devil himself.

"Good to see you," he said. He sat down on a white chair on the other side of the room instead of grabbing her and kissing her as he would have liked to do at that moment.

She nodded civilly. "You, too."

Cecile looked happy. The tension had lifted during the act of delivering the watches, an act comparable to tossing bread to a piranha. Her fear had temporarily receded, leaving her face clear, her demeanor placid.

"Come out to the patio and we can go over everything," she said.

Cecile started talking as soon as she sat down on one of the upright chairs in the patio. She passed Damien a packet of paperwork she had prepared. "Everything is here as far as expenses go. If you could have the reimbursements sent directly to the convent, checks made out

181

to the *Order of Our Lady of Good Counsel*, that will allow things to move along at home."

"Right." He took the papers, still bemused. It had always been normal for him to arrive home amid a flurry of contrived activity from the housekeeper, crying demands from his daughter, and a general sense of helplessness. Not so here. Here was tangible peace. Maybe he should marry a nun and bring some serenity to his life.

"I'll send off these receipts today. How's everything going?"

"Leonie's looking much better," Sister Cecile said. "I picked her up a few Florida clothes and she's been busy. Now, Damien," she dropped her voice, "I have serious business to discuss."

Cecile leaned forward and quietly told him the story of the ransom demand and the tale of the three diamond watches. "I just delivered the watches, so, that's all set. He's supposed to call me soon about the money. We only have three days."

"You actually bought three diamond watches and gave them to this Bobby Ortez? Today? And they cost how much?"

"Uh, something like $35,000.00. But I used the credit card, so it's okay."

"Okay? What do you mean, okay? $35,000.00 is okay?"

"It's money I can't really use for myself. I keep trying to give it away. I do give away a lot, actually." She looked perturbed. It was hard to explain that she was using the money to save a man's life so it was okay. Life was worth so much more than money.

"You just threw it away."

"No. It's to save Bradley Locke's life."

"You tossed all that at a man you don't know? Tell me about it?"

Cecile looked embarrassed. "It's a long story, but when I entered the order I was cut off from my father's money. He didn't care for religion so he wouldn't let any of it go to my order or anything to do with it. I can use it for other things, like diamond watches, cars, whatever. Just not religion. It's not really important, Damien, if it will save a man's life."

Damien felt sick. "If you left the order, could you get all his money?"

"Exactly," she smiled. "Now, I need some more cash for the job. I've had to bribe people, and I'm closing in on this. I have feelers out, and I made a deal for some good information. I just have to wait a day or so for things to solidify."

"I have the operations money," he nodded, wondering if he was crazy or what. He dug into his briefcase and pulled out five hundred dollars in cash. Had she really said $35,000.00? "Keep all receipts," he admonished, handing her the money. "You're sure you don't need to be reimbursed for the watches? Really?"

"No. It isn't necessary."

"I don't think the Agency would reimburse you for them anyway," he muttered and wiped his hand across his brow. "I don't know exactly what they would say."

"Then don't say anything."

"No. I guess not. Tell me, do you think this Dirty Bobby is behind the kidnapping or is he just a contact?" Damien asked. He was trying to keep his mind on business, but it was all so crazy. His gaze became caught up in Cecile's hair, soft, shiny curls blowing in a Florida breeze coming in off the Atlantic. She smelled clean, she looked beautiful. He should marry *this* nun. He would be rich, he could retire, and he'd already made her Leonie's guardian. He smiled, suddenly. It was fate. She was being much more amiable than she had been before. And he certainly did like her.

Cecile was strictly business. "I don't know if Dirty Bobby is party to the kidnapping, specifically. He has to go back and forth to these people. But I do believe Bradley's being held somewhere in the Everglades."

"Why?"

"Alligator meat. Bobby kept referring to alligator meat. That's where there are lots of alligators, right?"

Damien nodded. "They come out of the lakes, too. Canals sometimes. Matthison Hammock has them."

"Man eaters?"

Damien shrugged. He didn't know much about alligators. "When is this Dirty Bobby getting in touch again?" he asked.

"Thursday noon with instructions. Can you get the money? A million dollars?"

Damien looked out to the ocean. "I can ask."

"What do you think are the chances?"

"They aren't big on ransom payments. They do want Bradley back alive. He's a very important agent with a head full of vital information, but it would be cheaper to come up with an entirely new plan for the islands than to pay this money out with no guarantees. You understand, he could already be dead."

"I knew you'd say that."

Damien didn't speak for a minute, then, "Find him, Sister Cecile. What can I do to help?"

"I have three days to get this money, Damien. Dirty Bobby's going to call me later today about the time and place. We don't have much time. But I have a feeling about this prostitute who knew Bradley. I'm going to try her again."

"Don't bother." Damien shook his head. Cecile was talking about Violet, of course, and he felt a momentary surge of guilt. "She might tell you anything just to make you happy."

"Maybe she's reliable," Cecile said. "Prostitutes can reform."

"Like Mary Magdeline? Like drug overdoses, AIDS, bad pimps? Grow up, Cecile, prostitutes don't reform these days. They die." He stopped, turned to the positive. "This Dirty Bobby, he may be the connection. I'll check on him for you. He could be known in the underworld around here. Where did you run into him?"

184

"He works at the hotel where Bradley was last seen. I've already got feelers out, Damien. I should hear something soon. Maybe tonight." She sounded reluctant to talk about him.

"We have resources available to us that you don't. I'll research Bobby Ortez and get in touch by ten tomorrow. Maybe I can pull some known associates. Maybe we can run down some new connections. I'll do everything I can."

"Fine," Cecile said. "Dirty Bobby Ortez. That's his full name. And he lives on Fish Street."

"That should help. Meanwhile, how about dinner tonight?"

Cecile tilted back against the glass wall. He could see her hesitancy. This nun was not an easy project, but suddenly Damien was committed. He had fallen under her spell.

"Maybe you should take Leonie out for a pizza," she suggested.

"She looks like a case for Acne Control. Pocks. We can leave her. She's used to it."

"Damien, forget it. Have lunch with us here and talk to your daughter like you love her. Take her for a walk around the building, show her the weight room or something. She misses you."

Damien met the clear grey eyes of the nun and looked away. Cecile had that same look in her eyes that the prostitute had, telling him to provide for his daughter. They were right. "Maybe I'll take her out to Parrot Jungle. Think she's feeling up to it?"

"Yes. That would be wonderful. Raphael tells me she went for a long walk yesterday. Alone. She needs you, Damien."

"Needs me?" He'd never noticed that she'd needed him. Never. Leonie's emotions were as deeply hidden as his own. He wasn't even sure she had any sometimes. "Not likely," he said. "But there are times I feel as if I need her."

185

Damien took a long breath. It was so much easier to be an agent than a father. But he would try. "I'll take her out after lunch if you promise me dinner tonight."

Cecile looked hesitant for a moment, but he could see he'd gotten through to her. "Dinner, but Leonie comes too," she said.

"Leonie stays," he said with a crooked smile. "We'll be talking business."

Cecile turned away before she answered. "All right. Dinner. But first, Parrot Jungle. It doesn't have to be for long. Raphael said Leonie was exhausted after her walk yesterday. She's still not quite better. You be kind, Damien."

His lips twisted. "Kind? I do love her, Cecile. I'd do anything for her. What she really needs, though, is a mother." He looked directly at Sister Cecile. There was something highly suggestive about the look and he could see Cecile didn't quite understand it. She would, of course. Eventually. Later.

# 31

LEONIE and Damien left for Parrot Jungle right after lunch. Leonie looked surprised but happy. She carefully brushed her hair, put on a pair of knee-length blue and green striped pants and a matching top, and was well fortified with a healthful meal. She had even been seen cutting up small raw broccoli chunks and putting them in the salads and then actually eating hers.

"I think there's hope for her," Raphael said after father and daughter had left.

"I like her," Cecile said. "She has to learn to talk to adults, but I have a feeling that once she does, she'll never stop. And she does love her father."

Raphael nodded. "And he loves her. Fathers are so important. Damien isn't really that bad, Cecile. You act very hostile toward the man."

"I am. I had to bribe him to take Leonie out today, promised him dinner this evening, alone. Will you be here for Leonie tonight?"

"Where else would I be? I found some games for the computer. Maybe I can interest Leonie in a game. But I have to make that house inspection right now. Are you coming?"

Cecile nodded. "Yes. I want to do a run through, too. Then I'm going to drop by the Bella Vista Hotel and talk to Violet again."

The two nuns left to meet the house inspector at the old motel. Another world, no shadows here, just light. The site showed promise.

While the inspector walked through the buildings, studied the wires, the roofs, and the foundations, poked sticks through holes in walls, flushed toilets, sniffed in closets, and activated air-conditioning units, Sister Cecile tried to put Bradley Locke out of her mind. It didn't work, but the motel did. It would be perfect for the older nuns.

The nuns left, happy but hot. Cecile pulled up near the Bella Vista Hotel soon after, parking half a block down the street from the building. She sat in the car for a moment, the engine idling. The sunlight outside the tinted glass windows was bright. A steel blue sky demonstrated at least one aspect of eternity. Death was at bay.

"I hate to leave you in the car, Raphael. It might be dangerous," Cecile said. "So many muggers in this town."

"I thought I could come along inside," Raphael said solidly. Her hand was already opening the low slung door. The heat began pouring in.

"All right," Cecile said. "I'm going to ask Violet about the place near the Everglades that she mentioned. I have a feeling she knew more than she said. I have to find out where this place is. You just let me do the talking."

"Fine. You won't even see me."

Ken Newly resembled a slow-burning dump as the pipe smoke rose and lingered around him. He recognized Cecile and gave a nod through the haze. He pushed his magazine aside. "Help you?" He barely glanced at Sister Raphael, always invisible because of her age.

"I'm looking for Violet," Cecile said.

"So the hell am I. Haven't seen her for a couple of days."

Cecile felt ice reach her bones. Violet missing? "Really? Do you have her home telephone?"

He nodded. "Isn't there. Said she was going home early the other night and she never came back. I had a friend stop by there and she hasn't been around her place.

Answering machine is all filled up. Can't even leave her the word to call in."

"Could she have gone out on business, out of town, maybe?"

"Not likely."

"Does Violet have a room here? Maybe she left some information. I'm looking for an address out by the Everglades somewhere."

"Really?" Ken's lower lip turned down and he fingered off a small piece of soot.

"Does she have a room or something?" Cecile persisted.

"She's got a locker, keeps some stuff there. Ain't even locked. You can check it out. She won't care." He dipped his head to indicate a back hallway. "Down the hall, take a left, there's a big walk-in closet with some lockers inside. Her name's on it."

While they were talking, Raphael had wandered off and was looking around in the lobby, registering everything in her mind, the chairs, the few faces, the bar and lounge where Cecile had eaten lunch with Violet. As Cecile left to go search Violet's locker, Raphael returned to the desk to smile at Ken Newly, her old blue eyes noticing that the magazine he was reading was unsuitable for minors. "I'm just a friend of Sister Cecile's," she said. "You must know her by now."

"More or less. She's a popular lady. Still driving that car?"

"Yes. It's just a rental." Raphael bobbed her head in imitation of senility. "People really seem to like it." She let her eyes grow round.

"That dude went for her," Ken remarked. "She's got a real fan club, that friend of yours."

"How's that? What dude?"

"The dude that was here with Violet. He and Violet did some legal paper. Something to do with her. Used my copy machine." He nodded in the direction that Sister

Cecile had gone. Ken Newly was babbling, something people always did in Sister Raphael's presence.

"Really?" Raphael said. "You must have a copy. Did you make a copy?"

"Sure. Got it right here."

"Can I look? I won't say a word. I'm really the soul of discretion." Raphael babbled deliberately. She knew that the more one said the less was remembered, and this Ken would do well to remember her as a blithering old nun.

"No way. It's legal stuff." Ken loosed a fresh cloud of belching smoke that rose in a mushroom shape.

"But she's my friend. She should be aware of what concerns her. Is it a lawsuit?" Raphael was jabbing at stars. What could it be? She had to find out.

"Lawsuit? No. Something about being a guardian." He glanced down at his magazine impatiently.

"Well, I'll pay for the cost of a copy if you give me one," Raphael said. "I won't tell her a thing. I promise. Or just let me look at it."

"Copy? Costs money. Brand new machine. Ain't even paid for yet."

"Five bucks," Sister Raphael said, pushing it. Way too much, she knew. Copies went from three cents on up. But it was tough to set a figure somewhere between reality and bribery. She took out a five dollar bill and placed it on Ken's dirty magazine.

Ken Newly said nothing. He pulled open a drawer and tossed up a piece of paper. Sister Raphael read quickly. "Interesting," she said as though it was really very dull. "You should probably keep this. Who has the original?"

"Probably that dude."

"Well, five dollars for a copy is steep, but I'll pay. Just one copy, please."

Ken Newly ran off a copy while the nun continued to babble in the background. Five dollars was cheap for this information.

He handed her the paper and she stuffed it in her purse. "Thanks," Raphael said.

"Sure." Ken cleared the money off his magazine and turned a page. Sister Raphael couldn't help but see it before quickly averting her eyes. He stuffed his copy of the codicil back into a drawer.

"I think I'll sit and wait in your lobby. It's a very attractive place," Sister Raphael murmured and wandered back to settle into a wicker chair. She began to contemplate the paper she had just put in her purse. She had already decided she would not tell Cecile.

"Thanks, Ken. I found the locker." Sister Raphael heard Cecile's voice as the younger nun came out into the lobby.

"Sure. Any luck?" Ken asked.

"Not really. Some clothes, a lot of makeup. She's a very neat person," Cecile said.

"Wouldn't tolerate no slob."

"No. I'm sure. Could you let me know if she comes around? I'll leave you my number."

Raphael rose and started heading to the door, listening to Cecile's parting words. By the time she was at the hotel door they were together and as soon as they were outside Cecile began speaking quickly.

"I found a telephone number in Violet's locker."

"Whose?"

"Nina's. Someone named Nina. It has to be a friend of Violet's. I'll call the number when we get back and ask her about alligators, places they've been together, or whatever," Cecile said. "Maybe Nina went there, too. I'm assuming there's something, Raphael. Maybe this person has a lead. There has to be something."

There didn't have to be. They both knew it. Violet was missing. Violet could be dead. Sister Raphael didn't say a word. As they drove away, Raphael glanced sideways at Cecile who was driving straight ahead, resembling nothing so much as an angel in a barber's chair, waiting for the cuts of eternity. Raphael didn't say

191

anything about the codicil but it weighed on her mind. What if Damien died? What if Cecile should become a guardian? A nun could become a guardian. It wasn't unheard of, but it was difficult to contemplate. Raphael shook her old head, her brows bent down in a frown. What were the odds? Could anyone contemplate such a thing? Could God?

Back in the condo Cecile dialed Nina's number. Leonie had merely grunted a "hello" at the nuns' return. She had gone back to her room when Cecile mentioned she had to make a quick call. News of Parrot Jungle could wait.

When Cecile had finished dialing in the living room, Leonie picked up her bedroom telephone and covered the mouthpiece with a towel. She heard an indolent female voice answer the ring.

"A-One Escort Service."

"Is this Nina?"

"Might be."

"I'm looking for Violet."

"What for?"

"Uh, I'm a friend. My name is Cecile. Ken will vouch for me. I know her through the hotel."

"Sure, okay, what do you want?"

"Violet's been missing for a few days, and I was wondering if maybe you could help me."

"Violet? Haven't seen her. She okay?"

"I hope so, but she may be in danger. Can you think of any time she's ever been to the Everglades? Or some place where there are a lot of alligators?"

"Alligators?" The voice that must be Nina's laughed. "Violet's always up to her ass in alligators."

"I mean real ones. I'm very concerned."

"Like some place maybe she did a job?"

"That's possible. Any ideas?"

"I don't rat out my friends. See. I don't know you."

Then silence. It didn't show any promise of ending.

"Please." Sister Cecile didn't know what else to say. "Please?"

This time the silence was more thoughtful. Nina started in on a long "Mmmmmm." Finally she said, "Um, yeah. Was a place we did some work a while back. Going out toward the Redlands, near the 'glades. Bunch of animals had a party. Some place off the Tamiami. Head out, make a turn on a dirt road. Lot of noises in the bush, and someone said there was 'gators there. A shit hole," Nina said. "Mosquitoes. Fuckin' mosquitoes. Who'd you say you were?"

"I'm a friend of Violet's. We were planning to meet and really, it's so important. Off the Tamiami Trail? Can you think exactly where?"

"I can't think right off hand. My head's not on right today. Bad night. But there was something there. Some place, or something. It'll come to me. Everything's in my head, see. I might even have it on a piece of paper in my room."

"I'd be willing to pay for the information," Cecile said.

Leonie made a face at that. Cecile was being too eager. Leonie was tempted to break into the conversation. Didn't this nun know you don't bribe friends about friends?

Nina apparently felt the same way. "I said it will come to me. Don't be such a bitch."

"Sorry," Cecile whispered.

"Shit."

"I'm really sorry."

"You just damn blew it out of my mind. It'll come back. Gimme some time."

"Can I call you later? Maybe you'll remember."

"I'll think about it. She gonna be all right? Violet?"

"I hope so. I think so. I'll call you later. Maybe you can remember. My name is Cecile. Did I tell you that? I'll call."

"Okay, Cecile, you do that."

Cecile hung up. Leonie hung up. Then Leonie came out. "Oh, you're off the phone," Leonie said.

193

"Yes. Now tell me all about Parrot Jungle. Did you have fun?"

"It was cool," Leonie admitted. "But I'm beat to shit. We didn't stay long. Dad said to tell you he'd be by later. You guys going out?"

"Yes. We guys are having dinner," Cecile said, wondering if she should tell Leonie that shit wasn't a nice word. Maybe nobody had ever bothered to tell her that. But that wasn't really her job, so she merely added, "A business dinner."

"Oh," Leonie said. "One of them."

# 32

CECILE dressed carefully in an expensive dress. She regarded lay clothes as uniforms. This was a seven-hundred-dollar uniform. A dinner with Damien required that she be a professional and the dress was all of that. A clear beige that made her gray eyes come alive, a shimmering fabric that draped carefully over her curves in order to hide them. It succeeded in suggesting more than it revealed, and it had an astonishing impact, had she but known. She polished her gold cross and made sure it was clearly visible.

An hour later she was out, Damien was at the wheel of his rented car, something American with exceptional air-conditioning and plenty of soft room. A big Buick. They were going to a restaurant on Ocean Drive, not far from Paul's condo.

"How was Leonie today?" Cecile asked.

"Leonie's great. She got a little tired after a while so we just sat and ate junk food and talked about parrots. She's sweet. A lot like her mother."

"Yes," Cecile agreed. "I'm starting to love her. Leonie has a lot going for her. She's perceptive. Very much like her mother in that respect too." She paused. "I went out to the Bella Vista again. I'm honing in on some ideas. I think Bradley Locke's being held in the Redlands, near the Everglades, but exactly where, I'm not sure. I have some feelers out."

"Like what?" Damien was taking Cecile to a small, intimate restaurant, not at all businesslike. He didn't even want to talk business but he must. It was part of his strategy. Play it cool in romantic places.

"Someone who knows Violet. I have to call her later."

"You think it's a real lead?" It was eighty-five degrees out and his voice could have put frost on the car window. He sounded skeptical. He knew Violet and he hadn't quite forgiven her for making him write that silly codicil.

"Maybe," Cecile said. "Any luck rounding up a million dollars?"

"I called headquarters. They don't want to make a commitment."

"That means no?"

Damien was pulling around to the rear of the restaurant where there was a private parking lot.

"We can assume it means no. They operate by delaying the commitment until it's all over. My contact said it might prove difficult to come up with that amount of money, and considering the timetable we're on . . . Then he suggested we try Bradley's family. Unfortunately, I know from Locke's dossier that Bradley's family consists of one sister who lives in Phoenix, Arizona, and teaches third grade."

"Not a person to have a million dollars readily accessible."

"No." Damien got out and came around to open the door for Cecile. He would be the most gentlemanly person she had ever met. It was an act of will, he told himself. And love.

In the restaurant Damien was careful with her chair, making sure it was correctly placed, smiling at her least jest, giving her all the benefits of his knowledge of the Agency when it came to getting money for ransoms.

"I've heard the daiquiris are spectacular here. Would you like to try one? Or do nuns drink?" He asked it pleasantly. "Or mineral water?"

"Relax, Damien. I'm just a nun." She smiled disarm-

196

ingly and asked for a Blue Lagoon. "For research purposes," she said.

"Research. Of course."

"So Bradley's on his own, except for me," Cecile said, taking a delicate sip of her strange blue drink when it finally arrived. "Somehow, I have the feeling that no one really cares about this man. But Damien, I just had a thought. I set something in motion this morning and I forgot to call in about it. Could you excuse me a minute?"

Moments later she was in the restaurant's exclusive telephone booth putting in a credit card call to Paul on the *Short Tort*.

Paul himself answered.

"Paul, did you do it?" she asked after identifying herself.

"I caught a thirty-pound fish. Incredible."

"I mean, did you get Jean-Claude released."

"Yes. He's roaming the street as we speak. Let loose at seven o'clock, had a ride into town. He should land in Miami about eight. He's known as a wild man, this Jean-Claude, but they were going to release him soon anyway. Favors done, or something. My friend's call just expedited things. Cecile, what gives?"

"I'll tell you later, Paul. It's a long story. I'm in a restaurant right now and I can't talk."

"As usual. Enjoy your meal."

"Thanks. Bye."

Cecile returned to the table. "Okay, Damien, I should have some information on Dirty Bobby very soon. Want to take a drive to the Miami River after dinner?"

"Absolutely."

The meal was excellent. Cecile ordered white bean soup, saddle of mutton, cooked rare, and the spinach salad with garlic cloves.

Damien ordered cold lemon soup, Fondue Bourguignonne, the house salad, and a valuable bottle of red wine for them both.

"Nice wine," she said later as they ate and drank.

Damien liked the way things were going. She seemed happy and the food was seduction itself. He perceived her every action as a prelude to falling in love. Women did like him. They always had. "We'll have the brandies. And two blueberry puddings. All right, Cecile?"

Cecile barely seemed to hear him. "Excellent," she said, and when it all arrived, she drank her brandy and ate the pudding, and ten minutes after that they were outside, the meal over and she hadn't touched on her worry that Dirty Bobby wanted her dead. Over the pudding she had decided that Damien really shouldn't know because he was such a male. No matter how modern, men had ideas about women that never changed. People never discern reality, she thought, they only see their own opinions reflected back.

"Any leads on Felipe?" she asked as they returned to the car.

"None. I'm working on it with the FBI."

"Agent Walker?"

Damien chuckled. "Right. I'm looking into some Omega seven stuff."

"Tell me about it?"

"Omega seven," he explained in an obviously patient tone, "is the terrorist arm of the Cuban nationalist movement. There are several groups. Some are called Alpha, some Omega. They're into bombings, assassinations. They haven't been as active in recent years but this is the kind of thing they do. Felipe was closing in on something. I spent the morning going through his notes and there are some connections I'll be looking into."

"Raphael mentioned those Greek letter groups. But Damien, I don't think it was Omega seven that did Felipe in," Cecile said. "Everyone in the underground here knows Felipe. Everyone knows everybody, but they don't know what everybody is up to. I really think it was Bobby. And I think I'll have the proof as soon as we get to this place on the river. Now, how do we get to there from here?"

"This way."

They took the MacArthur Causeway, the closest route from the restaurant on Miami Beach to the Miami River. It was lovely with rows of palm trees like pillars holding up the evening sky. She was delighted when they just made it across the massive drawbridge before it began its ponderous rise to allow passing boats to go through.

The city was growing dark. Streetlights off the main road seemed dimmer. Although more frequent, not all were burning.

Near where the Miami River dumps into the bay is the land of homeless souls in shacks, of dark spaces and abandoned cars. Damien drove fast by the people living under the bridges in paper houses. There were small fires glowing like eyes, burning to cook pillaged meat. By the edge of a dark corner a man was bathing with a bucket of water. Local hygiene on the street. "We shouldn't be here," Damien grunted, tapping one hand on the steering wheel.

"It's not so bad where my friend docks. Up a ways, Damien. Keep going."

Louis Bojanis's houseboat looked empty when they hopped on board. Everything was hellishly black; even the neighbors were missing. The handsome dark man Cecile had seen before was nowhere in sight. The boat that Dirty Bobby had pulled himself up on was gone.

"Louis!" Cecile called. "It's me, Sister Rita's friend. I'm back!"

The stillness felt evil in its intensity. Damien grasped her arm. Louis had probably gone somewhere to drink rum and celebrate his friend's release from Krome Detention Center.

No noise.

"I'll knock on his cabin," Cecile said confidently.

Damien held her arm. "Wait."

199

The door burst open. A dull metal gun showed, reflecting almost nothing in the night.

"What have you done to my friend?" came the voice, a thickly accented English.

"Jean-Claude, is this you? I'm the person who had you released. Where is Louis? He had something for me."

"You have him killed for me?" The voice was strained, quivering. The gun held steady.

Cecile started to back away. A fist lashed out. Damien's. It struck the gun. The weapon spun off into the night. There was a heavy splash as the gun hit the Miami River.

Damien moved. Within ten seconds he had Jean-Claude in a restraining grip and had maneuvered the man down to a kneeling position. "You got a problem with my friend's questions?" Damien demanded.

"Hey, mon, no problem. My friend is dead, see, in there. I think maybe you come back for more. Someone killed Louis. Let me go. I done nothing wrong." His thin legs, bent at the knees, were quivering.

"Your name?" Damien asked.

"Jean-Claude Planier."

Cecile had moved inside the room and turned on a light. It flickered from the sporadic electricity coming off the generator. Louis Bojanis was there. What had been Louis Bojanis. He was dead on the floor, throat slit. She fell to her knees beside the dead man. "Louis, oh, dear God, I'm so sorry."

Blood was everywhere. Cecile forced herself to rise and turn, but before she did she noticed a small, white feather stuck at the edge of the pool of blood beside Louis Bojanis. It was enough to tell her everything.

"Damien, he's dead."

"You know who did this?" Damien asked. He was bending Jean-Claude's arm painfully.

*"Je ne sais rien,"* Jean-Claude managed. "I just got out half hour ago. They drove me here from Krome. I come here. Louis, he's dead. He been dead a long time.

He's cold. You check when they let me go, when this man dies, you see I cannot kill him."

"It's true, Damien, this man was just released from Krome an hour ago. I found out when I called my friend from the restaurant."

Damien let go of the man's arm. "Fine. Where'd you get the piece? The gun?"

"It was Louis's. Under his pillow." Jean-Claude stood up, rubbing his arm. Shaking. Crying.

Sister Cecile couldn't look back in the cabin. Another death. "Let him go, Damien. We can just call the murder in. I know who did it."

"Have you touched anything?" Damien asked, looking at Cecile.

"Nothing."

"How about you?" Damien asked Jean-Claude.

"The gun. Nothing else. The door was open."

"Then, we all leave. I'll take care of it."

It was well past midnight when Damien finally escorted Cecile to the condo door. "I won't come in," he said. "It's late."

"Fine, but I do think it was Dirty Bobby."

Damien laughed. "A chicken feather? That's not proof. I don't think we can have genetic codes checked on chicken feathers."

"Why not? Dirty Bobby has a white rooster."

"Everyone has chickens in this town. Go to bed, Cecile. Find Bradley tomorrow. I'll take care of this. Jean-Claude says for sure he knows the group behind it. Some of those Alphas or Omegas."

"Don't humor me. I *will* find Bradley. Good night, Damien."

There was a sudden silence. Sister Cecile was poised outside the condo door, key in hand. Damien took the key and opened the door for her. He paused, looking into her gray eyes intently. Incredible. The night hadn't exactly gone as planned, but there was time.

201

Here's hoping, he thought, took a step away and handed her the key. "Take care."

He touched her cheek, then turned so she could go in. He waited until he heard the bolt slide home and then he left. Her cheek had felt cool, beautifully cool.

# 33

Leonie heard Sister Cecile come in because she had left her door open, and she had left an empty garbage bucket full of metal utensils in the entry hall where Sister Cecile was sure to kick it. She knew about her father and women. He had brought women into the house regularly, ever since her mother had died. Sometimes a woman had spent the night, someone who would appear at the breakfast table the following morning, dressed in clothes from the night before. It wouldn't surprise Leonie to see Daddy there right now. With the nun. Nuns were people too.

Leonie had to find out how things went. Sister Cecile was pretty. Even a twelve-year-old could grasp the possibilities.

Leonie was out of bed in a flash when she heard Sister Cecile kick the bucket. It was a truly marvelous noise. She went to her door.

Leonie waited in the dark beside her half-opened door. She listened for some indication that things had gone well or badly for the nun. She expected a sob, or a giggle, or the sound of her Dad's voice. There had to be something. Leonie felt responsible for Cecile now. She had a serious obligation.

There were a few sounds in the kitchen. Maybe they were making love by the refrigerator. A cabinet door opened and closed, then she heard a chair scraping back. No voices at all.

Leonie came out.

Sister Cecile was sitting alone at the kitchen table, eating a bowl of cereal and reading from a small black prayer book she held in her left hand. "Hello, Leonie." She put the book down.

"What are you doing?"

"Eating cereal. Want some?"

Leonie looked at the Cheerios floating in milk. There didn't appear to be any sugar on the cereal. And there were tears in Sister Cecile's eyes. Leonie was sure of it.

"No, thanks." Leonie sat down at the table. She was wearing a long nightgown with a large picture of Minnie Mouse on it, one of the new things Cecile had brought her. "How's Dad?"

"Good. He seems to have recovered from Parrot Jungle."

"It was nice," Leonie said, staring at the nun. "He wasn't bad to you or anything, was he?"

Cecile stopped chewing and looked at Leonie for a moment. "No."

"You okay?" Leonie wasn't sure she believed the nun.

"Fine, really. We talked about the case we're working on, had a good dinner, went for a little walk. I just felt like a snack. I can't sleep sometimes."

Leonie looked doubtful. Her father always made a pass. She had seen it happen dozens of times from the top of the stairs. She had seen more than that.

"Dad's funny sometimes. It was nice to spend the afternoon with him."

"I'm glad."

Leonie nodded, satisfied that Sister Cecile was all right. "What about tomorrow?" she asked.

"Tomorrow? Another day. Mass in the morning, real estate business, things like that. I'll be in and out all day. You must be feeling better now?"

"I am." Leonie yawned. "It was nice getting out today. I like it here in Florida. It's warm."

"I do too." Cecile looked at Leonie as carefully as the

204

girl had looked at her. "You look like you should be in bed."

"Yep." Leonie stood up. "Good night," she said and headed back to her room.

Sister Cecile was okay.

The next day went much as Sister Cecile had said it would. After morning Mass the nuns dealt with banks and arranged for a termite inspection of the old motel. The purchase was under way.

Damien called at ten. "No luck with the million dollars," he said when he got Sister Cecile on the line.

"I figured as much. Is there anywhere else to go for it?"

Damien laughed dryly. "The rationale is that he's dead anyway, Cecile. Or, if not yet, he will be once they pocket the ransom. The government figures it's just money down the drain at this point. They're ready to pull you in and start all over again, change the plan, bring in new variations on the Cuba theme. They have the manpower."

"They would just drop Bradley? Forget he ever was?"

"I asked for another week for you. You have a week to pull off something. If you can't get the ransom, you have to find him. Bradley knows how it works. He's a good agent. He wouldn't expect us to come up with that amount. It's never been the policy of the U.S. Government to be blackmailed."

"I realize that," Cecile agreed. "But I'm sure there's plenty of blackmail in Washington."

"No doubt," Damien mused. "I wish I could do more. It stinks."

"Louis Bojanis knew what happened. That's why he's dead." Sister Cecile felt like crying again. "It's my fault."

"Not necessarily. He was into quite a collection of enterprises. I'm on to that. I got a lead on the terrorist group, Cecile. I'm ready to confront some nice Greek letter boys who already have murder warrants out on them. I know where they are."

"Damien, be careful."

205

"It's what I do."

"Damien, I'm going to find Bradley. There's more to this case than money."

"Please. Find Bradley."

"I will."

"Don't hesitate to call me if you need help, Cecile. For anything." The words were vaguely suggestive.

"I'll be in touch," she assured him.

"How's Leonie?"

"Wonderful. She loved going out with you yesterday. She's a dear child."

"Give her my love."

Leonie had missed the entire conversation. She and Sister Raphael were on level six of a computer game and it was tough to quit when you were ahead.

It rained with a sudden, dumping downpour as Sister Cecile and Sister Raphael headed out to the architectural firm. There they spent several hours hashing out plans and possibilities for the retirement home with a very competent architect. By the time they were done and the plans solidified, the sun reappeared and turned the rain to steam that rose like magic mists along the streets and sidewalks.

Miami was beautiful again.

# 34

DIRTY Bobby was sharpening his knife on a piece of Carborundum, watching the jewels of his new watch sparkle each time he moved his wrist. He held the blade up against a stream of light coming in the window of Olimpo's place. He ran the edge along his calloused fingertip and cut a sliver of his own coarse flesh. He resumed stroking the blade lightly on the sharpening stone. "So where we gonna pick up the ransom?" he asked. "I gotta tell the nun."

Nobody answered.

Satisfied with the edge, Dirty Bobby wiped it on his pants to remove the stone particles and then sliced a section off a mango, watching the juice drip out over the table. The knife was sharp. Like a razor. He took a bite of the fruit and let it dribble down his face until the sticky juice was mingled into the glossy darkness of his three-day beard.

"You're a pig, Dirty Bobby. Didn't your mother teach you how to eat?" Bajito was sitting at the same table fastidiously rolling cigarettes. No marijuana, just tobacco. His eyes kept straying to his new watch.

"Shut your mouth. Listen, I gotta call this nun about a million bucks. I gotta tell her where to go, where to take the money, where we'll bring him." He gestured to the rear of the shack where Bradley was incarcerated. "What you want me to tell her, Olimpo? I need some words. You're the word man here."

Olimpo was pacing back and forth, staring at the

morning sun out through the door screen. From where he paced, he could see a small alligator making its way along a swampy trail. It was already too hot out there and the pale green saw grass was showing heat fatigue. Olimpo was feeling restless.

"We take him to town, leave him in a warehouse a lotta miles from the money drop. That way, they screw up the money, we got time to take him somewhere else."

"Right. That's what we figured out." Bajito lit a cigarette and took a long drag. "We don't want no screw-up on this. It's got to run like a clock."

"I kill him later that night, then," Dirty Bobby said.

"He don't know *nada*," Olimpo said. "We already got that figured out. Nobody out there is looking for him but a nun in a fancy car. That's not government, that's just money. So we go for the money. We don't need to kill him."

"He knows you," Dirty Bobby said. "I think I gotta kill him, find out what he knows first. He's gonna finger you later if we don't. Might finger me."

"He never saw you. You just want to cut him up, Dirty Bobby," Bajito scoffed. "You like cutting holes in people. Think I don't know that? Left handed voodoo stuff. You're some kind of bokor, right? Want to split our prisoner's tongue, right? Make a zombie? You're crazy about all that blood."

"Shut up, Bajito," Dirty Bobby snarled. *"Cállate."*

"Give him some zombie cucumber, make him work in the fields, eh, Dirty Bobby?" Bajito was riding him, watching the pudgy man's face twist into an ugly mask.

Olimpo saw it and felt a shudder of fear run through him. Bajito might better watch it, he thought. *"Que te calles,"* Olimpo roared. "Bajito, shut up. Maybe we take a look at the man back there and think about it." Olimpo thought a minute. "And check the woman. And maybe we don't get the money, we sell him to somebody like Castro. That's what I wanted to do all along. I still got the word out for that. Maybe the *Cubano* comes to us. Then we really see some money."

"Cuba's got maybe fifty cents on the whole island. Shared between the whole place, Communist style," Bajito scoffed.

"Hey, shut up. Let's go look at the woman." Olimpo grinned and started walking toward the back room. "Wanna take a look? You seen her, Dirty Bobby? That skinny *puta* we had here a couple months ago come back snooping around so we stuck her back there with the *chico*." He had forgotten the prisoners weren't supposed to see any of them. The drugs did that to him.

"I seen her once," Dirty Bobby growled. "We gotta get rid of her. Can't have her running back shooting her mouth off some night when she gets high."

Bajito stayed in his chair and watched the other two leave. "I wish we never done it," he said to the empty room. "Dumb idea. Wrecked everything we ever worked for."

Olimpo unlocked the door to the prisoner's room. It swung wide to reveal Bradley and Violet sitting on the bed holding hands and staring at the wall. They were no longer stoned. Bradley had decided the first step to take with Violet on the way back to the real world was to be clean. Bradley was not a stupid man. But now they were floating in and out of a reality of their own making, singing old songs by the Eagles. Shadows glinted in their eyes, eyes fixed on the far wall as they recalled ancient lyrics. Bradley had strongly identified with Don Henley at one time. Violet had an ear for the twists in the melodies, and they were singing something resembling "Welcome to the Hotel California" as the door opened.

"Any line of gear," Bradley sang.

"She got a lot of tweety birds she calls friends," Violet warbled.

"Shit," Dirty Bobby said.

"The man is very twisted," Bradley said.

Violet smiled. "Can we leave yet?" A vine of light from the high window seemed to wind around her.

"We gotta get rid of her," Dirty Bobby snarled.

Olimpo barely heard Dirty Bobby. Instead he saw Violet, her hair fallen out of its twist so that it fell in a pre-Raphaelite vision of blonde curls down her chest, touching the exposed and rounded tops of her tank-top encased breasts. He felt a sudden melancholy at the couple's bemusement with each other and the song. He was half in love with her himself, just because she was there. "There is no reason to kill this woman," he said firmly in Spanish. "We will take our ransom and I will take care of her."

Dirty Bobby's disappointment showed. He was not a patient man. "Later, maybe, you get tired of her, I'll take care of her."

"Maybe."

They didn't know that Bradley understood everything. The agent wrapped a long arm around Violet. "I'll get double the ransom for her," Bradley said. "I will. You let her go with me. On my honor. You touch her, I'll kill you."

"Hero," muttered Dirty Bobby. "You think we ever let you go?"

"Shut up, Dirt Man," Olimpo said. He grabbed Dirty Bobby and dragged him back from the open door and slammed it shut, turning the dead bolt. "See, you don't tell him stuff like that, it makes him crazy. You like to kill the whole fuckin' world. Then where we gonna be?"

"He's already crazy, he's already dead."

"So, maybe we need him alive for the ransom, like we gotta prove he's still around."

"I'll do the *puta*."

"I just told you about the *puta*. I'm gonna keep her a while. You crazy, Dirty Bobby? You got one job to do, go call the nun, tell her the money goes in a brown sack out next to the mailbox on 178th Street. Friday noon."

"I don't like the noon part," Dirty Bobby objected. "I like night."

"Night? So, you set the time. What time you want?"

Dirty Bobby appeared to be thinking. "Two o'clock in the morning. Friday. Like real late Thursday night. By the mailbox. I'll tell her we pick the money up there on the dot. We have her man loose by three in the morning. We get the money, then we kill him. Dump his body in a canal."

"Yeah, sure, right. Call the nun."

Dirty Bobby walked back to the front room where Bajito was finishing what was left of the mango, neatly.

Dirty Bobby snarled wordlessly and grabbed his knife from the table. He stuck it in his boot. He walked out, slamming the screen door behind him.

Bajito wiped his mouth on the back of his hand. "That Dirty Bobby, he's gonna kill us all some day, Olimpo."

Olimpo sat down heavily. "Maybe he kill you, not me. Me, he's gonna love to death."

"I kill him first," Bajito replied.

"Yeah? You ever kill anybody for real, Bajito?"

Bajito nodded. "Yeah," he said. "I swat 'em down like bugs. How about you?"

It sounded like a lie.

Olimpo shook his head. "Never done it. See, they took my brother, shot him dead when I was a little kid. Never had no urge to kill anybody after that. I'm always thinking it's somebody's brother, like mine."

Tears came suddenly to Bajito's eyes. Olimpo's innate nobility touched everybody. "I know what you mean."

Olimpo continued. "So, I feel like getting the million dollars, see, and letting the man go." Olimpo spoke softly, ruminating over each word, knowing Bajito wouldn't agree. "That's what I figured when I brung him here."

Bajito shook his head. "Not smart, Olimpo. Fat fuckin' bastard Dirty Bobby is right. We gotta kill him. He seen you. They both seen you."

Olimpo turned away. Bradley Locke might be someone's brother, he thought to himself. "Sure," he said.
"We gotta kill him."

Olimpo stared out the screen door, seeing the bright
emptiness of the encroaching day. He wondered if the
lush sensuality of South Florida's rampant greenery
was something he could make love to. Sometimes he
felt that way, like it was all too much; he was swal-
lowed up by everything. He thought, not for the first
time, that maybe he should have done something else
with his life, because it was all out there, eluding him.
Or devouring him.

# 35

WEDNESDAY night was coming. Leonie made serious plans to go to the voodoo ceremony. First she found the spare keys to the condo, the two keys that hung inside the kitchen cabinet where the coffee cups were kept. Then she dressed carefully in pink shorts and a pink striped top and white sneakers. She put her hair up in an incredibly sophisticated hairdo. She put on lipstick and eye makeup, put on her best gold circle earrings and left. She looked exactly like a thin, pock-faced preadolescent.

Leonie asked the doorman for advice about hardware stores and was directed to a store within walking distance. She walked there in five minutes and had the keys duplicated. Then she asked the shopkeeper to give her directions to Fish Street.

"I've got a friend who lives there," she said ingenuously. "And she has chicken pox too, so I want to go see her. She just came down with them, and I'm all better. Is it near here?"

"You don't look so better," the man said, frowning at the girl's face. There was sweat on Leonie's nose and circles under her eyes, emphasized by thick, green eye shadow.

"These are just scabs," Leonie smiled. "It's better to have it when you're young. What about Fish Street?"

"Well, it's a ways. I'd take a car, get your mom to give you a ride. Shouldn't go alone."

"Mom works," Leonie said. She said that a lot, because

213

otherwise people gave her that look, like, you poor thing, your mother's dead. She really hated that.

"Take a cab, I guess. It's a couple miles, cross the bay."

"Um, yeah, good idea," Leonie said and pocketed her new keys. "Well, see you later. Thanks."

She hurried through the beating sun and returned to the condo, slipping the original keys back into the kitchen cabinet, putting her own, shiny ones in her pocket.

Leonie was sound asleep for a late afternoon nap when the two nuns returned. Raphael peeked into the girl's bedroom.

"Such an angel," Raphael said. "Sleeping like a baby. Poor thing."

"Actually, I think she's quite a resourceful child," Sister Cecile remarked as she filled a cup of water from the cooler. "There's quite a bit going on in that mind of hers. I suspect Leonie's going to be quite a terror when she starts feeling better. I'm growing very fond of her."

Sister Cecile cooked dinner. She baked potatoes, burnt the cheese sauce that was to go on them, and overcooked some pork chops until they were certified fat free. The broccoli was mush. It was not one of her better attempts.

"I'll cook tomorrow," Raphael said.

"Me too," Leonie added, flattening the broccoli to a green puddle with her fork. "This is heinous."

"I was distracted," Cecile explained. "I have a lot on my mind."

The dinner was eaten, more or less. They all cleaned up afterwards, and just when the last dish was put into the dishwasher the telephone rang. Cecile raced to the living room to pick it up.

"I guess I'm done, too," Leonie said, and slipped away with a faint smile, vanishing into her bedroom. Seconds later she had the telephone to her ear, and heard the last of Dirty Bobby's instructions. "Two o'clock in the morning, by the mailbox," he said in a gruff voice. "That's what they told me to tell you."

"Two o'clock in the morning. In a brown paper bag," Cecile repeated. "Are you sure? I thought you would be calling later. I thought I would have at least another full day for this."

Cecile's voice sounded wispy, or maybe she was feeling defeated because there was no way she could have a million dollars in less than forty-eight hours. "Who has Bradley Locke, Bobby? How do you get in touch with them? Couldn't we get together in the bar at the Place St. Michel and talk about this some more? My treat? Isn't there some time to negotiate? You really haven't given me enough time."

"No chance for more time, see. I just talk for these guys. They give me a call, I never seen them. I don't know nothin'. You want this guy, you get the money."

"All right, I'll have the money." Then she repeated his instructions: where to meet and what time. Leonie heard everything twice, memorizing it all.

Shortly after, Cecile took Raphael aside and told her that she would be going out late on business. "First I'll tuck Leonie in," she said. "Then I'm going to this place on Fish Street." She gave Raphael the address and a short summary of what she was up to, touching lightly on the fact that it was a voodoo ceremony of some sort.

Raphael started to flutter. "It's terrible, Cecile. They change people into zombies, you know. It's all caused by a deadly drug they extract from a South American plant. Daitura. This is an actual fact, Cecile. I've read all about it. Left handed voodoo. I'll be praying all the time you're gone. I promise."

"Good," Cecile nodded. "I don't want Leonie to know, so not a word. She could probably use an early night. These walks she takes seem to exhaust her."

"Right," Raphael said, very seriously. "I'll act quite ordinary. But, is this a reasonable trip?"

"Violet said it was important, and now Violet is gone. Maybe she'll be there! Plus the fact that she said maybe they'd have Bradley there. I can't pass up a chance to find him, Raphael. I'm supposed to have a million dollars by late tomorrow night and I'm being pulled off the case in a week. There *is* no million dollars, so in fact I have very little time. This may be my last chance to find him. I have to go."

At nine o'clock, when Leonie said she was going to bed, the two nuns exchanged tiny smiles.

"Good idea, Leonie," Cecile said. "Maybe we can go out to the beach tomorrow. I think I'll have some free time and you'll love the ocean. The saltwater should help your skin clear up."

"Sure," Leonie said. "Good night." She disappeared into her room and the two nuns breathed a sigh of relief. No explanations would be necessary. Leonie would be asleep.

"I've got to change," Cecile muttered and went into her bedroom to dig through her clothes. What do people wear to voodoo ceremonies? Something ethnic, something colorful so she could blend in. Cecile found white skirts, blue skirts, all kinds of nun clothes. Nothing would do. She came out to where Raphael was sitting, pretending to read magazines. "I've got to get some clothes. There's at least one store on the beach open until ten, so I'll stop there and get something appropriate on my way, a colored print skirt and a fancy scarf or something. That's what I see people wearing. Don't wait up."

Raphael's old hands were shaking on the magazine. "Don't worry, everything is under control. Good luck."

"Thanks."

Cecile left.

# 36

LEONIE heard everything, her ear pressed to the bedroom door. Clothes, she thought, she would need clothes too. She started going through her own new clothing and came up with a colorful, flower print cotton skirt and a matching blouse, just as Cecile had described, then sneakers without socks, a green scarf that looked like silk. She dressed and tied the scarf loosely around her head, did a few dance steps, and bowed to the mirror. She was ready. Now she just had to wait until the old nun went to bed. She felt a thrill go through her. "Neat," she whispered to the octopus and gave it a hug.

At ten o'clock Leonie opened her bedroom door and looked out. The living room was dimly lit, the off-white furniture cast ghost shadows on the pale rug. Sister Raphael was nowhere to be seen. She would give it another half hour and then leave.

Meanwhile, Cecile found only one boutique open, a small, expensive place where she had bought some of Leonie's clothes earlier in the week. In a rush, Cecile picked out an outfit identical to one she had bought for Leonie, a colorful print skirt with deep pockets for her keys and a matching blouse. She found an expensive green silk scarf to tie around her head and informed the saleslady that she would wear everything. She paid with her credit card. Then she drove toward Fish Street.

Sister Cecile deliberately parked several blocks away from Fish Street. She had taken the Ferrari because this might be a time she would need to move out fast. She said a prayer for its safety and left it under the protection of St. Rita, Patron Saint of the Impossible Cases. That should do.

Then she began to walk. By her own watch, she had close to an hour to kill, but she wanted to know the terrain. Having been there before helped. In case of emergency she wanted to know the best way out, fast. She took her time and studied the lay of the land, memorizing everything.

Fish Street held no surprises. It was hung over by small, scraggly trees whose roots were fed by soiled cigarette butts and dog urine. The scent of cooked onions, garlic, and annato was in the air. Trash containers were out. Two cats prowled, one a dingy white, the other pale gray, looking for scraps of edible trash. A few residents still lingered on door stoops getting a last gasp of evening air before going to bed in poor homes with dripping air-conditioning units or rattling fans. Halfway down the street groups of small warehouses grew like mottled beige mushrooms against a night sky.

Music came through an open window, something with a Latin beat that Cecile had heard before. There were shouts, yelling. Behind Dirty Bobby's home something was happening. Cecile could hear the sounds as she approached, men calling, cursing, bellowing numbers. She didn't know that it was a cockfight, timed as a preliminary to the voodoo ceremony, a way of adding to the atmosphere, a way of spilling blood. Getting in the mood. Cockfights happened in Miami.

Cecile had never seen a cockfight. She crept down a small alley between two houses to see what was causing the commotion.

"Dear Lord have mercy," she whispered, blessing herself. There was blood and feathers everywhere, men were yelling, their eyes glazed for the kill. She finally saw Dirty Bobby looking on, part of the group but somehow separate, as befitted a bokor, the person who would be

218

conducting a voodoo ceremony later that night, sacrificing an animal and drinking its blood.

In one hand Dirty Bobby held a beer, in the other a brown burlap sack with a game cock's head sticking out of it. It was the little white rooster from his house. Cecile saw the bird with a growing sense of horror. The poor dear thing was destined for death!

Dirty Bobby was crazy about cockfights and had located a power bird trained by someone who was rumored to create killer roosters. Tonight was a doubleheader. His bird was on as soon as the first battle was over. Dirty Bobby shook the bag to incite his bird, then stuffed its fluffy white head down out of sight with a vicious movement.

In front of him on the dusty lawn the first fight was half over. One bird was almost dead, a paltry, once-dusky white foul was fluttering for his life against a red and brown rooster. Dirty Bobby stood to one side, drinking his beer and yelling obscenities. Cecile had seen Dirty Bobby's rooster's head peeking out of the bag, and seen him stuff the bird's head down, now she only saw Dirty Bobby's face contorted into a mask of evil. The bird, in his bag, had been placed to one side out of the way of the mob.

"Sick," she whispered. "Extremely sick."

The dusky bird was making a comeback. The yelling grew louder. The group of men formed a closer circle around the cocks, the birds again ripping into each other with bloodcurdling efficiency. The men were shouting, changing money, drinking beer from aluminum cans.

Dirty Bobby had placed a bet on the brown bird. He was jumping on his pudgy legs, his lips flapping, covered with beer foam.

Sister Cecile was behind him, crouching against the wall of a crumbly stucco house, waiting and watching. She gazed in disbelief as the men stamped and clapped and yelled. The cocks were going at each other tooth and nail.

No, Cecile thought, still rational, they don't have teeth. "Help the roosters, Lord," she prayed softly as a riot of feathers rose into blood-spattered air. Her eyes returned to the burlap bag. It was a wiggly heap, almost at her feet.

The birds flailed and fluttered, gouging and maiming each other. Finally the colored bird prevailed, pouncing, pecking, ripping with razor sharpened talons and little, razor spurs tied diabolically above his feet until the loser was a limp, bloody pulp of mangled feathers.

The first fight was over. Nobody noticed Sister Cecile in her brightly colored print skirt and blouse. In the dark edge of the scene her clothing had blended in like a speckle of light and shadow. She felt invisible, protected somehow. Winners were busy collecting bets from losers. Dirty Bobby's rooster lay to one side, still thrashing in the burlap bag. Suddenly Cecile knew, if nothing else happened, that she was going to make at least one thing in this scene right.

She ran out from the edge and grabbed Dirty Bobby's rooster in its bag. She ran back into the gloom until she was in a neighboring backyard. She never looked back. She found a hole in a fence, raced ahead and made it through three backyards until another fence rose before her. She stopped, gasping for breath, sweat pouring off her face. Poor rooster? Cockfighting was an outrage!

Carrying the bagged bird, Sister Cecile saw a small dirt driveway and followed it back to Fish Street. Nobody had seen her. Five minutes later she was in her car, breathing hard and staring at her rooster, a black-eyed creature with fluffy white feathers springing from his head. He was a beautiful bird, but crazy.

"Thank you, God," she said with a grin. His head stuck out of the bag and it turned wildly in every direction, his sharpened beak pecked violently at the imported leather car seat. This bird could kill a Ferrari, she realized. She put the bag on the floor.

"Goofy chicken," she muttered and stuffed his head back down into the bag. The bag tied with a drawstring and Cecile knew it would be better for all concerned if the bird stayed in the bag, completely out of sight.

"Dirty Bobby is going to be furious," Cecile said out loud. "But I couldn't let you get killed, you stupid bird. I mean, the other poor creature looked like pillow stuffing."

The bag wiggled and thrashed as if in answer.

"But I don't know what to do with you, you dumb cluck," she continued. "So I'll take you home."

The bag wiggled again and a ferocious cackling sound came out of the loosely woven burlap. At least the bird was breathing in there.

"I know, you'd rather go free, but if I let you go now someone will catch you and turn you into chicken soup. Not a bad idea, actually, so don't count your chickens before they're hatched. You aren't free yet."

The bag began settling down as though Cecile's softly spoken words were being understood.

"Go to sleep, chicken. I'll be back."

She heard a final squawk as she left the car. The bag was out of sight on the floor. The bird would be fine for a few hours. She had things to do.

Sister Cecile made her way back to Fish Street. She was like a chicken coming home to roost, she thought. The expression "chicken shit," rose to her lips, and she mumbled aloud that she really shouldn't put all her eggs in one basket. "To find out where Bradley is," she said softly, forcing herself back to her objective. "He might even be here. Violet said as much. A bird in the hand," she confirmed sagely, "is worth two in the bush."

# 37

Darkness spread slowly from corners of the dingy neighborhood, crawling in like black sand. Leonie asked the cab to drive around the dismal area until she spotted the Ferrari amid the rows of parked cars. She asked to be let out nearby. She paid the driver, hopped out, and panicked. It was not her kind of neighborhood. Shadows, shadow smells, shadow people looking at her. This was not her thing. She looked for the cab to call it back.

It was gone.

"Batgirl," she muttered to herself, "is doomed."

Leonie ducked into a doorway, keeping her eye on the red car. She noticed something really odd. In the semi-dark of a low street lamp she saw Sister Cecile in the driver's seat, slightly bent over. Was the nun dead, or dying? She should have told the cab to wait. Really.

Leonie started to run closer, her heart in her mouth. Five car lengths away she realized that the nun was talking to herself. Sister Cecile's hands seemed to be moving in conciliatory gestures. Not dead. Not dying. From her vantage point, Leonie couldn't see the rooster. Apparently the nun had gone around the bend. Or maybe she was praying to the floor. Almost anything was possible with Sister Cecile. At least the nun was alive. Leonie breathed a sigh of relief at that thought.

She stood and stared at the nun, forcing herself to breathe long, slow breaths. She was struggling vainly to put the night into perspective.

Nuns were just odd, she told herself. From childhood

books she knew nuns in former times had resembled penguins, but no more. Modern nuns, she decided as she watched Sister Cecile from a distance, her scarf-wrapped head bobbing up and down in the car, were more like chickens.

Leonie moved back behind an old Chevy truck. From there, she watched Sister Cecile come out of the car, look left and right, then head toward Fish Street. The nun walked fast and glanced down at her watch. Leonie did the same. It was close to eleven o'clock, close to the time the voodoo ceremony was to begin.

Leonie followed Cecile. Something else was odd about the nun. What? Leonie's fear was at bay. She had her father's analytical mind, and it was working again. Leonie puzzled over the feeling that something else was wrong as she crept from behind one car to the next, in case Cecile should glance behind her. The nun really should look back. Imagine not checking for a tail! Then Leonie looked down at herself and realized that she was wearing the same clothes as Sister Cecile had on. That was what was wrong. She almost laughed. It was nothing at all. No big deal.

The nun had been right. People did wear clothes just like this. Lots of them.

The bad neighborhood grew worse as Leonie walked farther. Soon she heard a low drumbeat ahead, strange atonal sounds, and the sounds of people. Low cries of people murmuring, occasionally pierced by a loud shriek.

"What the heck," Leonie muttered. "I'll have to save Cecile again. Batgirl is *called*!" It didn't take an amateur to see that Sister Cecile was heading into deadly trouble.

The street was so poorly lit there was really no danger of being seen. Thick, heavy darkness slowed the girl's walking. Heat radiated off of every building. Constant city noise hummed and rumbled and from somewhere ahead the muffled sound of the drum grew more insistent.

She watched Cecile ahead of her, pausing before one

of the houses, looking down a driveway, looking behind a car. Leonie stopped when the nun stopped. She moved when the nun moved. It was like a kid's game. Her sneakered feet felt glued to the pavement. She saw the nun start up again, casually because there were other people appearing out of the darkness, all going in the same direction toward the row of small, dark warehouses.

Cecile paused as if she were turning and Leonie retreated into a shadow. A spider web wrapped itself around Leonie's face and she repressed a scream. Shadows crept up behind her. She turned and looked back. Nobody! She was not being followed. She started again, forced to scurry. Cecile had vanished. She had lost Cecile.

The cockfighting scene had broken up early when it was discovered that Dirty Bobby's renowned fighting cock had mysteriously vanished. Dirty Bobby had been furious when he discovered his bird had disappeared. He had drawn his knife in a wild display of anger, and the crowd had melted into the shadows. Now Bobby was left alone with the dead rooster from the first fight, only Dirty Bobby, stabbing the air and kicking the corpse.

Dirty Bobby was shaking with rage. His mouth worked in a frothy motion. Still kicking at the dead bird, he turned to look for his equipment, the raffia bag of items he needed for the ceremony. He had placed it to one side of the cockfight. It was still there. He picked it up.

Calmer now, he walked deliberately to where the voodoo rite was to occur, keeping out of sight by going beyond the warehouse and approaching from the rear. The people would come back. There were others involved in this. He would wait. He always made a sudden appearance, as befit a bokor. Unseen and malignant, he stood in a shadow and watched.

There were already several women arranging items

procured from a nearby botanica: horses' tails and coarse statuary, the weird corruptions of Catholic imagery adopted into a syncretic persuasion, saint statues with painted blood dripping down splayed and martyred plaster flesh. Religion gone mad. Nearby a live chicken waited to be sacrificed. A fire glowed in a brazier. The mambo was bossing other women, move here, do this, do that. A huge female priestess, dressed in a long black shirt and black blouse, her voice was mellow, almost beautiful. Her fleshy, wrinkled neck was draped with a massive collection of beads. Her hair was long and tangled into knots. Rasta hair on a light-skinned woman. The billowing black clothes appeared to be a diabolical tent moving every time she did.

Everyone watched the mambo. Sister Cecile arrived, invisible and silent. The nun moved cautiously to the edge of the ceremonial area. She felt invisible. She was just another small female figure in a scarf and print skirt. She could see the strange articles arranged on a platform in the dim light, and the huge mambo moving about in a trance-like pattern. Others arrived and set up bottles of wine, intricately carved bowls, and a ritual sacrificial knife. Some of the men from the cockfight had already filtered back into the area. Still drinking, they gathered in small groups around the edges of darkness. The fire burst into livid flame now and then as someone threw something volatile on it, casting satanic light. It looked like Hell.

Cecile almost gasped aloud when she saw several children playing with the sacrificial chicken. Apparently the children didn't know or didn't care that the bird would soon be dead. She saw a goat tethered nearby. A child was feeding it handfuls of grass.

Smoke. The drum changed tempo. Faster.

"Babalawo-bokor here," a woman called when she saw Dirty Bobby emerging from the shadows. More people appeared, rushing by her to gather in the gloom.

Cecile joined a small group to the rear, her features covered by her scarf, her face shadowed by the warehouse.

Cecile was relieved to see that she had dressed properly. The full skirt was much like what other women were wearing. She settled alongside a group of women, looking left, then right, then straight ahead. But she made one mistake: she failed to look behind her. Had she done so she would have seen another person dressed in a skirt and blouse identical to her own, a small person, a girl.

Leonie had found her.

Leonie crept behind Cecile. She was shaking. She was enough of her father's child to know that she could be in danger, but she needed to be here, and that was all. Her heart began to beat in time with the drum. Her hands clenched into small damp fists. Be calm, she told herself, because everything depended upon her. She was the only one who knew what was really happening. Cecile's life was in her hands. Again.

The ceremony began with talk, a speech, or perhaps a chant, because the words of the mambo were tied to the rhythms of the beating drum. The mambo began to twist slowly around the platform, her movements unhurried and subtle, caught up in the beginning of a dance that could last for hours. She moaned about mysteries. She called on Obatala to preserve and protect them. She babbled and mumbled and howled.

Suddenly, Dirty Bobby emerged into the firelight, and the drumbeats grew faster. His eyes were wide open. In one hand he grasped a huge beef tongue. He walked up to the platform, took the sacrificial knife, and made a deep cut in the tongue, invoking the spirits. Finally he took the opened tongue and called for money. Dazed people came up and handed him bills, ten-dollar bills, twenty-dollar bills. All the while the mambo kept up her circular dance, now and then stopping to toss something on the brazier, causing the flame to leap higher.

Dirty Bobby stuffed all the money he had collected into the pocket he cut in the tongue. Then he took a large, threaded tailor's needle from the platform and began sewing the beef tongue together where he had cut it open, making a bulging pillow of meat stuffed with money.

People chanted. A second drum joined the first and more people glided around, dancing to the hypnotic beat.

Cecile looked for Bradley Locke. She half expected to see him, drugged, pushed forward and forced to eat raw chicken or drink dangerous drugs. It didn't look that way. They had a chicken to kill. There was absolutely no sign of the missing agent.

She lost track of time, hypnotized by the drums and the swirling bodies that swayed and jumped to the feverish beat. The scent of blood filled the air, blood and raw sweat and fear. She couldn't move.

Behind her, where Leonie was standing, several other young girls jumped into the circle and began spinning wildly, stopping by the fire for a moment to pick up live coals with their hands. Leonie gaped at the girls who appeared to be possessed by some evil spirit. Her eyes riveted on Dirty Bobby, who tossed the beef tongue on the platform and grabbed the sacrificial chicken from the children. He seized it by the neck and waved it in the air. The doomed bird's loud squawks incited the moving body of people to gyrate faster. The mambo took the bird from him and held it while Dirty Bobby drew up the knife and slit the animal's throat.

Mad dancing. People began crying, moaning louder. Blood flowed into a cup held steady by the mambo. The bird was drained. Dirty Bobby sliced off pieces of chicken, passing unplucked, raw flesh to members of the group. He took the cup and called the children up, pushing it to their lips and forcing them to drink. People began yelling in high-pitched whines, coming for the cup, wiping bloody mouths on their sleeves and joining the dance.

The drumbeats continued.

Sister Cecile took a final look around. It was definitely time to leave. Bradley Locke was not here.

Abruptly the girls who had carried the hot coals began to gyrate faster. They stopped before Cecile and screamed that a cursed one was among them. Cecile jumped back as the girls approached her and then she began to run, weaving among the people. They had known she was different.

Leonie stood paralyzed. Dirty Bobby had recognized Cecile. He brandished his knife and began pursuing the nun in Leonie's direction. The nun tripped and fell head first into a pile of rubble as she tried to jump over an upended trash can. She was as good as dead.

Leonie screamed. It had worked before by the Miami River. Besides, she couldn't help it. It just came out, shrill, high, riveting. She had to distract Dirty Bobby or Cecile was finished. Leonie raced out into the center of the yard. "I'm going to steal your money!"

Leonie ran up to the makeshift altar and grabbed the beef tongue, flaunting it above her head in a wild gesture, howling. The drummers kept beating, madness was a natural part of the night; Leonie fit in.

Dirty Bobby saw everything through the haze of his own night madness. He stopped, unable to comprehend that the woman in the flower print outfit who had vanished into the dark had returned, metamorphosed into a child in the same clothes, a strangely marked, speckled child who was howling like a banshee and waving hundreds of dollars over her head. Devils had intruded, somehow. He didn't even suspect it might be angels. The Dirt Man turned and raced back to the altar in confusion.

The knife was high above his head. Someone had to die.

# 38

SISTER Cecile never knew what saved her. For the rest of her life she was convinced that an angel had intervened. She knew that Dirty Bobby had spotted her and was only a few yards behind when she had taken a dive into the trash barrels and had her breath knocked out of her. But something, or someone, had stopped him, and he had turned back. His bellowing still echoed in her ears. He had sounded like a crazed animal, a wild bull perhaps, about to gore her. Then he was gone.

When Cecile was able to move, she found herself in the dark. The crowd was focused back on the drums and screaming. Cecile picked herself up and ran away. She never looked back except for a quick glance to make sure Dirty Bobby was not on her tail. She could barely breathe. Her hands were cut and bleeding from a broken glass bottle that had been on the ground where she landed.

She arrived at the Testarossa, car keys still safe in her deep pocket. She fumbled, unlocked the car, and fell inside with a wail.

The rooster began to squawk.

"Oh, bird, oh, bird," Cecile sobbed. "I never should have gone there. At least I saved you."

She wiped her face on the hem of her skirt, shook her head to clear away the fear, and drove home. No Bradley, no salvation, only a rooster and bloody hands on the steering wheel. It took the whole trip home to breathe normally again.

Seen from the underside, Miami was hot and deadly. Seen from the car, trapped behind tinted windows and air-conditioning, the city was a dream. Sister Cecile had discovered both parts.

Leonie was still spinning and screaming when Dirty Bobby came racing back to the circle of true believers. She had taken ballet since she was four years old and she knew how to spot. She kept her eyes on Dirty Bobby as she turned, her screaming became gleeful as she watched him. She was twelve years old and hence, immortal.

Dirty Bobby had first thought the woman in the print skirt and blouse was Sister Cecile, that oddball nun he planned to kill. But it wasn't. This was a magical apparition, a small, blond girl who drew all eyes to her, hypnotizing everyone as she danced and spun like a dervish. She must be a spirit, he thought wildly.

The other girls joined her, their spinning less controlled, more lunatic. Voices rose in unison like wind before a storm. Others were drawn to dance until there were men, women, and children circling to the drumbeat.

Dirty Bobby tried to keep his eyes on the donations in the beef tongue as it whipped round and round in the air, still clutched in Leonie's hand, but somehow he became lost in the cadence of the drums and spinning people. He was their leader, stuck in his own production. His eyes opened wide, his lips foamed, and he began to turn. The drums developed new patterns and rhythms, and the crowd danced.

Leonie almost got trapped in the delirium, but slowly, gradually, she drifted to the edge of the crowd until she was able to slip away down the dark alley and on to Fish Street. She didn't stop until she came to the end, where it intersected with the main drag. She stood by a pile of trash cans and gasped for breath. Sweat poured off her face. Her hands were still clutching the gross piece of meat in a death grip. "Blech," she said. "Blech." She dropped it on the ground.

That crazy voodoo guy was going to wake up to what she had done, she realized, but she didn't want to leave him all the money. She looked around. The distant drum still pounded in the night. Heat still rose from the pavement and up her legs. She was standing in fire, gasping for air. She delved into a trash can and pulled out a small plastic bag of trash. She dumped the trash onto the street, stuffed the tongue into the bag, and wrapped it around into a sticky package. She tucked it under her arm.

"Outta here," she muttered, and moments later she was at the telephone booth she had spotted on the way in. Twenty-five minutes later an obliging cabby let her out in front of Paul's condo. She paid him and turned to look around for the red car, then realized it was probably in the underground parking garage. She wiped her face with her sleeve and boldly walked up to the door. Her downstairs key worked like a charm.

The lobby clock read one A.M. Cecile had to be back by now, Leonie thought, and she took the self-service elevator up to the sixth floor, got out, and went to her door. Carefully she inserted the key, turned it, and paused to listen. Not a creak of hinges. Not a sound. The upstairs key worked, too. All the lights were out.

Grinning, she walked boldly in and looked around. All the bedroom doors were closed, her own was shut as she had left it; she heard the sound of a distant shower. Probably Sister Cecile was getting cleaned up. She should after falling in the dirt like that, Leonie thought. What a mess.

The nuns probably assumed she was in her room too, out for the night. Like all good secret agents she had left a wad of blankets neatly arranged to look like her body, peacefully asleep.

Moments later Leonie was in her room, sitting on her bed. The pile of wadded blankets was intact. The packaged beef tongue stuffed with money rested on her lap. She unwrapped it, took out the money, and brought it into her private bathroom where she washed the bills in a sink of warm water and spread them out on a towel to dry. She re-wrapped the tongue and stuffed it in a corner to deal with later. She rinsed herself in scalding water, put on her new Minnie Mouse nightie, and cried herself to sleep.

Dirty Bobby's night was done for too. When the spinning was over and the drumbeats stopped he did his usual vanishing act, hand clutching a full gallon jug of Sarde Valley Red Wine. He staggered up to his room, cursing at the loss of his night's take, but through the haze of gore, wine, and madness, he didn't even care. Tomorrow he would have his share of a million bucks. Drunkenly he reeled into his bedroom, drinking from the bottle with a grand arm movement. He was snoring loudly within minutes.

# 39

"It was the worst experience of my life," Cecile said to Sister Raphael the next morning. "If nothing else, it showed me what kind of people I'm up against. I'm absolutely certain this particular voodoo is just another twist on Satanism. Nothing else could explain what went on there. It was very evil. Very ugly. Christian symbolism all tied up in a lot of satanic ritual that really makes me want to throw up. The things they made those little children do! It was child abuse. Imagine making a child drink chicken blood."

"Terrible," Raphael murmured sympathetically. "You'll have to be careful. And you're all right now, thank God."

"Thanks to Divine Intervention. There's no other explanation. I'm still not sure what made Dirty Bobby turn back." Cecile sighed and looked Raphael in the eye. "I'm thinking about carrying . . ."

"Carrying what?"

"A gun, of course. This isn't the first time I've been in danger. The only reason I got out of it alive was because of a miracle. Really. All those prayers you were saying. God sent an angel. Two angels."

"Fine. Maybe we should just work on more miracles and forget the gun. I don't like guns, Cecile. He who lives by the sword, and so on."

"I was really winging it last night, Raphael," Cecile argued. "I felt like I was playing chicken with a bunch of madmen."

"I still don't like it."

233

Suddenly Cecile laughed. "Speaking of chickens. Have you been in the front bathroom today?"

"No. I use the one off my bedroom."

"Let me show you."

Sister Cecile first went to the kitchen and found a piece of bread. Then she beckoned Raphael to follow her. "I call him Chucky. He was a little incoherent last night, but I saw him this morning and he seemed just fine."

"Chucky?"

"Come and see."

Cecile opened the bathroom door a crack and there was a sudden flurry as the rooster jumped up on top of the shower curtain. "Come here, Chucky," she said softly, crumbling the bread into small pieces and scattering the crumbs on the floor.

"He's a little upset from everything, and I believe he's been trained to kill, but only other roosters. He's cute, isn't he? He's a game cock."

Sister Raphael's old blue eyes opened wide, then her mouth burst open into a grin. "Why, he's just beautiful! Wait until Leonie sees him!"

"I know she'll love him, but he's not really a pet. They train these birds to attack other birds. I don't quite know what to do with him, but that horrible Dirty Bobby was about to put him in a cockfight, and poor Chucky could have easily been killed." She shuddered as she remembered the other birds: the winner, and the loser. The memory was going to fester a long time.

"I don't think it was stealing, taking him. More in the nature of liberation. Do you have any thoughts about where we could take him?"

"We'll think of something. Meanwhile we can keep him here," Raphael said. "But, it's late. Mass is in less than ten minutes."

Cecile poked a head into Leonie's bedroom before they left. "Dear child. She's sound asleep. Such a sweet face," the young nun whispered. "She'll be just fine. Let's go to church."

234

Moments later the nuns were gone. In the bathroom Chucky flew down from the shower curtain and began to peck at the bread crumbs Cecile had tossed on the floor. In his little bird brain he was sure he had died and gone to bird heaven because Dirty Bobby had kept him in a small box and poked him with a sharp stick now and then, forcing him to attack in order to eat. It had been a horrible life. Here he had water in a small bowl that Cecile had left in the bathtub, food was plentiful, and there was room enough to actually fly.

After he had eaten his fill of five-grain health bread, Chucky flew up onto the back of the toilet and let out a glorious cock-a-doodle-do.

Leonie heard it in her sleep.

Then she heard it again.

"Cock-a-doodle-do!"

"Chickens," she muttered, and put the pillow on her head and went back to sleep for five minutes.

"Cock-a-doodle-do!"

Leonie thumped out of bed and came out into the living room, still half asleep. "I hear chickens," she announced, but there was nobody there. Then the rooster crowed again and this time Leonie heard exactly where it was coming from. She marched over to the bathroom door and opened it cautiously. Chucky jumped up on the edge of the bathtub and gave her a baleful eye.

"Oh, a cute little chicken," Leonie said. "Where did you ever come from? You must be hungry. Wait a minute."

Closing the bathroom door behind her, she went out to the kitchen and looked into the refrigerator. Leonie did not have a clue what chickens ate. She pulled off a few collard leaves from a bunch Raphael had bought and began to tear them up. "Green stuff. You probably like green stuff. All those nuns do. If you eat it, I won't have to."

She brought the greens back into the bathroom and

went inside. "This is a real treat," she said and held out a leaf.

The rooster got ready to attack.

Leonie knelt there, hand outstretched, collard greens dangling. Had she but known, chickens and roosters love collard greens. Chucky began to dance, an evil light in his eye. He could mangle a human hand with that razor sharpened beak.

Leonie began to sing. "Here little chick, chick, chicken. Breakfast time for youuuu."

The rooster stopped his death dance and looked at her. The song must have struck a chord in his miniscule brain, or maybe it was the fact that he had already eaten that day, because he became still and stared at the girl.

"Come on," Leonie said. "Good green stuff. Prevents cancer, or something." She tossed the food down on the tile floor. Chucky came forward and began to peck.

Leonie smiled and watched the bird gobbling. Then she reached down carefully and stroked the fluffy white feathers that stuck up from his head. "You really are a beautiful chicken," she whispered. "Where on earth did that nun ever get you?"

And then she remembered the night before.

"Oh, there," she said, and turned pale. "She saved your life, didn't she? They were going to chop you up and eat you, weren't they. I guess that Sister Cecile really is a nice person even if she is a nun."

Leonie closed the bathroom door behind her and went back to her own bathroom where she took a very long, very hot shower to wash away everything from the night before. She dried herself carefully, dressed in another of her new outfits: a pair of tan Bermuda shorts and a striped shirt. Then she took all the money she had left out to dry the night before and counted it. "Six hundred and fifty dollars," she said in awe. The money was dry now and she looked around for a place to put it. It fit nicely in a pocket of her suitcase, so that's where it went. Then she remembered the beef tongue that she had stashed in a corner of her room. It was very gross but at least nothing disgusting had leaked out of the plastic bag she had re-wrapped it in the night before. She picked it up carefully and went out to the kitchen and stuffed it down into the bottom of the trash barrel. It had already begun to smell, but the nuns might think it was the fish remains from the other night. Maybe she would even volunteer to take out the trash today.

Leonie left the kitchen and made a survey of the condo. She paused before a hall mirror and checked her face. Definitely better today. In a week she would be considered cured and probably sent back to Washington, D.C. The housekeeper would be back, her father would be either here or there, and life would go on as it had.

What a bore. She made a face in the mirror. Even after last night's terror, she liked it here. She might even like the nuns, she thought. Besides, they really needed her. "I must like them. I wouldn't have done that crazy stuff last night, otherwise, would I?" She studied a chicken pock on her neck. "No, I would have done that for anyone," she decided. Then she turned away and went to visit the rooster.

# 40

"I have to call the other prostitute," Sister Cecile said as the two nuns arrived back at the condo from church that morning. "Nina said she might remember something. I should have called yesterday, but I had too much on my mind."

They stood in the hall outside the apartment and talked. Some things shouldn't be said in front of Leonie.

"I can't imagine she could be any help," Raphael said.

Cecile shook her head. "It's a last hope. Nina was going to try and remember an address for me, a place they had gone to do a job once, and I think it may be the place where Bradley is. Violet told me about a party out there with Dirty Bobby and some of his friends. It's a last resort, Raphael. I don't know where else to turn."

"Maybe so," Raphael agreed. "Time is running out for Bradley Locke."

"Not only that, but I know what Dirty Bobby is capable of now." A vivid picture of the chicken Dirty Bobby had sliced last night flashed before Cecile's eyes. "I think he actually enjoys cutting things up. Like people."

Raphael opened the door to the condo. "Call her right away. I'll see to it that Leonie is out of the room."

Leonie was in the bathroom playing with the rooster when they stepped inside, but she came right out when she heard their arrival from church. "Cool bird," she said, and then, as if she didn't know, "Where'd he come from?"

"Uh, from a friend," Cecile replied. "The rooster's name is Chucky. I have to find him a home."

Leonie looked down at her new shorts. "I know. I sat in some chicken shit."

"Rooster droppings," Raphael corrected. "Don't say shit. Maybe you should go change."

"I do have a call to make," Cecile said to no one in particular.

"Uh, yes, I'll change right away." Leonie vanished into her room and Sister Cecile went triumphantly to the telephone. Nina's number was on a slip of paper in the drawer of the telephone table and Cecile pulled it out. She dialed.

Nina answered.

"Hello, Nina? This is that friend of Violet's. My name is Cecile. Remember me?"

"Sure."

"How are you?"

"Cut the crap. You want to know that place down south, right?"

"Right."

Neither of the women heard Leonie pick up the receiver in the other room, but Leonie heard them. She heard the directions to the house in the Redlands, on the edge of the Everglades, and she wrote everything down in her small notebook. Sister Cecile would probably need to be rescued again.

Leonie was beginning to wonder how the nun had ever survived without her.

"Go out the Tamiami, couple miles maybe. Then you start looking for this place, Duke's Restaurant, see. Take a right turn there. No, it's a left. You get on this dirt road and keep going. You'll be there. Watch out for these guys. Real bastards, especially the fat slimeball. He's mean."

"I'll watch it."

"Do that."

"Thanks, Nina, you may have just saved a life."

"My pleasure. I'm doing this for Violet."

"She'll appreciate it."

"Sure. 'Bye." Nina hung up.

Cecile hung up and came out into the living room. "Okay, Raphael. I've got it."

Leonie hung up too. Then she changed her pants, tossing the shorts into a growing pile of laundry. The nuns were talking seriously when she came out.

"I should call Damien," Cecile said.

"You should. No place to go alone," Raphael said, she was trying to be cryptic.

Cecile pulled out another number from the telephone table drawer and dialed it. Damien picked up the call immediately.

"Damien, this is Sister Cecile. I have a possibility. An address out on the edge of the Everglades. I'm planning on going there tonight and check it out." She was conscious of Leonie in the room and tried to be mysterious. From the corner of her eye she saw the young girl leave for the kitchen.

"Good. Go for it."

"I thought maybe you should come too."

Damien frowned. It showed in his voice. "I've got a lead on the Felipe killing. I've got plans."

"You don't think this is important?"

"It may be. I'll send a man along if you want. It's good to have backup in any case."

"Who would it be?"

"Local talent. I'll pull someone in. A man will come to the condo and get behind you. You won't even see him."

Sister Cecile didn't like it. An invisible stranger for backup didn't instill much confidence. "I'll be leaving late. Maybe eleven-thirty. Should I wait for this backup?"

"No. He'll be there. Count on it."

"Right. What's with Felipe?"

"Apparently Felipe wasn't clean."

"Oh. You mean bribes."

"It happens. Anyway, I've got a place to go tonight. A

240

meet. Word from one of his connections came in. I can't ignore this."

"Oh."

"You'll have a bodyguard. Don't worry." Damien sounded anxious to hang up. Cecile sensed he had already given Bradley Locke up for dead.

"Fine," she said. "But I do know who killed Felipe. *And* Louis Bojanis. I'm sure it was Dirty Bobby."

"I have a direct lead from the Agency," Damien said. "An excellent lead. I have to follow it up." His laugh was a kindly sound, meant to give her hope, she was sure. Purely patronizing.

"Thanks, Damien." Basically, she would go it alone. Local talent guarding her? More likely whoever it was would mess things up. "Want to talk to Leonie?"

"Sure."

Cecile put her hand over the mouthpiece and called Leonie from the kitchen. "It's your father."

Leonie came over and took the receiver. "Hi, Dad."

"How are things going with those nuns?"

"Okay."

"You like them?"

"Yeah, fine. Really."

"Um. You know I tried to set it up nice for you there. I was worried about leaving you alone."

"I know, Dad."

"You know I love you, Leonie."

Leonie looked startled. "I love you too, Dad."

"I'll talk to you later, Leonie. Take care. Listen to the nuns."

"Okay. 'Bye, Dad."

# 41

CECILE and Raphael heard Leonie's half of the conversation between father and daughter. Cecile was surprised at the words of endearment. She felt a shudder go through her body, an ill wind. She shook it off. There was no reason to worry about those two.

Raphael, on the other hand, was suspicious. Words of love between the Drails were clearly not common. She thought of the codicil. "Is he coming with you?" Raphael asked.

"No, he's following a lead on the Felipe Klondacki business. He's sending a bodyguard, someone I won't even see."

"Not quite a guardian angel type," Raphael murmured, eyeing Leonie who had wandered off to the kitchen and was pulling collard greens out of the refrigerator. Most of them were dropping on the floor. "But better than nothing."

"I was hoping Damien would come with me. I could really use a backup with a gun, right beside me."

"What exactly did Damien say about this bodyguard?"

"Just that he would get some local talent. He doesn't really think I have a lead. I could tell."

"It's a gender thing," Raphael said. "When will men ever learn."

"They won't. Meanwhile I feel exposed."

"I know who could come along."

"Who?" Sister Cecile asked.

"Me," Raphael said. "I may be in my seventies, my

*early* seventies, but I'm very agile and I could drive the getaway car. The Testarossa. I'm good at it."

"I jog," Cecile said. "I'm fast. And I won't bring you. I could give Paul a call but no telling where he is. He has a gun in Boston. Maybe he has one here."

"I don't like it. Call Paul. I don't trust local talent. Meanwhile, I think Leonie is feeding Chucky all the collard greens."

"Good. I hate collards. And, yes, I'll see if I can reach Paul."

Sister Cecile called the number of the boat Paul was on only to reach an answering machine. She left a message asking Paul to give her a call as soon as possible. Then she turned to Raphael. "He's out. Probably at the Bamboo Convention. Could you give him the message if he calls, Raphael? I *would* feel better with him along. Tell him I need him."

"Need? Doesn't sound good. You know Paul. He'll think you want to get married."

"Raphael, you know what I mean."

The old nun smiled. It was the least she could do in a situation that was becoming tense. "I'll take care of everything. Don't you worry about a thing."

"Right." Sister Cecile began jingling her keys.

"You're going out?"

"The car needs gas. I have to be ready for anything."

Sister Cecile spent the rest of the day on the telephone, and using Paul's fax machine to prepare for passing papers on the motel they were buying. The closing date was set for just weeks away and there was a tremendous amount of paperwork to be done.

Leonie napped for most of the afternoon, giving the nuns reason to believe that she really wasn't over the chicken pox. They didn't know, of course, that Leonie hadn't gotten to bed until almost three o'clock in the morning and she was just plain tired.

The three of them had dinner together at six o'clock, a

243

concoction of beef, plantains, and coconut, stir fried, served with side dishes of Minute Rice and fresh pineapple for dessert.

"I was talking to a Jamaican at the grocery store," Raphael explained as Leonie dissected her plantain slices. "They use plantains like we use potatoes, so this is something like a Southern Hemisphere Beef Brunswick Stew. They're also very good for ulcers."

"I never much cared for ulcers, or Brunswick Stew either," Sister Cecile said.

"I don't much care for this food at all," Leonie said, poking at her food. "Although the meat isn't bad. It's this mucky stuff. Maybe Chucky would like it."

"Well, I thought it was a good idea," Raphael said and proceeded to eat all her plantain slices, chewing diligently and wearing a very serious expression on her wrinkled face. Then she spoke again. "Broadening one's horizons, trying new foods and all, but, actually, I think I should have put the pineapple in it and left out this mucky stuff."

"I had plantains the night I ate with Felipe," Cecile recalled, staring at her gluey pile. "Ugly."

"Heinous," Leonie muttered, then finished everything on her plate except for the plantains. "What's for supper?" she asked.

"Chucky ate all the collards, or we would have had them too," Cecile said. "I fed him the rest of them while you were sleeping."

"I know, I went in and talked to him just before supper. There was green stuff all over the place. I think he had a fight with it." Leonie looked worried. "What are you going to do with Chucky? He doesn't much like living in the bathroom. It's starting to stink."

"I don't think Paul would like him in there either," Raphael said. "What if Paul shows up tonight and finds a rooster in his main bathroom?"

"Maybe a pet shop would take him," Cecile said. "Although, Paul is very understanding."

"No pet shop. Someone would put him in a fight," Raphael said firmly. "Chucky was trained to fight and now I think he'd just be killed if he were put up against a bad rooster. Or someone might just buy him and eat him."

"He needs freedom," Leonie said.

"Maybe I can find a farm somewhere," Cecile murmured.

Raphael looked skeptical. She made a sound resembling a "cluck," and began to stack the dishes. She picked up the pile and carried it over to the sink. "I'll think of something," she said and turned the water on hard.

Cecile paced the rooms as she waited for darkness to fall. Paul hadn't called and nobody answered the boat's telephone. She would be forced to go south with an invisible person as backup. She was worried.

Her plan was simple. Drive out to the house. Hide the car, sneak up. She would distract the occupants, then she could release Bradley from where he was being held captive. Simple, really. Of course Bradley Locke might not be there at all, or he might already be dead, but those were scenarios that Cecile refused to accept. She had been hired to find and save this man, and she would, one way or another. This might be her last real chance to find him. Time was up.

She continued to pace. She was afraid. Of course she was afraid. But she wouldn't let it show.

Leonie ignored her, feigning interest in a pile of comic books Raphael had bought for her.

Raphael fluttered around from one room to the other, finally drawing Cecile aside. She spoke in a whisper. "I want to come. This is too dangerous."

"No. I have a plan."

"One woman against how many?" Raphael's voice was shaking. It wasn't Damien who was going to be killed; it was Cecile.

"Oh, one or two. I just have to get the kidnappers out,

maybe start a fire somewhere for distraction. Then I sneak in and get Bradley."

Raphael turned away, angry. "I hope he's not there. I hope you get lost in the swamps. I hope you trip over an alligator." She stopped, then started again. "I hope you survive, Cecile. Really. I'm worried."

"I know. I'll be just fine."

Sister Raphael turned away. She didn't look Cecile in the eye and she didn't say another word.

# 42

IT was still early evening. Leonie found it easy to pretend she knew nothing about Sister Cecile's upcoming trip to rescue Bradley Locke. She immersed herself in a comic book and rarely looked up. But she wasn't reading.

Her thoughts ran something like this:

"Gosh, Uncle Doddy, we've got to save the nun."

"I don't know what we can do, Batgirl. She's stubborn. Smart, too. But she's in way over her head this time. She's going to *die*."

"I'll give you a hint, Doddy, she won't die. Not with *me* on the job."

"Chill out, Batgirl. She's *dead*."

*The future is rather bleak for Sister Cecile. Abominable before, it is about to get decidedly worse.*

*Maximum Grimm* continues in MONSTER GONE MAD, volume no. 10. WRUUUUF! SHEEEE! WOOMP! HURRY!

While Leonie invented comic book dialogue, the two nuns watched *Jeopardy*. Raphael was pleased to have most of the answers. Cecile claimed she was distracted and shouted out several incorrect responses.

"I would like some serious prayers," Cecile finally announced when a commercial came on. "If you two ladies could oblige."

She flipped off the television; sudden silence fell on the room.

247

Leonie looked up from the comic book and frowned. She couldn't recall praying. *Batgirl* never prayed.

"We'll say a rosary," Raphael said and proceeded to lift her old black beads from a pocket.

Leonie watched as the two nuns prayed, sitting silently while the words drifted through the air. It wasn't as bad as she thought it would be.

Finally the prayers were over and Cecile stood up. "That should do it," she said. "Now I'm ready. I think I'll go talk to Chucky for a while and then I have some reading to do. You can have the remote, Raphael."

Raphael and Leonie watched Sister Cecile go to the rooster's bathroom.

"She's nervous," Raphael said. "It doesn't always show with her, but after a while it's easy for me to spot. Most people don't have a clue about Cecile."

"I'm like that too," Leonie admitted. "I don't think there's anyone in the world who can tell when I'm worried."

"I'm worried myself," Sister Raphael said in a whisper. "Cecile is going to go out and do something dangerous tonight." Raphael's blue eyes sparkled.

"Really?"

"Very foolish. She wanted your father to come along. I know you heard that telephone conversation. Did you get the gist of it?"

Leonie tried very hard not to look guilty. "Well, sort of," she said. "What was it about?"

"He wasn't able to go with her tonight on a very perilous mission. And she won't allow me to go with her. She thinks I'm too old. And Paul isn't back from his Bamboo Convention."

"Oh, but will she . . ." Leonie stopped in mid-sentence as Cecile came out of the bathroom.

"I need some bread crumbs," Cecile said and walked by them on the way to the kitchen. She found some slices of bread and went back, barely noticing Raphael and Leonie who were both staring at her.

Leonie waited until she heard the bathroom door close. "I don't think she should go alone either," Leonie whispered. "I think we should go too. She's going to need us. I'm afraid for her. We should go after her, Raphael. She might be killed."

"I don't think it's possible," Raphael said. "There's no way I could follow her without being seen and I don't know where she's going except it's out toward the Everglades somewhere."

"I know where," Leonie said. "I just happened to pick up the telephone, and I heard the directions. I never forget things I hear."

"You just happened to hear?"

Leonie nodded. "Really. It just happened. I do have a telephone in my room. The receiver just sort of fell off, and I picked it up. I couldn't help hearing."

"It happened. I see." Raphael was thoughtful for a moment. "But she told me not to go with her. We have a rule of obedience, so I can't follow her."

Leonie put an angelic look on her face. She had a devious mind not unlike her father's. "Maybe we should take Chucky out to the Everglades and let him go tonight. Good idea? He needs freedom."

"Oh," Raphael said. "Chucky? Take him out and let him go? I'll have to think about that for a while. Seriously think on it." She flipped the television back on, and when Sister Cecile came out of the bathroom for the second time Raphael and Leonie were totally involved in the Movie of the Week.

Cecile stood there for a few minutes watching them stare at the flickering images. Finally she sat down and stared with them.

"How's Chucky?" Raphael asked at the next commercial.

"Getting fat. I think he needs a bath, but I don't think roosters take baths," Cecile said.

"Chucky needs to be free," Leonie said.

"Yes," Raphael said. "I really think we should take

him to a nice wild place and let him loose. Maybe near a farm somewhere. At least he'll have a chance at a real life."

Cecile nodded. "I agree. He needs a life."

Raphael beamed triumphantly and turned the television off with a flourish. "Well, that settles it," she said. "Chucky needs a life."

"Right," Cecile said and wandered off to her room, too concerned with her own upcoming troubles to register the conspiracy that had just received her blessing.

Jacob and Esau had nothing on these people.

By unspoken agreement, Raphael and Leonie didn't speak about anything of consequence for the rest of the evening. Eventually Leonie found a Scrabble game and set it up and invited the nuns to play. They did until Cecile formed a series of words: dead, bloody, and kill. At that point she rose from the table and excused herself, vanishing again into her bedroom.

"I'm glad we're going," Leonie said in a whisper.

"Shhhh," Raphael warned.

"I think I'll go to bed early," Leonie said loudly as Sister Cecile returned to the room. "I'll read for a while. Good night, Sister Raphael. Good night, Sister Cecile."

"Good night, darling."

Cecile nodded a second good night as Leonie passed by. The evening sky had turned a heavy yellow ochre, and Cecile was staring out the huge window wondering if the world might be coming to an end. Finally, at nine o'clock Raphael said she was going to bed early too, and Sister Cecile was left to herself, with Raphael's final words ringing in her ears. "Be careful. Maybe you should call Paul again."

Cecile continued to pace.

"Right," Cecile muttered two hours later. "I'll be careful. Very, very careful."

She dug through all of Paul's drawers looking for a weapon. Nothing. He still hadn't called. "Paul really

250

should have a gun somewhere," she said to herself. He had a gun in Boston, but apparently not here. And this was Miami. What was the matter with him?

Sister Cecile dressed in dark clothes, a pair of sweatpants and short sleeved top she used for jogging in Boston and had packed for pajamas. She picked up the keys for the cheap little rental car. It was invisible. Much as she would like to have a fast car, it was a time for discretion.

Maybe Bradley was already dead. Maybe Damien hadn't gotten anyone to follow her. Maybe this was a waste of time.

At eleven-thirty, Sister Cecile walked out of the condo. She was very careful to close the door softly so she wouldn't wake Leonie or Raphael.

Sister Cecile's decision to leave the Ferrari behind effectively eliminated her bodyguard. The agent had been instructed to look for an attractive young woman in a red Ferrari. When Sister Cecile drove out, the agent barely gave her a look. Cheap rental cars were like mosquitoes in Miami. One tried to avoid them.

Sister Cecile was alone.

Moments later Leonie and Sister Raphael were in the living room, grim at the task they saw ahead, but still bubbling with repressed excitement.

"How long should we wait?" Leonie asked. She felt prickly all over, and for once it wasn't from chicken pox.

"Give her ten minutes. She probably took the Testarossa," Raphael said, looking at Leonie carefully. The girl had put on the old jeans she had arrived in, a dark cotton top, and her old sneakers. Raphael had on a navy skirt and a white blouse. "I think I need something dark to wear," the old nun said. "I'll look in Cecile's closet."

She vanished while Leonie went to the kitchen to get some bread to bring for Chucky.

Sister Raphael emerged wearing a dark plaid shirt

251

tucked into her skirt. She wore black oxford shoes, serious nun shoes with thick rubber soles.

"I'll get Chucky," Leonie said.

"I'll get the keys," Raphael said.

They left, two conspirators with a rooster in a burlap bag, casually taking the elevator down to the parking garage. Raphael was almost giggling because Cecile had left the keys to the Testarossa.

Sister Cecile's backup, patiently waiting across the street, was looking for a young woman in a red Ferrari. When he saw the red car pull out, he was quick to check the occupants. An elderly nun and a girl did not match the description. He knew there were a lot of Ferraris in Miami. He would keep waiting for the right one.

"I'll have to restrain myself," Raphael said. "Good thing I've had some practice driving this thing. I was really good, Leonie, you should have seen me. Now, what were those directions?"

"Ferraris are cool," Leonie said, ignoring the question and leaning back on the leather seat. She took a deep breath of Ferrari Testarossa. "I want a car like this."

"Hang around with Sister Cecile and you just might," Raphael said, but then she remembered the codicil, and her words seemed dangerous. "You do love your father, don't you, Leonie?"

Raphael stepped down on the accelerator as she spoke and the car lurched forward onto the main drag heading for downtown Miami. It took Leonie a minute to speak, fighting to get her words out from the acceleration.

"Why? I mean, sure. Everyone loves their father."

"Good," Raphael said. "Now, the directions. Where are we supposed to go?"

"Tamiami Trail all the way to Duke's Restaurant. Then we take a right. No, a left. It should be a dirt road, so we should park somewhere off it and sneak up. We can let Chucky go whenever it looks nice and wild. There should be plenty of things out there for a rooster to eat."

"Or that eat roosters," Raphael said.

"Chucky will be fine. He's a fighting bird, right?"

"Right."

They drove for a while in silence. Miami slipped by, its tall buildings hanging like colored reeds among the stars. Stoplights, perpetually red, delayed their way, but Cecile was probably going slowly too.

Leonie looked at the car clock and saw that it was almost midnight. She looked down at the burlap bag at her feet. It wiggled as Chucky tried to get loose from his dirty prison, crud from his other life reminding him of where he'd been. If roosters can remember.

"Soon, Chucky, soon," Leonie whispered.

# 43

NOT long after she left, Cecile found herself on the endless stretch of road heading west, a long, dark ride. Calle Ocho was the Tamiami Trail, a long haunt of shops that turned into the Everglades. Eventually she found the left-hand turn at Duke's Restaurant and drove down the straight, narrow road.

Bad thoughts entered her mind. Fear of dying. Fear of failure. The fear washed into her, making her cold. She turned off the air conditioner and opened the window. Night noises screamed, obscuring everything. It was too loud.

Finally, way ahead, she saw the dim lights of a house, set back in the scrubby growth of palmetto brush. That had to be it! She slammed on the brakes where she was, dimmed the lights, backed up the car, then parked in brush. Gingerly she stepped out into weeds and pushed the car door shut.

A spasm, like a gunshot, went through her. She started walking.

For a few moments, all she saw was the darkness. Even the stars didn't help light the land, darker than black with the warts of tropical shrubs covered with exotic vines surging out of the undergrowth. More noises, sounds of late night bugs and birds. The dirt road was clear now. The heavy sky of earlier had passed but the air was thick with heat and the scent of living things gone bad. Cecile stumbled only twice before she saw the house again. Nina's description matched perfectly. A low, small structure with a few crumbly outbuildings; it stood in a grassy patch of solid ground, a hammock between the hiss of canal alligators and the sea of grass. She could feel the pulses in her wrists. Her stomach drew into a knot.

Sister Cecile followed Violet's route. She moved cautiously around the building, stopped near the dark room where Bradley and Violet were sleeping. She stood for a long time and listened before she climbed up on the trash container. Balancing carefully, she peered through the window.

Bodies! Barely visible, two under-dressed figures breathed deeply, slumbering on a small cot. Could that be Bradley? And who was that female?

Sister Cecile stared long and hard at the woman's face. It was Violet, she thought with a strange and terrible feeling. It really was Violet. Violet. And Bradley Locke? Yes. She had his photograph back at the condo. Violet and Bradley.

Bradley was smiling in his sleep. One of Violet's arms was wrapped around his neck. They both seemed to be purring, bodies rising and falling in deep sleeping breaths. Cecile knew she should feel scandalized and avert her eyes, but she didn't. They looked sweet, happy. Even Violet looked happy, and Cecile had a feeling that men ordinarily didn't make Violet happy at all.

Cecile stepped down carefully and continued to move around the cabin. She crept up on the window to the front room. She felt cold in all the heat. This was not going to be easy. Maybe she could attract her backup somehow and get help. But she hadn't seen a car behind her. There was nothing, nobody but herself. Damien had failed.

Low sounds and yellow light coming through the screen indicated that people must be still awake inside.

Raising herself on tiptoe, she gazed through the screen. She heard the ceiling fan hum and grunt. Dirty Bobby was sprawled back on a bench, going through a deck of cards, playing solitaire. Sister Cecile watched him flip

255

through the cards once, shift a card, then run through the deck again. He was cheating. The Dirt Man was a cheat. He had a beer beside the cards and took a pull at it every so often. Bajito was sound asleep on the greasy daybed. Olimpo was leaning back in an old rocker staring at the clock. It said two o'clock. Cecile glanced at her watch. It was closer to midnight.

"I'm gonna sleep," Olimpo grunted. "We gonna be rich real soon. I gotta get some sleep for it. One hour, I wake up rich."

"Yeah, we pick up the money in a couple hours. You ready for it?" Dirty Bobby glanced at his diamond watch. "I'm going into town now; I'll meet you at the money at two-fifteen." His lips split out sideways, his idea of a smile, then he scooped up his cards and tapped them into a rectangle.

"Do you believe this? We're gonna be stinkin' rich," Olimpo chortled. He looked at his diamond watch and held it up to the light.

"These things are real diamonds. I checked," Dirty Bobby said. "I took it to the pawn shop and he said so."

"Me too," grunted Bajito from the cot, opening one eye. "Means the nun's real. Real million bucks."

"Real jewels," Olimpo said. "Soon as this stuff is over we're gonna have one party. Maybe keep the *puta* around for that."

Dirty Bobby grunted and shook his deck of cards together. He stuffed them into his shirt pocket. "Sure. We have a good time. *Mañana*. Now I'm going." He grunted and headed out the door so fast Sister Cecile barely had time to duck. For a heavy man he moved fast.

Outside, Dirty Bobby saw the movement of shadows as Cecile scurried back around the house. He stood stock still. He was used to fleeing bodies, an expert at tracking them down and dragging them back. He stopped for only a split second, then took off around the opposite side of the building, and there, just below Bradley Locke's window, he came face to face with Sister Cecile.

*"Hermana!"* he said in a voice loud enough to wake up Bradley and Violet.

Sister Cecile took off for the brush behind the building. Too late, she knew it was a dumb move. She should have headed for her car because she was a fast runner and Dirty Bobby was fat. Fat but fast. Before Cecile had even fallen on the rubbery earth, trapped by a tangle of low vines, he was on her, grabbing her wrist and clutching her in a death grip just as she started to drop. She fell back against Dirty Bobby's grasp, then righted herself and stood for a second of paralyzed fear. Caught.

"So what you doing here?" he rasped, his eyes thin black slits.

For once, Sister Cecile was speechless. There was absolutely no explanation for why she was here that would make any sense at all to this man. So she screamed the loudest most bloodcurdling scream she could.

Dirty Bobby pulled her up to him. She was still screaming, struggling, fighting, howling like a banshee. Suddenly she stopped. His mouth was too close, his eyes too evil, and his hand was twisting her arm around into a horrible position. All she could do was whimper.

Bradley and Violet had waked together from sound sleep. They stood on the cot and looked down through the high, narrow window.

"It's the nun," Violet whispered. "The poor damn fuckin' nun. She come to save us and look at that."

Bradley took a good look then got down and sat on the bed in the dark room. "Shit. She was our only hope."

They heard Sister Cecile being dragged around the building, heard the door slam shut and voices rise in the front room. Violet sat close to Bradley in the dark and took his hand as though she were blind, clutching him tightly. "She's a crazy nun," Violet said. "Maybe she's got backup."

"Like a bunch of saints?" Bradley shook his head. "Not likely."

"She was connected," Violet said. "I think she might have backup. I do. I know her."

"You ever see any backup?"

"That other guy knew her," Violet mumbled.

"What guy?"

"I dunno. Some guy."

Sister Raphael drove competently and fast. "Leonie, keep your eyes open. Policemen see a car like this and they immediately assume something, like you're speeding, running drugs, or something. Ordinary people just don't have cars like this, so it presents a serious obligation to be well within the law."

"Slow down."

"I can't. It doesn't go any slower. The fuel pump will choke."

"Why does Cecile have this car? I mean, she's a nun."

"She's not ordinary."

"Why not?"

Raphael pursed her lips. "The thing is, she's got background, and I read a lot. We don't belong to a cloistered order. Our order was established primarily to educate, and part of education is to keep up on things. So I read. She drives fast cars because of her lawyer. I drive her fast cars because they're there. It's a matter of humility. Humility means living humbly with what you have. Even if it's a Ferrari."

"Um," Leonie said. "Well, there's a cop at the next intersection. See the shape of the headlights? Cops drive those big American cars with lights like that, so slow down."

Raphael slowed down. Sure enough it was a police car. "Headlights?" Raphael asked. "How do you know that?"

"You can always spot a cop car. There are things that everybody knows."

Eventually Raphael pulled the car into the dirt road to the left of Duke's Restaurant and bumped along until they

258

found the spot where everyone else had backed off into the bushes. The house was just visible ahead. Raphael turned off the ignition, stuffing the keys into her skirt pocket. "This looks good. Far enough from the house so they won't hear us."

They got out quietly and looked around. Leonie had the rooster bag in her arms. She moved under a small tree and carefully untwisted the old burlap. The bag dropped on the ground. Chucky let out a small squawk.

"Hush, Chucky, I got some bread here. Be quiet, now."

The rooster poked his white feathered head around and peered into the darkness with his little black eyes. He took a tentative peck at the bread in Leonie's hand.

"Check it out, bird. You're free." There was a catch in Leonie's voice as she felt his little heart beating rapidly through the feathers. Somehow the creature had learned to trust her, but she knew she had to let him go. It wasn't going to be easy. She stroked the feathered head. She could hold him for a while longer, anyway.

Sister Raphael watched from the side. She could see the emotion in Leonie's face, but uppermost in her mind was Sister Cecile. Raphael barely heard Leonie's fond farewell, the words floating softly in the night air.

"Good-bye little bird. You have a nice time here in the Everglades. You'll have lots to do and there are plenty of good bugs to eat." Leonie was babbling softly, wiping a tear from her eye. "I love you, Chucky."

Chucky looked at her and seemed to nod.

At last Leonie walked toward the old nun. "Okay, I think he's going to be just fine. I really do. Let's go find Cecile."

The old nun and the young girl walked quietly along the dirt road, Chucky still under Leonie's arm.

"You should let him go, Leonie," Raphael whispered. "I mean, what if we get there and he makes a racket."

"In a minute. He likes me carrying him. He won't squawk as long as I hold him. I don't want them to know we're coming either."

They continued on into the night, the darkness surrounding them like velvet. Cricket sounds filled the air, a splash of water came from one side as a frog jumped, a rustle came from the other as a turtle slithered beneath some dry grass beside the road.

Cecile's screams could suddenly be heard, coming from far ahead.

"Cecile," Raphael gasped. "It's her. That's her voice. Has to be!"

"Hurry, Raphael. Run!"

Raphael and Leonie began to run pell-mell down the road. Chucky began to flap wildly under Leonie's arm, jostled into activity. "Bawk, Bawk!" he squawked adding to the myriad sounds. Leonie clutched him harder.

"That *is* Cecile. It is!" Raphael huffed as they ran. "Please God, let us help her!" She was gasping, and Leonie tugged her to a walk.

"Raphael, slow down or you're going to die," she whispered in an unsteady voice. "So they caught her. Now we've got to have a plan. Chill out. Don't just run in there!"

"Yes, yes, I know. Dear God, what am I going to do?" Raphael was breathing hard and tears started running down her face. Leonie shook Raphael's arm with one hand, still clutching Chucky with the other. She was finally getting through to the old nun. Raphael stopped blithering and stood in the dark, forcing herself to listen to a screen door slam shut and voices rising in the distance.

"Raphael," Leonie continued, "we've got to hide. What if they come out looking for other people! Come on." Leonie dragged Raphael into some brush. "Now, think. We need a plan."

"I wish I had a gun," Raphael said, finally getting control of herself. "I'd go in there and shoot 'em all up."

"No you wouldn't," Leonie said.

"No, I wouldn't. You're right. Listen. They're shouting."

Leonie strained her ears. Raphael held her breath and

listened, but all she could hear was a roaring noise. "What are they saying?" Raphael asked.

"Somebody wants to kill her. They're fighting about it. Somebody does, somebody doesn't. Now they're just yelling. They don't get along very well." Leonie was shaking but she knew she had to act calm for the sake of Sister Raphael. It was all up to her.

"Listen, Raphael, they're bringing her outside. Look, that blubbery man has her." Leonie was whispering, pushing Raphael back into the shadows. "Get out of sight, into the bushes." Her voice was frantic with urgency as she dragged Raphael back further into the brush.

"I'm here. They can't see us. What can we do?" Raphael's old voice cracked with pain.

Suddenly Leonie recognized Dirty Bobby from the voodoo ceremony. No good. Really evil. "Oh, shit, Raphael. Shit." Leonie started to cry quietly, hugging Chucky to her chest. Sister Cecile didn't stand a chance against that man.

"Don't look, Raphael," she sobbed quietly. "There isn't anything we can do."

# 44

LEONIE and Sister Raphael moved silently up, maneuvering through the edge of the bushes, their feet becoming wet in the damp area off the road. Finally they were close enough to see everything clearly. They saw Dirty Bobby dragging Sister Cecile across the yard. They felt tangible, heavy despair.

Chucky began to wiggle and twist against Leonie's tight grasp, and she looked down at the little bird who was suddenly becoming agitated from the noise and the commotion. He had a savage look now, little black eyes glinting wildly in the small, feathered head. Dirty Bobby had tortured him and trained him to kill. He was ready. The little rooster's heart began to pump double time. His entire life had prepared him for killing.

Chucky began to thrash in Leonie's arms in a frenzy, his feathers puffing out, making him look twice as big as he really was. He had suffered torment, his feathers had been plucked. Dirty Bobby had filed Chucky's claws and beak razor sharp. Leonie felt them now as Chucky struggled against her stranglehold. Chucky wanted to kill! And there was Cecile with that man, that horrible man. Leonie could see the knife, a quick glint in the darkness. Chucky began to bounce against Leonie as though he wanted to get away, to fight! Suddenly Leonie knew exactly how to help Cecile, battered and almost unconscious in Dirty Bobby's grasp.

\* \* \*

262

Inside the cabin Olimpo was still yelling. "He's gonna slice that nun up. Shit, Bajito, I don't like that nun-killing stuff. These people, all they want to do is kill the nuns. Shit. I never shoulda started this. I never shoulda brought that Bradley home. I want to get out of here."

Olimpo was totally out of control. His enormous voice rose to the ceiling. His big fists pounded on the table. He had finally hit the bottom line. Olimpo Olarte-Rodríguez was not a killer.

It was too late.

Bajito laughed.

"It's not funny!" Olimpo roared.

"Hey, the game's over. The nun's here. No million bucks. Just a dead nun." Bajito looked down at his diamond Piaget watch and shrugged. Then he smiled broadly, showing all his silver dental work.

"So, let him go," Bajito said with a shrug. "There's still time."

"Let who go?" Olimpo didn't understand.

"That *fulano* in the back room. Let him the fuck go. Like, you're gonna be his hero. If you don't let him go, then Dirty Bobby's gonna want to kill him and the girl too. He's already got the nun."

The could both hear the nun yelling, and then a sudden silence.

That was all Olimpo needed. He raced to the back room and slid the dead bolt. "Move those Anglo asses into gear or that crazy bastard's going to slit you up." Olimpo was almost crying with relief. His conscience had been killing him ever since he'd imagined Dirty Bobby chopping Bradley into pieces for alligator meat, and slicing up that beautiful woman in there. That was the kicker. Olimpo couldn't bear the thought of seeing Violet die. She was a woman. "Split, you guys, I mean, really split!"

Then Olimpo turned to Bajito. "And you keep your mouth shut. I know you aren't nobody's brother."

Bradley and Violet stood up together. They were in

shock, dressed only in the minimum of clothing. The door was open.

Bradley gave a swift glance at the woman by his side and grinned. He grabbed Violet's hand.

"Let's go."

Dirty Bobby had Sister Cecile down on the ground in the front yard near a wild tamarind tree. Olimpo had been right. Dirty Bobby was ready to kill. Nobody could save Sister Cecile from that. Cecile was dying right on the dirt in the front yard.

It was happening. The blade was cutting a razor thin line on Cecile's left arm. The blood was coming out like a red drawing, almost black in the night. Nun blood. Dirty Bobby was sitting on her, grinning. He was going very slowly. It was going to take a very long time, but she was going to die. She wasn't screaming much. She was limp, mostly because he'd batted her on the head a few times to keep things under control. Her forehead was stained with blood from the blow, but she wasn't hurt badly, not yet. Give her a minute and she'd start to fight again.

Dirty Bobby anticipated the struggle. Her eyes were flickering open already.

He picked up the blade to start on the other arm when Leonie came blasting out of the bushes and tossed Chucky right at the man. Chucky hit Dirty Bobby right in the eyes, legs extended before him, claws out. Chucky's claws were still razor sharp. He had been living in the bathroom where everything was neat and smooth. The claws hadn't worn down a bit.

Leonie hadn't known when she had readied the bird for the toss, but roosters always went for the eyes.

Dirty Bobby screamed. The sound lasted a full thirty seconds, ending in a gurgle as blood flowed into his mouth from his eye.

That was just the first scream.

Gouge, peck, squawk. Chucky was fast. Dirty Bobby didn't know what hit him. His screaming was horrible. He

264

flailed his arms aimlessly, grabbing at feathers. He was fighting off the devil while blood dripped down his face.

Chucky backed off, then came in for another attack. The left eye was gone, the other one was bleeding badly. Chucky hit the right eye with both claws, digging in, pecking madly with his beak at what remained of the left one before flying back again.

When Cecile had seen the wild flash of white feathers, she started to roll, pushing at Dirty Bobby as she scrambled on the ground to escape. Her push had saved Chucky from being grabbed when he had first been thrown and begun his attack. Now the rooster was on his own. He didn't need any help.

Dirty Bobby rose up squealing. He gripped his knife with one hand, reached for his eyes with the other. He was blind. He stabbed at nothing as Chucky went in for the kill. This time the bird flew at the back of Dirty Bobby's head, pounding at the left ear with beak and claws. Dirty Bobby turned in circles, screaming. Then he stumbled over his own feet and fell on the knife. What Chucky couldn't finish, Dirty Bobby did himself.

Cecile saw it happen from where she lay in the dirt. A man destroyed before her eyes. Dirty Bobby toppling into darkness, dashed against dry earth hungry for blood.

Bradley and Violet saw it happen from the steps of the crumbling house where they stood, hand in hand in their underwear.

Raphael and Leonie saw it happen from the shadows.

"Lord save us all," Raphael murmured.

Leonie said, "Splat," when Dirty Bobby hit the earth.

The screaming ended. The land was silent. No bugs, no birds.

Cecile rose, staggered away, and puked in the bushes.

Olimpo and Bajito didn't see a thing, but they had heard the screaming, first the nun's, then Dirty Bobby's. They looked out when it stopped and saw a defunct heap, a pile of death. There was nothing left of Dirty Bobby. His soul had gone directly to hell.

"We maybe ought to go someplace," Olimpo said softly, his voice catching an eerie quality from the stench of death. "I think the Dirt Man is dead."

"I got a real nice spot we can hang for a while," Bajito agreed. "I was thinking maybe we go into real estate some place else. We can go out the back door here."

Bajito beckoned with his head and the two men slipped away into the night. Their obsession with riches was dead, like Dirty Bobby. Only Violet noticed the two dark figures creeping away.

Chucky knew he had won. He fluffed out his feathers and flew on top of Dirty Bobby's head and crowed. "Cock-a-doodle-do!"

The sound traveled through the trees. A chicken who lived in a shack a half a mile away heard it, shivered with delight, and ruffled her brown feathers. She began to cluck. Moments later she laid an egg.

"Cecile, you're all right!" Raphael cried and ran to the younger nun who was emerging from the bushes.

Cecile's face was a mess of blood and vomit. She pulled up a corner of her shirt and wiped her mouth before she spoke. "What are you doing here?" she asked. Her eyes struggled to focus. She was still afraid. Her arm dripped blood. "Where's my backup?"

"Chucky. I can't believe what he did." Raphael pushed the words out. Leonie came up beside them, tears rolling down her face. "He saved you, Cecile."

"Chucky," Leonie sobbed, "It was Chucky. Really, it was my fault. We were just taking Chucky out to let him go."

"You said he should be free," Raphael added. "We've got to get you to a doctor, your arm needs stitches. Dirty Bobby's dead."

"My arm." Cecile looked at her arm, then looked around her in the dark. She was almost in shock. She couldn't feel the pain yet. The arm could wait. She had things left to do and she forced her brain into a familiar channel. This was her case and it was complete. She had found Bradley Locke. Her eyes passed over the shade of Dirty Bobby, dead on the grass, and she saw Bradley and Violet standing and staring at the three women. Things almost came into focus.

"Bradley Locke?" Cecile asked.

He smiled and stepped forward. Violet came along behind him. "I presume you are Sister Cecile?"

"Yes. I'm afraid things didn't work out as planned, but it's wonderful to meet you. Alive." Sister Cecile walked up and they shook hands, her bloody arm held at an angle behind her. He didn't look at the arm and Cecile didn't look down at his plaid boxer shorts or even seem to notice his bare feet and naked chest. She met him with a firm handshake and looked him in the eye. She was tough as nails, doing everything by rote. "And of course I already know Violet," she said formally.

Violet came up and gave Cecile a small, dainty hug, not quite crushing the blood and vomit on the nun's tee shirt. Violet had seen worse.

"Things were starting to look real rough," Violet said. "Glad you made it. Glad you had some backup."

"My friends," Cecile said and beckoned for Leonie and Raphael to come up. "Meet my friends."

Chucky squawked from somewhere behind.

It took a few minutes for things to be sorted out. Bradley took a moment to ascertain that Dirty Bobby was really dead. He was. Then Bradley suggested they all head back to Miami, and everyone agreed that might be a good idea.

"But what about the men in the shack?" Cecile asked. Things were not as clear as she had thought. Dark images seemed to flit in and out of the darkness around them, hazy thoughts, hazy people. "There were two other men."

"I saw them leave," Violet said. "They went right out and ran on by the edge of the water over that way," she gestured widely, almost losing the tank top. "I don't think anyone's gonna see those boys for a while. Olimpo, he wasn't so bad. I think he and his buddy might just go set up shop some place else, but you sure as hell won't find them around here."

"They're definitely gone," Bradley agreed. "If you'll excuse me, I'll get my clothes. Violet and I have business back in the city. And I've got to call headquarters immediately."

"They're anxious," Cecile assented. "Tell them I found you, please."

"I will."

Leonie gave a big yawn. "Let's go home."

They all agreed to that idea, but first made plans to meet at the condo the following day. Cecile knew the telephone number of the FBI. "I'll call them right away about Dirty Bobby's body," she said. "That John Walker person. He was anxious to do something with this case. Or maybe I should try to get Damien. Whoever I can contact first. Dead things smell quickly in this climate. And there are alligators."

"And you need stitches," Raphael said again.

Violet discovered her car was exactly where she left it, keys and all. She and Bradley left in that. Raphael drove Cecile and Leonie in the small rental over minor objections. Together they decided that the Testarossa could wait until tomorrow, although it seemed almost sinful to leave it alone in the bushes.

"Chucky's gone," Leonie said to Raphael when they were halfway back. "I didn't see him anywhere after that last squawk."

"I think he knew what he had done," Raphael said with nunlike certainty. "I think he's done what he was supposed to do."

Sister Cecile didn't say a word. She had seen Dirty Bobby die only inches away from her. She had seen Chucky when he had crowed triumphantly. She had seen enough.

268

# 45

By the time the moon sank and the light appeared in the east, Cecile had slept for a very few hours and was awake again, sitting in one of Paul's huge chairs, facing the sea. She had done everything the night before, it seemed, but she couldn't rest. Her arm hurt dreadfully; each stitch felt like barbed wire, put in at one-thirty in the morning by a haggard resident in Jackson Memorial Hospital's emergency room.

Dirty Bobby's death rested badly in her mind. Out the condo window she could see a white sea slowly turn gray-green as the day began. No one else would be awake for several more hours and she was grateful for that, letting exhaustion and the red coals of pain clean her. It was one of those moments when she felt terribly Biblical, like Isaiah.

"There was no one at your father's motel," Cecile said later to Leonie, when the day had formally begun. "I've been calling all morning. I'll keep trying."

"Yeah, sure," Leonie said. It didn't seem important to her. She had been jolted by what she had witnessed. It had been nothing like television or books. It had been serious reality. She was covered with mosquito bites now as well as rapidly healing but itchy chicken pox. She was spread out on Paul's couch looking small, flipping through comic books.

"I still don't think you two should have come," Cecile continued, this time speaking to Raphael. "I told you not to follow me."

Raphael didn't even look contrite. "I distinctly heard you say that Chucky needed freedom, and Leonie mentioned to me that she knew about a place near the Everglades. I figured there would be people nearby for Chucky to discover, and really, you never told me where you were going. It was just luck that we should come upon you as we did."

"Pure chance," Cecile said dryly.

"Chucky saved your life."

"I saw him."

"The person who was supposed to be with you never showed up. You would have been dead."

"And Dirty Bobby would have been alive. I wonder what happened to Damien and the man he said he was sending. Maybe he could have stopped the death."

"I think," Raphael said finally, "that one never can second guess these things. Besides, you may have more things of value left to do in this world than Dirty Bobby could even dream of. Most people would agree. Now don't start on John Donne about one man's death diminishing me, and all the rest of those words, because I know that already. And God loves us all, and . . ."

The telephone interrupted her grand speech. Raphael picked it up.

"Hello."

There was a moment of silence and then Raphael said quietly, "This is Sister Raphael. We're together here. Yes. Go ahead."

For a while Sister Raphael listened intently to the speaker. Her face seemed to quake. Anxiety passed like a strong wind over her wrinkled features. She looked at Sister Cecile, still tangled in her chair and the terror of last night. She looked at Leonie, pale and tired. More bad news. Could they take it? Sister Raphael's responses were soft, almost whispers, and her head turned away from the others in the room.

"I'll tell her. I'll tell them both."

Raphael paused and listened to more words. "It was a

major connection with a drug cartel? Astounding. And he left notes on the case. Yes, I've heard of plastique. Yes. . . . yes. I know. But what's the prognosis? You did find the codicil? Where, did you say? . . . I do know her guardian. She's in good hands. Absolutely. I'll take care of it. And you will call with more information in an hour? Please. Don't worry, I'll see to everything."

Raphael put the telephone down. She looked from Leonie to Cecile and took a great gulp of air as all the wisdom of her years seemed to desert her. Damien, she thought, his name scratching across her brain, the man who was Leonie's father. Damien. Guarded condition. Near death.

Was it possible that Sister Cecile would become a guardian? No. He would recover. She would storm heaven. Damien would survive. He didn't stand a chance of dying, not with all the nuns she knew, all those prayers. Damien would be just fine. She smiled confidently and turned to her friends.

The telephone rang again. Raphael picked it up. It was Paul, back from the Bamboo Convention. "Paul, could you come over right away?" Raphael asked in a whisper. "We may need you."

She hung up quickly, took a deep breath, and began to speak.

"Leonie, your father was hurt. He's in the hospital but he will be fine. Just fine."

It wasn't until morning that Chucky came down from the high tree where he had flown after taking care of Dirty Bobby. He had been shaken by his own violence. His feathers were still ruffled and bloody, his sharpened talons encrusted in blood. From his perch he had seen the FBI agents come for Dirty Bobby's body at dawn. The agents had been all aghast at what had been done to the dead man's face. Chucky had no understanding of the mutilation he had accomplished, how it

271

looked as though a demon had attacked. Perhaps Chucky would have been proud, had he understood, but he was only a bird.

In the days that followed, Chucky made his home near Olimpo Olarte-Rodríguez's empty house. The rooster was washed by rain and combed by the bushes and the sawgrass until he became clean again. He ate palmetto bugs. He crowed every morning, and stared, now and then, through a window into the building. He gazed at the shiny face of the clock that never changed.

Eventually he began to roam. One day he discovered another shack where a group of migrant workers holed up when there was no work on the lettuce and bean fields. He discovered the workers' little brown chickens and he moved in, welcomed because the hens had no rooster before he came. There he had a home and finally a family of his own. Chucky had a life.

Olimpo Olarte-Rodríguez and Bajito Suarez fled to Tampa where Bajito was able to find work for them both in a small cigar factory. They sold their diamond watches and rented a place in a nice section of Tampa.

Bradley Locke and Violet were married by a justice of the peace at a small ceremony in the lobby of the Hotel Bella Vista. Bradley's cat, Bismarck, had fared well at the kennel, having been removed from his cage by the kennel master's daughter after the first week and brought into the house. While Bradley and Violet were honeymooning in Ecuador, Bismarck had kittens. When the newlyweds returned to Washington to begin their life together, mother and kittens came home. Violet named the liveliest kitten Cecile.

Damien Drail, who had been injured in an explosion in a cafe in Hialeah, made a miraculous recovery and was soon reunited with his daughter.

* * *

Peace returned to Miami for a few moments, and the nuns had time to wrap up the purchase of the old motel on Miami Beach. "I think we're going to be here for a while," Sister Cecile remarked to Sister Raphael after the deal was complete. "Someone's got to supervise the new retirement community. I think it's us. I think Miami is in our future."

"Miami?" Sister Raphael looked out the window at the distant ocean, then closed her eyes for a moment. "Heaven," she said with a sigh. "And hell. With a swimming pool."

# GLOSSARY

*Bajito*—Spanish for "short" or "Shorty," as in "Hey, Shorty."

*babalawo*—a priest in the Yoruba and Santería religions.

*boca de gusano*—Spanish, "maggot mouth."

*bokor*—practitioner of left-handed voodoo who does rituals for money.

*botanica*—a small retail store that sells objects used in the practice of Santería and Cuban voodoo.

*cállate*—Spanish for "shut up."

*chocolates*—Spanish slang for hashish.

*El Chulo*—"pretty boy, pimp."

*fulano*—a very old Spanish word for someone of uncertain identity, a so-and-so, a whatzisname, also *fulano; zutano; mengano*, as in Tom, Dick, and Harry.

*Guapo*—Spanish for "handsome, good-looking" (masculine).

*Left-handed voodoo*—the darker side of voodoo, associated with evil.

*mambo*—a female priest in voodoo.

*paca*—Spanish for a tightly compressed brick of marijuana.

*Pompano*—a prized fish of the genus *Trachinotus*.

*puta*—Spanish for "prostitute" (slang). Lit. whore.

*que putada*—Spanish for "What a fucking disaster, bloody shame."

*que te calles*—Spanish for "shut up already."

*Sapo*—Spanish for "frog," also the name by which Manuel Noriega's secret service men were known.

*syncretic faith*—a religion formed by combining ideas from several different faiths.

Discover...

The Christine Bennett Mysteries

# by LEE HARRIS

Even after leaving the cloistered world
of St. Stephen's Convent for suburban
New York State, Christine Bennett
still finds time to celebrate the holy days.

Unfortunately, in the secular world
the holidays seem to end in murder—
and it's up to this ex-nun
to discover who commits
these unholy acts.

## THE GOOD FRIDAY MURDER

Ex-nun Christine Bennett has only just begun settling into her new life in suburban New York State when she finds herself volunteering to investigate a murder that happened on Good Friday—forty years ago.

## THE YOM KIPPUR MURDER

When Christine Bennett discovers that her friend, a lonely widower living on Manhattan's West Side, has been murdered, she is determined to solve the crime.

## THE CHRISTENING DAY MURDER

Christine Bennett is looking forward to attending the christening of her friend's baby—until the skeletal remains of the victim from a thirty-year-old murder are found in the church basement.

## THE ST. PATRICK'S DAY MURDER
Police officer Scotty McVeigh is one of New York's finest, until he is shot on St. Patrick's Day. Speculating that his murder may be connected with the deaths of other off-duty cops, Christine Bennett begins to pursue a killer.

## THE CHRISTMAS NIGHT MURDER
When a priest never arrives at his Christmas night party at St. Stephen's Convent, the worried nuns invite Christine Bennett to investigate. But nothing turns up—until an old scandal involving the priest and a novice resurfaces.

## THE THANKSGIVING DAY MURDER
Natalie Gordon vanished a year ago at the Thanksgiving Day Parade, and still the police have no leads. Christine Bennett feels compelled to investigate Natalie's mysterious disappearance—and her equally mysterious past.

## THE PASSOVER MURDER

For fifteen years, Iris Grodnick's murder during Passover has remained a troubling mystery. Chris Bennett reluctantly consents to look into it for Iris's family one last time—and soon suspects that some of the relatives are not telling her the whole truth.

## THE VALENTINE'S DAY MURDER

Three friends disappear after a Valentine's night walk across frozen Lake Erie—and later two are found dead, with the third suspected of the murders. Chris Bennett is offered the difficult task of finding the third friend and proving his innocence, but when she closes in on the truth, she finds herself skating on very thin ice.

## The Christine Bennett Mysteries by Lee Harris

Published by Fawcett Books.
Available in your local bookstore.